Pearl Wilson is a journalist who has worked in print media and public relations both in Australia and the United States. During her early career as a journalist she wrote five books – a medical series for children and two local history books, some of which were published in Australia and the UK. The publications were *Broadway and Beyond, Oakleigh's Golden Days, Katie Goes to Hospital, If You Knew Nicky* and *Mummy Why Can't I Breathe?* She wrote the narrative for *Winter Orbit*, a slow cinema production about the Covid-19 pandemic. Pearl teaches creative writing and organises literary events. She has facilitated a writing group for the past twelve years. Several of her short stories are included in the anthologies *Woven Words* and *Reflections* published by the group. *Ticket to Paris* is her first novel.

TICKET TO PARIS

Pearl M Wilson

BAKERS ROAD
ENTERTAINMENT

Published by Bakers Road Entertainment
Victoria, Australia

pearlmwilson.com

First published 2023

 A catalogue record for this book is available from the National Library of Australia

ISBN 978 0 6489553 9 9 (pbk)
ISBN 978 0 6489553 8 2 (ebk)

Cover photo by Shutterstock
Typeset by Helen Christie, Blue Wren Books
Printed by Ingram Spark

For Isabella and Sophia,
remembering all our imaginary trips to Paris
when you were little girls.

1

Nothing looked real as the taxi crawled through the heavy traffic. Annie pulled her cardigan across her chest, trying to take it all in. Paris was so big, so beautiful and she felt so small huddled there on the back seat. Formal gardens in front of her stretched out towards the Arc de Triomphe, and in the distance the Eiffel Tower stood like a mirage on the horizon. Sun reflected off a glass pyramid in a crowded plaza.

The driver smiled when he heard her intake of breath. 'Is this your first time here?' he asked, his French accent caressing the words.

'Yes,' she whispered, 'but I never imagined it would be like this.'

'A lot of people say that,' he nodded, steering around the Louvre.

They drove by bridges with ornate streetlights and green bookstalls lining the banks of the river. Sun sparkled on olive-green water while tourist boats trailed long ribbons of foam.

She rolled down the window, breathing in Paris. Trees in blossom flashed by, reminding her of ballerinas in pink tutus. Footpaths were a kaleidoscope of people, shop fronts, flower sellers and outdoor cafés. As the taxi rounded a corner, an artist stood painting the streetscape like a scene from a postcard.

She craned forward, trying to see the canvas before they crossed a bridge to an island in the middle of the river. The taxi rattled over cobblestones, driving into another world resembling a provincial village. Paris seemed to disappear as she gazed out at streets only wide enough for one-way traffic. They passed apartments with wrought-iron balconies and rows of miniature shops.

Somewhere close by, bells chimed as if heralding her arrival. She sat back, rubbing the goosebumps on her arms while the stirring chorus reverberated through the car. When they reached the end of the street, the taxi stopped in front of a hotel with red awnings.

The driver glanced around. 'We're here,' he said, pulling on the handbrake. 'This is your hotel, Madame.'

Annie sat riveted to the seat, remembering all the tears and angry words leading to this one moment. The bells were now silent, replaced by her own pulse pounding in her ears. She was a world away from everything she knew and unsure if she would ever make it home again.

2

Months before Paris, on a Melbourne summer morning, Annie stood in a sea of knee-high weeds, as if waking from a trance. She looked out across her parched garden, struggling to process what she was seeing. A dead mouse by the front gate swarmed with ants, and drifts of junk mail lined the fence. She glanced back at the verandah littered with leaves blown across from the garden, wondering how her life had come to this.

'Why are you out in this stinking heat?'

She spun around, squinting at the blurry face peering over the palings. 'I can't see in this glare – is that you, Jess?'

'Well, it's not a movie star,' the old woman cackled. 'What are you doing over there?'

'Wondering how I'm going to clean up this mess.'

'It's too hot. Come over for a cuppa.'

'Sorry, not now.' She shielded her eyes with her hand in the shimmering heat. 'I might start weeding before it gets any hotter.'

'You'll get sunstroke,' Jess lectured. 'Stop being so stand-offish. I'll put the kettle on and expect you in five minutes.'

Annie swayed in the heat haze, her red hair a halo of damp curls. Trickles of sweat pooled in her bra and the beginning of a headache jabbed at her temples. She closed her eyes; there would be no way to get out of this.

Everyone knew a conversation with Jess could be tricky and sipping tea in the neighbourhood busybody's stifling kitchen was the last thing Annie intended to be doing when she'd dragged herself out of bed that morning. She'd never meant to talk about anything more than the weather, but an overwhelming need to confide in someone marred her better judgement. Later, she would blame her lapse on the heat.

It started when she mentioned she wasn't sleeping well. Jess pounced on the morsel of information like a bird with beady eyes. Before she could even finish her tea, Annie found herself answering the old woman's string of prying questions.

'I really shouldn't be telling you any of this,' she whispered.

Jess ignored the comment, leaning across the table. 'You'll feel better when you get it off your chest.'

A clock in the corner ticked away the seconds while Annie grappled to find the right words, her eyes bright with tears. 'I'm having horrible nightmares and they never change,' she finally said, trying to keep any emotion out of her voice. 'They started after Leo died.'

'What are they about?'

'I'm on a balcony with my yellow tote bag. I stand on it so I can get my leg over the side of the railing. While I'm teetering there, I look down at a rose garden.'

'Where's the garden?'

She knew where it was but admitting it would be a step too far. 'I'm not sure, although it seems familiar.'

'That doesn't sound like a nightmare.'

'It is to me. I let go of the railing and hit my head when I fall over the side. I can taste blood and hear my skirt snapping around me as I scream for forgiveness.'

'To God or your daughters?'

'I'm only trying to tell you what I've been dreaming.' Annie glanced away, twisting her wedding ring. 'Anyway, God doesn't listen.'

Jess crossed herself. 'How can you say that?'

'Because I'm not even sure there is one.'

'What do Mia and Lucy think about it all?'

Annie's heart began to race. 'They don't know. It's been hard enough for them losing their father. If you see them, please don't mention this. They don't need anything else to worry about.'

'My lips are sealed.' Jess patted her mauve perm. 'I won't breathe a word.'

'Let's talk about something else. Have you heard if there's going to be a cool change?'

'Wait.' Jess put up her hand. 'What happens at the end of those dreams? Do you ever hit the ground?'

'No, they always end with the rose garden rushing at me before I wake up. Now I'm afraid to close my eyes at night. You can understand why I don't want the girls to know any of this.' She glanced around the spotless kitchen, wondering how to escape the interrogation. The only way out would be to cut and run.

'I once saw a film about a man living the same day over and over again,' Jess said, interrupting Annie's exit plan.

'What's a film got to do with anything?'

'It's like you on the balcony every night in your dreams. Eventually he stopped trying to fight it. Maybe you should, too.'

'My life isn't a film, and these aren't just little dreams. You don't seem to understand how disturbing they are.'

'I'm trying, dear.' Jess smirked across the rim of her teacup, arching an eyebrow. 'You should see a doctor to get something for your nerves. I'm sure some medication would help you forget your troubles.'

'I don't pop pills.'

'Maybe it's time to start. You need to make an effort. You've let yourself go, not to mention your poor garden.'

Annie swallowed her hurt feelings with the bitter stewed tea. What would Jess know anyway, she thought. Mrs Suburbia in her neat little house, living her safe little life.

A week later Jess rang for an update. Annie flinched when she heard her neighbour's high-pitched voice.

'How are you today? Still upset?'

'I'm fine,' she whispered, guessing Jess had already told most of the street about the nightmares.

'But you weren't last week.'

Annie leant against the kitchen bench, resolved not to co-operate with another grilling. 'I'm on my way out and can't talk.'

'Where to?'

'You sound like a detective.' The comment didn't register as Jess rushed on to what she'd been fixated on for days.

'Before you go, have you seen a doctor yet? You know, one specialising in mental problems.' The question hung between them, stretching out in a long silence. 'Are you still there?'

'I can't believe you're asking me this,' Annie gulped, the words almost choking her.

'I only have the best intentions. It's been days since I saw you and you should've at least made an appointment by now.'

'I think I'm entitled to be upset. I don't need a shrink; I need Leo.'

'But he passed over months ago and you have to get used to life without him. Shouldn't you be moving on?'

'How can I move on when my life's already over?' Annie blurted, clutching her chest.

'Don't get dramatic; you have to pull yourself together.'

Annie began to answer her but clicked off the phone instead, shoving it into her pocket. The old woman's words churned up doubts she already had about her own sanity. Tears streamed down her face as she lurched across to the stool by the sink, wishing she would keel over and end it all on the tiles. She didn't know where to turn or how to ask for help, her reasoning dulled by lack of sleep and the sad memories haunting her every waking hour.

3

Lucy could see her sister trying to cross Chapel Street. Each time she stepped off the kerb, the break in the traffic disappeared, forcing her to jump back. Her skin-tight skirt and high-heeled sandals made her antics even more precarious in the heavy traffic. It was agonising to watch.

Lucy reached for her phone. 'Mia, I can see you. I'm already at Coco's. Go up to the lights before you get flattened.'

'Sorry I'm late!' she shouted over the street noise.

'Do you want me to order for you?'

'Awesome. Ask for something cold; I'm boiling. See you soon.'

Five minutes later a waiter slid her iced coffee on the table as Mia hurried into the café still clutching her phone. 'How brilliant is that!' she said, flashing a dazzling smile at him. She plonked on a chair and puffed out her cheeks, dropping her bag at her feet.

'What's up? You look a bit wasted.'

'You always get to the point,' Mia grinned. 'My mother-in-law had a pool party for her sixtieth last night. It went on until well after midnight. I'm just a bit tired.'

'It's lucky you don't have to teach today.'

'I know, I got to sleep in. And by the way, thanks for meeting me. We don't get to do this often enough.'

Lucy shrugged. 'Closing the shop for just an hour won't matter much on a Monday. There was only one customer this morning.' She swirled a straw in her lemonade. 'Why did she have the party on a Sunday?'

'Now she's retired she's forgotten anyone else has to work. She's going through her cashed-up retiree stage. You know, yoga, meditation, vegetarian cooking classes in India; she's having a ball.'

'I wish we could say the same about our Mum.' Lucy watched Mia's smile fade as she spoke. 'No yoga or meditation for her.'

'Sorry, I didn't mean to sound so insensitive. Do you think I shouldn't have gone to the party?'

'I'm not saying that, just don't mention it to Mum. You know how she doesn't want us to celebrate anything this year.'

'But she can't dictate that about anyone else. I still think it's all a bit over the top.'

'It's her call; we can't change anything now.' Lucy shook her head. 'She's too fragile.'

'Someone told me it'll get better after this first year. Do you think that will happen?'

'Who knows; this is all new to me. All I want to do is get through Dad's first anniversary. I think that'll be the toughest day of all.'

'So do I, but at least I have David's shoulder to cry on.'

'Lucky you.'

Mia reached out for her sister's hand. 'You know I'm always here for you.'

'Yeah, whatever.'

'Are you sure you're okay?'

Lucy glanced away, avoiding her sister's pitying eyes. Now wasn't the time to discuss how much she was hurting. 'I'm fine. I don't need anyone's shoulder.'

'Mine is here if you change your mind.'

'Give it a break; can we talk about something else?'

Mia sat back in her chair. 'Did you speak to Mum on the weekend?'

'Only briefly. She didn't want to talk. It's like all the lights have gone out in her life. She keeps telling me she feels like a person without a country. Stateless.'

'I should've called her,' Mia sighed. 'I ran out of time with all the party preparations. When I went around to see her last week, she was talking to herself in the garden. She didn't know I overheard her. The garden was a mess. It's all so sad.'

Lucy rubbed the muscle knotting in her neck. 'Sometimes I worry that she won't survive without Dad. If only she'd gone back to work after the funeral, things might have been better by now. At least all those little kids at the kindergarten would've been a distraction from the grief.'

'She says her nest egg is keeping her going, but it has to eventually run out.'

'Maybe when it does, she'll be forced to at least get back to her art for some extra cash.' Lucy frowned and looked out the window. 'I don't think she's even picked up a brush since Dad got sick.'

A tram trundled by and they fell silent, watching it sway along the tracks in the busy street. The waiter returned with their lunch, breaking the silence. Mia unfolded her paper napkin, leaning across the table.

'We should give her something to look forward to.'

'Like what?'

'I don't know, but it would need to be pretty cool. What about a trip somewhere? My mother-in-law sometimes goes to France and loves it. She says Paris mended her broken heart after she split with David's father. Remember? It was just before our wedding and he didn't show up for his own son's big day. She went to Paris later that year.'

'I remember when they divorced, but not any details. Did Paris really help?'

'She seemed better when she got back. Maybe the City of Light might help Mum, too.'

'I'm not so sure about that.'

'Why don't you ask about a few prices at that travel agency near your shop?'

'I guess it would save trolling through the internet, although I think a trip overseas would be a problem with her thing about flying.'

Mia giggled. 'I forgot about that. What a way to start her honeymoon, vomiting all over the groom as soon as the plane took off.'

'That one rough flight to Tasmania doomed us to all those camping trips when we were kids. All because she wouldn't get back on a plane. It's ridiculous when you think about it now.' Lucy rolled her eyes. 'God, I hated camping.'

'It would've been a lot easier if they hadn't been such purists. I could never understand why it was so important to camp in the bush away from civilisation. Remember Dad sending us out in the dark with a torch, shovel and a roll of toilet paper to do a poo?'

'Don't mention it,' Lucy shrieked. 'Can't you see I'm eating here?'

'You brought it up,' Mia grinned.

Glossy posters of European river cruises, African safaris, North American train trips and tours of China were all vying for attention in the travel agency window. An Eiffel Tower poster stuck on the glass door advertised Bastille Day.

A young woman with a pixie haircut looked up from her computer when Lucy walked in. 'Are you browsing or do you need some specific help?'

'My sister and I want to organise a trip for our mother, but we don't have time to do it ourselves.'

The young woman walked across to her. 'As you can see, we can arrange trips for anywhere in the world,' she said, pointing to a display of brochures on a long shelf. 'What kind of holiday do you have in mind?'

Lucy glanced back at the poster on the door and the young woman smiled, reaching for several glossy brochures. 'Good choice, everyone loves France.'

'You read my mind,' Lucy laughed, 'although I'm not sure if we can afford this.'

'Why don't we check out a few prices? There's no obligation to book anything, but if we look at places and availability now, you'll at least have a better idea. We actually have a few good European deals going at the moment.' She pulled out a chair in front of her desk. 'Take a seat. By the way, I'm Deb.'

'And I'm Lucy.'

'Can I make you a coffee before we get started?'

'No thanks, but I might need a strong espresso after I see the prices.'

'Now, what's your mother's name?'

Lucy smiled as Mia's idea took wings. 'Her name's Annie, Annie Green.'

Two days later Lucy rang her sister, armed with a stack of glossy travel brochures and a long list of prices. 'Mia, it's me. I thought I'd catch you between classes. Got a minute?'

'I don't have long. Where are you?'

'At the shop. It's a bit quiet at the moment.'

'Have you been to the travel agency yet?'

'Yep. Are you sitting down?'

Lucy told her about the prices for a month in France. 'So, now you know how expensive this would be, are you still asking for my blessings? Or is it more like my money and my blessings?'

'Come on, Lucy, stop joking around. I can't do this alone. Maybe we should cut it back to three weeks. That would be more doable.'

'I know we have to try something, but I'm not convinced this will work.'

'A trip away could make a real difference.' Mia's voice became breathy as she pitched her idea. 'We could tell her on Dad's anniversary to get her through the day. It would be worth the cost if it helps.'

'It's not so much about the money, I just doubt if Paris could fix anything. But since you're all fired up, we might as well get on with it now. I'll email the travel agent and get things rolling. Listen, kiddo, someone just walked in the shop and I've got to go.'

'Why don't we go over everything on your birthday? We could have breakfast at the botanic gardens.'

'I thought birthdays weren't on this year.'

'I don't think we can call breakfast a celebration. I'll meet you at our usual spot about ten. I might bring a cupcake with a candle on it.'

'Try to find an Eiffel Tower candle,' Lucy laughed.

Sunday morning traffic inched around the Royal Botanic Gardens. Lucy could see families with picnic baskets and people walking dogs while she did two slow circuits searching for somewhere to park. By the time she slid into a tight spot fifteen minutes later, she was late. She hurried along a track on the perimeter of the gardens, dodging joggers powering towards her. When she reached the main entrance, Mia was slumped on a retaining wall while she waited, her long hair the colour of corn in the morning sun. Lucy called out to her twice before she looked up.

'Hey, you were away with the fairies,' she smiled, sitting next to her. 'Sorry I'm late; the parking's chockers.'

'No stress. Anyway, I'm still half asleep.' Mia kissed her cheek, handing her a paper bag. 'Happy birthday, big sister. I couldn't find the candle you wanted, but I managed a French vanilla cupcake.'

'I never really expected you to. Thanks.' She propped the bag next to her on the wall. 'Are you all right?'

'You drive me crazy; I can't hide anything from you,' Mia said.

'What's wrong?'

'A bit of friction on the home front.'

'It shows; you look like shit.'

'Thanks a million.'

'Want to talk about it?'

Mia looked out to the gardens. 'David isn't impressed with the Paris trip. When I told him about it, he accused me of being secretive.'

'When did this happen?'

'A few days ago. I guess I should've discussed it with him first before I paid for my half.' She pulled at her hair as she talked.

Lucy studied her sister's pinched face, unexpectedly grateful she didn't have a partner to justify anything to. 'There wasn't anything secret about it,' she offered. 'Did you tell him we would've missed a great deal if we didn't book before the deadline?'

'I tried to, but he wouldn't listen. Not even when I kept telling him I'd cover it all with extra hours in the after-school program.'

'Did you use a credit card?'

'There was no other way to pay for it,' she said, shaking her head. 'He was awful and kept lecturing me about how we're battling to save for a deposit on a house. In the end, I said the wrong thing.'

'What was that?'

'That I'd ram the card up his bum after I paid it off. Now he won't talk to me.'

Lucy stood, grinning down at her. 'He'll get over it; try not to worry.' As they began to walk, a jogger brushed by them, forcing them to jump sideways to get out of his way. 'Watch where you're going!' Lucy shouted at the Lycra-clad man.

'You're a bit edgy today.'

'Sorry, I can't help it. I keep thinking about my birthday last year. Remember how Dad insisted on getting out of bed for that little afternoon tea Mum organised for me?'

'He was so weak. I don't know how he did it.'

'I still can't believe it all went so pear-shaped the next week.'

'Everything will get better.' Mia reached for Lucy's arm. 'It just has to.'

'I need a coffee. By the way, where're we going?'

'The café near the observatory – my treat.'

'Thanks, kiddo, we can eat while we figure out how to get our darling mother on that plane.'

$$4$$

Alone customer ordering coffee glanced over his shoulder when Annie opened the glass door of the café. She stood behind him at the counter while a young waitress in a black apron fiddled with the controls of a hissing coffee machine. Annie tilted her head to get a better view of the pastries displayed near the cash register. She didn't want much, only something to help her face this terrible day.

On the far side of the café, a glass cheese room displayed rounds of yellow delicacies stacked on marble-topped tables. Behind her were shelves lined with tins of imported tea. She could smell coffee and pastries, licking her lips while she tried to decide what to order. When the customer walked away with his coffee, she stepped forward as a young woman flounced into the café in a cloud of pungent perfume. The waitress's face lit up.

'Wow, where'd ya get that bag?' she squealed.

Annie blinked. 'Me? Are you talking to me?'

The waitress ignored her while the young woman elbowed up to the counter in front of Annie.

'Cool, isn't it?' she said, stroking her over-sized bag covered with metal rings and chains reminiscent of a leather biker's jacket. 'Got it in Bali. Came back with loads of stuff. Give me an espresso; I need a kick-start after last night.'

The waitress leant across the counter, still ignoring Annie. 'What happened?'

'I'll tell you later.' The young woman fanned her face, her red nails a vision of acrylic artistry. 'Let's just say it was all hot.'

'You're such a naughty girl,' the waitress giggled.

Annie looked around at the empty tables wondering what she needed to do to be heard. She fidgeted with the buttons on her cardigan while the young woman with the over-sized bag gushed about her trip. Finally, she put up her hand. 'Any chance of getting a coffee?'

The waitress still ignored her as if she didn't exist. Defeated, she stepped back against the display of imported tea, realising too late the shelves were behind her. A row of tins clattered to the floor, the noise exaggerated as they skidded along the tiles. She now had the waitress's full attention.

'Look what you've done,' she screeched from behind the counter.

'Sorry,' Annie gulped, trying to fish out the tins from under a table with her outstretched foot. As she moved a chair to reach them, it upended, crashing into the shelves.

'Leave them,' the waitress fumed while another row of tins bounced across the tiles.

'I'm having a bad day.'

'Yeah?'

'You don't understand.' Annie's voice trailed off. 'I'm not myself.'

'Oh dear,' the waitress sneered while the other woman flicked her hair at the unwelcomed interruption. A star tattoo on the side of her neck peeped out with each toss of her head.

Annie's cheeks burned as she backed away from the glaring women. She couldn't remember where the door was as she hurried around the shelves, her heart racing. She came to a dead-end near the cheese room and backtracked, all the while knowing they were still watching her. When she finally found the door, her shoulder bag clipped a display of gourmet bread as she rushed by. Several loaves toppled over, scattering across the floor. She sidestepped them, glancing back at the mayhem before bolting outside.

She panted across the street to her ancient car, ignoring the tightness in her chest. Her fingers fumbled like they didn't belong to her while she tried to unlock the door. She put her shoulder bag on the roof and when the key finally turned, she fell into the driver's seat battling unshed tears of humiliation. There had been tears in the car before and she picked up a crumpled tissue from the pile on the passenger seat, dabbing her eyes before groping for her keys.

Her car sputtered and backfired while she reversed, the unsecured seatbelt rattling on the side window. When the forgotten shoulder bag slid down the windscreen, her fight for self-control dissolved in a flood of tears.

The deep wound of grief was bleeding again, the scab ripped off as she walked into the hospital. She bowed her head, weaving through the crowded foyer, overwhelmed by the memory of the last time she'd been there. The idea to honour Leo's anniversary where he'd died now seemed all wrong. She bit the side of her lip. She shouldn't have come.

The image of herself in the hospital chapel begging for a miracle was still vivid even now a year later. That morning her knees had throbbed, but she had kept kneeling, sure some higher power would intervene at the last minute and rescue him. Pain had eventually forced her back on a pew where she slumped across the polished oak, still waiting for a whiff of smoke or a clap of thunder, anything that would have given her a sign some divine force was listening to her prayers. But no sign had appeared and after months of denial, the brutal truth had become clear to her. Nothing would save him because God never listened.

He'd died in her arms an hour later while lunch trays clattered in the other rooms. The Leo she knew had vanished into a void without a word and all she could do was hold him while it happened. When two nurses had begun switching off the monitors next to his bed, she had taken flight, running through the ward like a wild animal. She'd barged out through a balcony door near the exit, tripping over and skidding along the cement on all fours. Her knees had been bleeding when she staggered to her feet and limped across to the railing. She'd stood sobbing with blood trickling down her shins, the world she'd known and everything she believed in collapsing around her.

The dark memory consumed her as she walked through the hospital foyer. Time became fluid, the past merging with the present, and when she stopped in front of the lift, she automatically pushed the top button. Her grip on reality slipped away as the doors hissed open and she stepped inside. When it reached the seventh floor, she stood facing the oncology ward, unsure if it was Leo's anniversary or the day he'd died.

The stuffy ward smelled of sickness. The long corridor, pale green walls with worn handrails and scuffed tiles she knew so well, only added to her confusion while she tried to distinguish which day it was. A young nurse on the phone didn't look up when Annie reached the nurses' station. She stood back against the wall, still disorientated as she listened to the nurse complaining about the air conditioning.

'My unit manager wants it fixed today. Not Monday – now.' Her lips puckered while she listened to the reply, a portable phone wedged between her shoulder and ear. Tendrils of blonde hair cascaded from her long ponytail as she talked. 'Environmental services must have someone to help us. Please, it's roasting up here.'

The pleading conversation faded as Annie walked into the empty room across the hall. She stood with the harsh light of the ward behind her, trying to get her bearings. The curtains were drawn against the morning sun, the room laced with the smell of antiseptic and fresh linen. Gauges lined one wall and a coil of plastic tubing hung from a blood pressure monitor in the corner.

She eased herself into an armchair, the movement making a crunching noise while she squirmed on the frayed vinyl. She reached out and touched the empty bed, listening to the familiar sounds of the ward. Across the hall, the nurse slammed down the phone on its charger and Annie sighed. So much for the air conditioning.

No one noticed her until a flustered cleaner rushed into the room. The woman crashed her cart against a cupboard. 'I won't be long. I'm running a bit late, but you're welcome to wait there while I finish off the loo.' She pulled out a bucket of cleaning products from a shelf at the side of the cart. 'The surgery is probably finished by now.'

'Surgery?'

'Yeah, I was bum up, head down doing the bathroom when they came for him. I cleared out while they got him ready for theatre. Are you a relative?' She frowned when Annie didn't answer, annoyance spreading across her face. 'You know you shouldn't be in here if you aren't. This is the high dependency unit of the ward and the only visitors allowed are family.'

Annie hauled herself out of the chair, her mind clawing back the months to the present. 'I did have a relative in this room,' she whispered, acknowledging what she'd subconsciously denied for the past twelve months, 'but he's gone now and never coming back. Ever.'

The cleaner stepped towards her and she backed out of the room, nearly colliding with an entourage of nurses. Behind them a porter pushed a bed festooned with monitors and tubing. A bag of blood swayed from a pole while an oxygen bottle puffed life into a man cocooned in the bed. She tried not to look at him, hurrying down the long corridor and out to the balcony that wrapped around one side of the ward. She stood against the concrete wall sucking in fresh air, remembering how she'd taken refuge there the year before, now in no doubt what day it was.

A gnarled peppercorn tree swayed in the breeze, the branches moving with the currents of hot air swirling over the top of the hospital and down through the garden atrium in the heart of the building. She thought of all the times she'd stood at Leo's window in the oncology ward gazing down at the tree dancing in the wind. He'd laughed at her when she called it her friend. Now it seemed to be waving hello. A breeze lifted her tangle of red curls while she watched its shadows play a game of tag with flashes of sunlight.

She inched towards the railing and looked down at the rose garden. From high up on the balcony the blooms looked like tiny blotches of colour on an artist's palette. Her hands trembled as she thought of the nightmares, a lone tear sliding down her cheek. She now understood. The nightmares were showing her the way. Leo left her a year ago today and now she would follow him. All the suffering would soon be over for both of them. She ran her fingers along patches of peeling paint on the railing, wondering how to pull herself up without her tote bag to stand on.

The muffled sound of her ringing phone broke her concentration. She waited for it to stop, but the ringing persisted. The phone seemed to have a life of its own as it rang and vibrated, forcing her to fish it out of her shoulder bag. She froze when she saw Mia's name displayed on its small screen.

'Mum, is that you?'

'Yes, it's me,' Annie whispered.

'You sound funny.'

'How could I be funny today of all days?'

'I meant funny, odd.'

'Mia …' Annie's voice trailed off while she looked down at the roses, gripping the railing with her free hand.

'I know you said you didn't want any fuss on Dad's anniversary, but Lucy and I need to see you. I've taken the day off work and she's closing her shop.'

'I want to be alone.'

'You know, we loved him, too.'

Mia sounded like a little girl and Annie started to cry, struggling to speak. 'I'm not at home.'

'Where are you?'

'At your father's hospital.'

'What's happened?'

The panic in Mia's voice cut through her fog of emotions. 'I just needed to be here. I went back to his room, but I couldn't find him. I don't know what happened, I'm a bit confused.'

'Mum, he's dead,' Mia said.

Annie began to sob, unable to utter a single word.

'Oh God, listen to me. I want you to go out the front and wait until I get there. It'll take me about twenty minutes. Talk to me; where are you right now?'

Annie looked down at the roses. 'I'm on my way to have a coffee.'

'I should be there before you finish it.'

'I'll be near the glass doors.'

'Mum, I love you very much. See you soon.'

Annie silenced her phone and dropped it back in her bag, wiping away tears as she looked down at the peppercorn tree. 'I'll have to be going soon, old friend,' she whispered, and the branches swayed in the breeze.

5

Two men in dressing gowns were smoking in front of the hospital when Mia drove to the main entrance. One of them on a drip leant against a five-minute parking sign while he dragged on a cigarette. She pulled on the handbrake; her mother wasn't there.

A car parked in front of her was taking the only space. She drummed her fingers on the steering wheel as a pregnant woman struggled out of the passenger seat and shuffled towards the glass doors. When the car left, she drove into the space before sprinting into the hospital.

All the tables were taken in the café at the far end of the foyer. A team of baristas in matching red shirts juggled cups with assembly line efficiency while a stainless-steel coffee machine the size of a small car whined above the din. Doctors in surgical overalls, patients in dressing gowns, executives in suits and frazzled mothers with screaming children waited at a counter for their coffee. Mia scanned the café before rushing back outside.

A security officer with a crew cut stood looking at her car, his hands on his hips. She ignored him, turning her back to ring her mother. Her call went to voicemail and she hurried back to the foyer still gripping her phone as she joined a queue at an information desk. A man at the front was complaining about parking fees. She half listened to his heated conversation while fidgeting with her phone, willing it to ring.

'I don't make the rules,' the woman behind the desk kept reciting, her voice as expressionless as her face. 'If you're unhappy with the rates, you can park in a side street or take public transport.'

The man looked out across the foyer and back to the woman. 'I'll never forget this place and it will be for all the wrong reasons.' He stormed off and the woman behind the desk motioned the next person to step forward.

Mia fought back tears when it was her turn. The woman behind the desk kept nodding, her face blank as Mia tried to explain about her missing mother.

'Is she in the emergency department or a ward?'

'She's not a patient. She came here on sort of a pilgrimage and now I can't find her. Can you please make an announcement for me?'

'Sorry, we don't make announcements for visitors.' The woman looked over Mia's shoulder, nodding at the person behind her to step forward.

'Wait a minute, I need to get this sorted,' Mia pleaded, putting out her arm to keep her place. She could hear the desperation in her own voice. 'Please, won't you make one announcement?'

The woman shook her head. 'Why don't you go to security? It's over there.' She pointed to the end of the foyer and Mia backed away.

The security officer behind a counter was the same one she'd seen at the front of the hospital. She knocked to get his attention. 'Excuse me, I need some help,' she gulped, trying to quell her rising panic.

He looked up from his computer. 'What kind of help?'

'I've lost my mother.' For a split second she felt like a child again. 'I'm worried something has happened to her.' He stood and grabbed a notebook from his desk, scrawling across one of the pages as she told him about Annie.

'I'll need to make a phone call; you can wait inside.' The counter had a concealed door and he flicked a switch underneath to open it. 'Take a seat; I won't be long.'

'I can't thank you enough. You're so different from that woman at information,' she said, sitting on a stool beside his desk. 'It felt like talking to a robot.'

He glanced down at his notebook. 'That's Marg; she's due for retirement soon. Everyone gets like her when they've been here too long. It's self-defence from all the misery.'

'That's no excuse.'

'I guess not,' he shrugged, picking up the phone.

A bank of closed-circuit television monitors lined the back wall of the office. As Mia stared at them, she saw a familiar looking woman. When the woman turned her head, she recognised her. She jumped up and pointed at the screen.

'There she is. Look, on the balcony.'

The security officer put down the phone, studying the monitor. 'Are you sure?'

She squinted at the screen. 'Positive. It's her.'

He picked up the phone again and she listened to him giving directions. Minutes later another officer appeared on the monitor, walking towards Annie. She was leaning over the railing.

'I don't know what she's doing up there,' Mia said, flopping back on the stool.

The security officer crossed his arms. 'A lot of people go out for some fresh air, but we try to keep an eye on them. We sometimes get jumpers.' He nodded as Mia gasped. 'Unfortunately, we've had two in the last few years. We stopped the others in time. That's one of the reasons why the railings are so high and there's no furniture to stand on. It makes it harder to jump.'

'How awful. What would make someone want to do that?'

'It's usually bad news about themselves or someone close to them. They get caught up in the moment and their emotions take over. It's not common, though, most people only need to get out of the hospital environment for a little while.'

'Mum tripped and hurt herself on one of those balconies last year after my father died in the oncology ward. When I got here, they were patching her up in the emergency department. I missed saying goodbye to him. It was the worst day of my life.'

'So why is she back here now?'

'It's his first anniversary today. I guess she needed to come back one last time.' Mia thought of telling him about Annie's search for her dead husband, but changed her mind, glancing back at the monitor as her mother followed the other security officer into the hospital. A few minutes later they were standing at the counter. She seemed surprised when she saw Mia.

'Mum, I've been looking everywhere for you. You said you'd

be at the front entrance. I rang again. Didn't you listen to your voicemail?'

Annie bowed her head without answering. The officer with the crew cut looked at Mia, raising his eyebrows while he activated the switch to open the counter.

'Thanks for your help,' she said, joining her mother on the other side. Annie looked back and forth as they talked, hugging her shoulder bag.

'That's what we're here for. Will you be okay getting to the car park?'

'Actually, I'm out the front near the main entrance.'

'The silver sedan?'

Mia nodded, rubbing the back of her neck. 'I never expected to be so long. Sorry. Have I copped a ticket?'

'It's on your windscreen,' he smirked. 'We did make a couple of announcements for it to be moved.'

'I'm sorry, I missed them. Under the circumstances, would there be any chance you could tear it up?'

He shook his head and she grinned at him. 'I guess you can consider it a donation for my gratitude. She turned to her mother. 'Come on, Mum, it's time to go.'

'I'm parked in a side street; drop me off there,' Annie said when they reached the entrance doors.

'We can get it later. Right now, I think you need to get home.' When they walked outside, Mia looked across to her. 'Why were you up on the balcony?'

'How did you know I was there?'

'You were on a monitor in the security office. That's how I found you. So why were you there?'

Annie winced. 'I wanted to see an old friend again, someone you don't know.' The words caught in her throat. 'Leo's gone,' she whispered and Mia grabbed her hand.

'Yes, Mum, I know.'

The kitchen benchtops were piled with dirty dishes and a frying pan soaked in the sink. Mia wrinkled her nose as she filled the electric kettle, trying not to look at the pieces of food floating in the greasy water.

While the kettle boiled, she found a tray in the walk-in pantry, wiping off the crumbs with her sleeve. She glanced around, trying to take in the confusion of crockery and food packets scattered on the shelves. She pulled out an unopened bag of biscuits from behind a plastic canister and tore the cellophane, scooping out a few pink wafers.

When the tea was made, she tucked an envelope of travel documents between two mugs and went out to her mother on the back verandah. The crockery clattered as she slid the tray across a cane table.

'This is for you. It's such a sad day, but it might help,' she said, handing over the envelope as she sat down.

Annie turned it over. 'What is it?'

'Something special.'

She touched the illustration of a blue wren on the front of the envelope and looked at her daughter.

Mia smiled. 'It's like the one in your painting.'

'You remember.'

'How could I forget the first painting you ever exhibited? I must have been about ten and thought it was so cool having an artist in the family.'

'And I didn't know your father bought it until the next day when I saw it hanging in the dining room after the exhibition closed.' Annie's face lit up. 'I'd seen the red dot on the frame, but no one at the gallery would name the buyer.'

'I guess they were all in on Dad's surprise.'

'They sure were. I sold a lot of paintings after that. That bird became my lucky charm.'

'Whatever happened to it?'

'It went the way things go. I think it might be under the bed in Lucy's old bedroom.'

'I thought of it when I saw the envelope in the newsagency and couldn't resist it.'

'Sorry, I'm all thumbs today,' Annie said, fumbling with the seal. 'You open it for me.'

Mia tore the envelope, her smile strained as she unfolded the printed ticket. 'This is for you from me and Lucy,' she said, handing it back to her mother. 'We hope it will help after all you've been through. Lucy will be here soon, but she didn't want me to wait to give it to you.'

Annie recoiled, the ticket fluttering to her lap. 'I can't accept this. It's too much.'

'Mum, you deserve it. We've arranged for you to stay in London on the way to Paris and booked some lovely hotels in both cities. There's even a tour to Giverny. We know how much you love Monet's paintings. Remember when you did the art history course and would tell us about France?' She fished in the envelope again, trying to sound upbeat. 'Here are the vouchers for everything and an application for a passport. All you need are a few photos. You can get them done at the post office.'

'I can't be thinking of passports and trips away, especially to somewhere like Paris with all those terrorists.' She tossed the ticket on the tray. 'This is insane. Whose idea was this?'

'I forgot the milk,' Mia squeaked, jumping up from her chair.

'Don't change the subject.'

'I'll be back in a minute,' she called out, rushing inside to ring her sister. She glanced out through the screen door as she grabbed her phone. Her mother was still staring across at the ticket.

'Where are you?' she demanded when Lucy answered, pacing up and down the lounge room with her phone.

'I'm almost there. There's still plenty of time to get to the cemetery. How's Mum?'

'I'm not sure, I found her about an hour ago.'

'What's that mean?'

'I'll tell you later.'

'Have you given her the ticket?'

'Yes, a few minutes ago. She hates the idea.'

'I told you.'

Mia was filling a milk jug when Lucy walked into the kitchen and threw her bag on a benchtop.

'Fuck, look at this place; it's almost as bad as the garden.'

'You should see the rest of the house. Now I know why Mum always wants to meet at a café instead of at home.'

Lucy glanced over her shoulder. 'Where is she?'

'She was on the verandah, but I only looked out a minute ago and she wasn't there. She must be somewhere in the garden.'

'So, what's going on?'

'I'll tell you later.'

'You said that before, tell me now.'

Mia slid the jug on the table. 'When I rang to tell her we were coming over, she was at the hospital where Dad died. She was looking for him.'

'Far out.'

'I never expected this. It's terrible.' Mia crossed her arms and told Lucy what had happened. 'When that guy in security said people sometimes jump from those balconies, it made me wonder if she tried to do that last year.'

Lucy whistled, shaking her head. 'Do you think she went back today to finish the job?'

'I thought the same thing, but she seemed calm enough when I saw her. Maybe she only needed some fresh air. She said something about seeing an old friend. I'm not sure what she meant. It was all weird and I didn't want to ask too many questions.'

'What did she say on the way home?'

'Not much; she seemed exhausted. I think she's been in denial all year and the anniversary has forced her to accept what happened.'

'What about Paris?'

'I'm starting to think it's a huge mistake. You should've seen the horrified look on her face when I gave her the ticket. It's obvious she isn't in any shape to go away. While we've been plotting over tours and airfares, she's been going downhill.'

'I knew this wouldn't work. Didn't I tell you right at the start?'

Mia grimaced, reaching for the kettle. 'Don't start rubbing it in. Maybe we should let her think about it for a few days, but we may end up having to cancel the whole thing. You go out first; she asked about you on the way home. I'll make more tea.'

'I need something stronger than that.'

'Stop thinking about yourself.'

'Don't crack the shits with me because your big idea has gone arse up.'

'Go see Mum, will you?' Mia snapped, turning on the tap.

6

nnie watched Mia disappear into the house. She glanced across to the ticket; the flight was leaving in five weeks. Her heart raced as she pulled herself out of the deck chair, escaping to the garden. She lurched down to the ruins of the old woodshed near the back fence, flopping on a stump. Dappled rays of sun filtered through the branches of the gum tree above her as she sat camouflaged in the shaded corner of the garden.

A trail of ants marched around her feet while she stared at them like a benevolent giant hunched over on the stump. As they trekked over the carpet of dead gum leaves, she could hear a lawn mower whining somewhere down the street and children laughing on the other side of the fence.

She squinted up to a patch of blue sky in a corner of the gum tree's canopy, trying to make sense of what had happened earlier in the day. Although it was only mid-afternoon, she'd already behaved like a mad woman in a café before completely losing it at the hospital, almost swan diving off a balcony. Now a ticket to Paris. She sighed, wondering what could happen next.

She'd only planned to light a candle for Leo in the hospital chapel, knowing she could never face going to the cemetery, but she'd begun to unravel as soon as she parked in a side street near the entrance. Her knuckles had been white as she gripped the steering wheel battling for self-control. When she'd finally found the courage to go into the hospital, she'd stood frozen at the open door of the chapel, unable to step inside. She squirmed on the uncomfortable stump, remembering the flickering tea lights on the altar and her sudden realisation she'd returned to the place where her prayers had never been heard.

She peered down at the ants, unsure of how she'd ended up in the oncology ward. All she knew was the ward had felt like her true north and she had seemed to materialise there on the spot after she left the chapel. When she'd pushed open the ward's double doors, she had been swallowed by it all, sliding into another dimension.

She wiped away tears thinking of how she almost ended it all, fuelled by a tidal wave of sadness and the relentless nightmares chipping away at her night after night. 'Leo,' she whispered, 'will this day ever end?'

A twig snapped and Annie looked up from her perch on the stump as Lucy fought her way through the hydrangeas. The bushes pulled at her skirt, scattering tiny blue flowers in her wake. When she broke free, she staggered as she steadied herself in her stilettos on the uneven ground and wobbled towards her. Annie tried to smile and put out her arms.

'What are you doing down in this jungle?' Lucy asked, giving her a hug. 'You'll be eaten alive by mozzies.'

'I'm thinking. It's been an awful day.'

'Mia said you were at the hospital. You gave her a fright.'

'I don't want to talk about it.' She looked down at the shredded tissue on her lap. 'I want to forget it ever happened.'

'I'm not sure what you're referring to.'

'Don't interrogate me.' She started to cry again, wringing her hands.

'Come on, stop it or you'll get me started.' Lucy squatted down, facing her on the stump. 'I closed the shop early. I thought we'd all go to the cemetery and get flowers on the way.'

'I can't,' Annie whispered, wiping her cheeks. 'It's too sad.'

'It'll always be sad, but we have to go on together. There's no choice. We're all stuck here without Dad and he would want us to keep living for him.'

'I hate that stuff about moving on.'

'I didn't say move on, I said go on together.' Lucy shifted her weight to balance herself in the awkward position.

'Stop playing with words; it means the same thing. Moving on sounds like we've forgotten him.'

'We'll never forget him, you know that.'

'I hate the other word, too.'

'What word?'

'Closure. There'll never be closure.'

'Mum, my legs are killing me. I'm going to fall over if I don't stand up. Can we go back inside to talk about this?' Annie didn't answer her. 'You know, Mia and I aren't feeling too crash hot either. I think if one more person tells me time heals all wounds, I'll punch their lights out.'

Annie smiled through her tears. 'So, I'm not the only one hearing that.'

'No, you're not. Come on; Dad wouldn't want to see you down here like this.' She steadied herself and stood, pulling her mother to her feet. They walked back to the house arm in arm. Before they went up the verandah steps, Annie stopped and turned towards Lucy.

'I'm not going to Paris.'

7

A week later, Annie lugged a plastic basket of groceries around the supermarket, half listening to the monotonous music playing in the background. Crowded aisles were bathed in harsh light from fluorescent tubes strung across the rafters. She juggled the heavy basket from hand to hand as she browsed, trying to concentrate on the shelves in front of her. Nothing registered, only the airline ticket and the possibility of actually going away. The exhilarating idea of Paris competed with the shadow of grief and she was worn out from both extremes of emotion.

She was in the biscuit aisle examining a bottom shelf when she felt a tap on her shoulder and looked up into Jess's beady eyes.

'It's obvious you still have that sweet tooth; you've stacked it on,' Jess observed, pursing her lips. 'So how have you been? I haven't seen you in months. How's work?'

Annie stood, bracing herself for one of Jess's interrogations. Her nostrils twitched at the scent of mothballs clinging to the old woman's clothes. 'I'm having a year off,' she gulped, pressing her back against a shelf of chocolate biscuits.

'But it's more than a year now, isn't it? You know, since he passed over.'

'His name was Leo and it's been twelve months and one week.'

'Of course, I know his name,' Jess spluttered, fidgeting with her shopping list. 'I just didn't want to upset you.'

'How could his name upset me?'

'Still prickly, are we?'

Annie gave up. 'Yeah, like a cactus.'

'So, what do you do all day if you're not working?' The old woman tilted her head back, peering at Annie with one raised eyebrow. 'I guess you could try bingo on Mondays down at the community centre. It's not my cup of tea, but I'm sure you would love it. I've heard a lot of lonely people like you go there.'

Annie later wondered if it was Jess's smug expression or her tone of voice that made something in her mind slip sideways. Whatever the reason, she spoke without thinking. 'Actually, I'm getting a few things ready for a trip.'

'Where to?'

She tried to answer, but Jess talked over her. 'Harry and I only came back yesterday from two glorious weeks in Lakes Entrance.' By now her sharp features looked birdlike as Annie stared at the white whiskers on her chin. 'I wanted to ask you to collect our mail,' she babbled on, 'but I thought you wouldn't be up to it. We love a long road trip. I guess road trips are over for you now, you poor thing. Where could you possibly go, Rosebud?'

'Oh, I'm going a bit further than that. I'm going to Paris.'

Jess's top dentures momentarily dropped. 'Paris, France?'

Annie nodded. 'It won't be Lakes Entrance, but the weather will be just as glorious. It'll be spring. I'm staying in London for a few days to unwind after the flight.'

'Who's taking you?'

'No one, I'm quite capable of going alone. I might even get in some sketching at Giverny.'

'Giverny?'

'Monet lived there. You know the artist, Claude Monet?'

Jess jutted out her chin. 'Of course, he's the one who cut off his own ear. I have one of his paintings of sun flowers on a tea towel.'

'You have the wrong artist,' Annie grinned, her eyes dancing. 'Monet's famous for painting water lilies. Vincent Van Gogh painted sunflowers and cut off his ear. Although there's a new theory he may have lost his ear in a knife fight with another artist.'

'Sunflowers, water lilies, they're all the same,' Jess snapped. 'Don't let me keep you, I can see you're very busy.' She shoved her trolley and it took off down the aisle without her.

Annie laughed as she watched her chasing it. 'Bye,' she called out. 'I'll have a coffee for you on the Champs-Élysées.' She picked up the shopping basket at her feet, muttering to herself. 'Well that's done it.'

The deck chair on the verandah creaked as Annie eased into its folds of faded canvas, a glass of red wine in one hand and the long envelope in the other. She drained the glass before pulling out the airline ticket. If she didn't go now, Jess would never let her hear the end of it.

Her daughters wouldn't take back the ticket despite her protests and it had sat on her dressing table all week while she tried to ignore it. Each morning when she dragged herself out of bed drenched in sweat from another nightmare, the envelope with the blue wren was there, propped against the perfume bottles. At night as she curled under the doona fighting sleep, her last thoughts were of the streets of Paris she'd seen in her glossy art books now stacked somewhere in the garage.

She was still staring at the ticket when the phone inside rang. She rocked back and forth to pull herself out of the low-slung chair, finally rolling forward to her feet before hurrying into the kitchen.

'Yes, hello,' she whispered, perching on the stool by the sink.

'I'm so glad I caught you.'

'Who's this?'

'Muriel. Didn't you get my last two messages?'

'I haven't been checking my voicemail. Sorry.'

'I rang on Leo's anniversary and again a few days later.'

Annie looked at the greasy pots in the sink. 'I'm surprised you remembered.'

'Of course I remembered. I thought of you both on that day. I haven't seen you since the funeral. That's a whole year. When my emails bounced, I sent cards. Did you ever get them?'

'It's been a hard time. I closed my internet account months ago. The only mail I open is anything that looks like a bill. I just can't face anyone.'

'But we've been friends since we were kids.'

'There's no point trying to explain how it is, even to you.' Her voice drifted off as she looked out the window. 'Actually, there's no point in anything.'

Muriel persisted. 'I wanted to send roses on Leo's anniversary, but when I couldn't reach you, I thought you might have gone away.

I did come over about two months ago. I rang the bell, but there was no answer.'

'Well, I'm still here for now.'

'What do you mean?'

'I've done something really stupid and I don't know what to do about it.'

'Would you like to meet somewhere for a coffee? We could talk it over like old times.'

'I don't have the energy to go anywhere.'

'Put the kettle on; I'll be there soon with chocolates. Dark or white?'

Annie's mind raced, her ability to socialise even with those once close to her now gone. She shifted her weight on the stool, trying to think of a diversion.

Muriel interrupted her thoughts. 'Are you still there?'

'I'm thinking about the chocolates.'

'So, what will it be?'

'Do you have to ask?' she smiled.

'Dark it is. Get out the Earl Grey.'

'What about a red? I've raided Leo's wine rack.'

Annie stood at her bedroom window watching Muriel walk up the driveway. A multicoloured scarf wound around her neck matched her jeans and tunic. Long silver earrings glinted in the sun. When the doorbell rang, she hurried to answer it, checking her reflection in the hall mirror. She touched her round face, remembering Jess's cutting remarks in the supermarket. The doorbell rang again and she pulled in her stomach before opening the door.

Muriel burst in like a whirlwind. 'I've missed you so much.' She put down her basket and gave Annie a bear hug. 'I've brought chocolates and a lemon tart,' she grinned when she let her go. 'Do you think that's enough to keep us going while you tell me what you've done?'

Annie picked up the basket, closing the door. 'Let's go out on the back verandah.' She saw Muriel wince as they walked through the kitchen. 'Sorry the place is such a mess,' she offered. 'I can't seem to get my head around housework these days.'

8

Muriel frowned, taking another sip of wine. 'Never mind what you told your neighbour, how could going to Paris ever be stupid?'

'I've hated the idea since the girls gave me the ticket,' Annie shrugged. 'I don't know whatever possessed me to tell that old biddy I'm going when I've no intention of travelling anywhere. Somehow I've got to take back what I said.'

'Why would you want to reject this generous thing your girls have done for you? I loved Paris when I went and so will you.'

'I know you did, but I don't want to go. Why would I with all those mad terrorists running around? I'm really annoyed with them for doing this. They've paid for everything, but the damn trip has put me in a terrible position.'

'I can understand why you're spooked by those attacks in Paris, but you would be really unlucky to get caught up in something. Anyway, it could happen here too, and we can't let it change the way we live. Why are you so worried about this?'

'You wouldn't understand.'

'You know you can tell me anything.'

Annie stared across to the towels hanging limp on the clothesline in the still afternoon. Her eyes welled with tears when she looked back at Muriel. 'It feels like I'm being smothered by all the memories in this house.'

'What's that got to do with Paris?'

'I don't know myself anymore,' she whispered. 'I think I've gone a little crazy.' Her voice trailed off as she thought of the hospital balcony. 'I can't sleep and I spend most of my time in a fog. There's no way I could go anywhere, especially Paris, by myself.'

Muriel leant forward. 'Is the insomnia that bad?'

Annie glanced away, avoiding another confession. 'I keep waking up and only get a few hours' sleep each night.'

'It's grief playing with your head.'

'When my parents died so close together all those years ago, Leo helped me through it, but it was never like this. It's like part of me died with him. It's hard to explain this to you; you've never lost anyone.'

'Yes, I have; what about our stillborn baby girl?'

Annie blinked. 'I'm sorry, I don't know why I forgot. It was so long ago.'

'Exactly; life has gone on and to be precise it was twenty-five years ago. Each year on that day I imagine how we would've been celebrating her birthday.'

'You and Paul were so devastated.'

'And you were there to support us during that horrible time even though you never went through something like that yourself. I'm here now, like you were then. I haven't lost my husband, but I'm trying to understand.'

'Let's forget it.' Annie wriggled in her chair. 'I don't want to talk about this anymore.'

'Why are you acting like we're strangers? I've never seen you so withdrawn.' The question hit a raw nerve.

'Have you been talking to the girls?'

'No, but maybe I should.'

'Is that some kind of threat?' Annie demanded, twisting out of her chair.

'Why would I threaten you? For Christ's sake sit down; you're getting all fired up about nothing.' Annie started to cry, crumpling back in the chair and Muriel grabbed her hand. 'A lot of people love you to bits. We all loved Leo, too, but he's gone, and you have no choice now. You have to dust yourself off and keep going.'

'I'm sick of hearing that,' Annie sobbed. 'I'm sick of it.'

'But it's true and you have to listen. You need a break from all the sadness and your girls have given you that chance. You should sell up if it's so hard living here, but first you have to get away. It's time for some happiness.'

'But that's just it; I don't know how to be happy again. I feel like there's a hole right here in my chest and it won't go away.' She clenched her fist over her heart, tears streaming down her cheeks. 'I can't get over what happened. And I've thought about selling up, but I wouldn't know where to even start.'

Muriel dragged a chair next to her, putting an arm around her heaving shoulders. They sat huddled together, bound by grief. When the mournful sobs eventually stopped, Muriel stood, pulling out a small packet of tissues from her handbag. Annie looked up at her as she took one and blew her nose.

'I'm pretty screwed up, aren't I?'

'No, you're not; it's called being grief-stricken.'

'It's horrible; I feel like my life is over.'

'Unfortunately, you have to go through it all before you can get better. When I lost our baby, someone told me my grief was like wading through a stream. To get to the other side, I had to keep going. I couldn't turn back. Even after Jason came along two years later, I still felt like I was in the middle of the stream. I did get to the other side, but it took years.'

'I'll never get to the other side. I know it.'

'Yes, you will. You've already started.'

Annie began to speak, but stopped as Muriel sat down again, taking another sip of her wine. The lavender hedge in front of the verandah swarmed with bees in the hot sun. They sat listening to the buzzing symphony, both women lost in thought. Muriel finally broke the silence, reaching for the box of chocolates she'd brought with her.

'After we've knocked off a few of these, we should go out for a meal,' she said, fingering through the dark selection. 'What about that Indian place in Richmond?'

'I haven't been there since Leo got sick.'

'Let's go see if it's still there.' Muriel smiled, handing Annie a chocolate.

'We can have a vindaloo for Leo,' Annie sniffed, popping the large truffle into her mouth.

'Maybe we'll just have one for you since Leo isn't here.' The simple statement got an instant reaction.

Annie flushed hot with rage as she stood. 'I know he isn't here,' she shrieked, bits of chocolate spraying from her mouth. 'He's in the ground rotting, that's where he is. While you're sitting here lecturing me and downing his wine, another piece of him just turned to mush.'

Muriel jumped up, grabbing Annie's arm, the box of chocolates tumbling from her lap. 'Don't do this,' she begged.

'Leave me alone and go back to your perfect life.' Annie jerked her arm away. The glasses went flying as she crashed into the table on her way back inside.

She was leaning against the kitchen table sobbing into her hands when Muriel chased after her through the shards of glass.

'You can't get rid of me like this; we go back too far. Take down your hands and look at me,' Muriel demanded.

Annie shook her head.

'Okay, don't look at me, but I'm going to stand here anyway and tell you a few home truths whether you like it or not. You're so wrapped up in your own grief you aren't thinking of anyone else. You've never once mentioned how the girls must be feeling after losing their father. All you've done is berate them for trying to help you. You said you don't know who you are anymore and frankly neither do I.'

Annie turned, running from the kitchen.

'Ring me when you come to your senses,' Muriel called after her. 'I'll be waiting for the real Annie to come back.'

A streetlight filtered through the lace curtains in the dark bedroom. Annie rolled over on the creased doona and sat up, her body aching from sleeping in an awkward position. Her shoes were still on and she kicked them off before padding across to the window. She thought she'd heard a car door slam in her fitful sleep, but she couldn't be sure as she stared at the deserted driveway. Maybe it was all another nightmare.

When she went back to the kitchen, a light had been left on and the shattered wine glasses were in the bin. A note was propped against the untouched lemon tart. She read the brief message before screwing the paper into a ball, shoving it into her pocket. It wasn't a nightmare.

She squinted out to the dark garden, her dishevelled reflection in the uncovered window making her look away. Muriel's note said she would always be her friend, but Annie doubted if she could ever face her again. She plonked on the kitchen stool, dissecting their angry words while she unconsciously twirled a curl around one of her fingers. When the phone rang, she was still trying to focus through her haze of troubled thoughts.

Mia's voice sounded chirpy. 'How are you?'

'I'm fine; Muriel's been here.'

'There must have been a lot to catch up on. I know you haven't seen her since Dad's funeral.'

'How do you know that?'

'Didn't she tell you? I bumped into her at Parliament Station.'

Annie's eyes narrowed. 'She never mentioned it.'

'It was ages ago. We only stopped for a minute. I never thought to tell you.'

'So, you were talking about me.'

'Of course we were talking about you. Why do you make it sound like something nasty? She said she was worried about you.'

'What did you tell her?'

'I only said you were feeling low. I told her we all were.'

'Did you mention Paris?'

'Paris wasn't even on the radar then. We hardly said much; we were both in a hurry to catch a train. Why all the questions? Are you sure you're okay?'

'I'm as good as I'm going to get. And by the way, I've made a decision.'

'About Paris?'

Annie could hear anticipation in her daughter's voice, finally recognising her own ungratefulness.

'You're going,' Mia giggled. 'I can tell by your voice that you're going.'

'Yes, I'm going.' She touched Muriel's note in her pocket. 'And I don't think I mentioned it before, but I really appreciate what you've done for me. Both of you.'

'We thought you hated what we did. We've been really bummed out about it.'

'I never hated it,' Annie laughed, trying to hide her real feelings. 'I was only surprised.'

'When did you decide?'

'This afternoon in the biscuit aisle.'

'What?'

'I'll answer with another question. Why don't you come over? I have a lemon tart sitting here and I'll tell you everything while we eat it.'

'I could bring something else if you haven't had dinner yet. David's working tonight and I'm getting take-away. Any preferences?'

Annie smiled, pulling the crumpled note out of her pocket. 'What about a vindaloo? I'll steam some rice when you get here.'

'Make sure you don't start on that tart.'

'Don't be too long or I might. See you soon.'

She put down the phone and tossed the paper ball at the bin, watching it bounce on the rim before dropping on the broken glasses. Images of the emotional day spun around her as she made a mug of tea and went into the lounge room to wait for Mia.

Her paintings were on all the walls, the giant canvases overpowering the mishmash of furniture that once belonged to old friends and relatives. Leo had often referred to their home as a memory palace, although now as she looked around the claustrophobic room, it seemed more like the local op shop. She slumped on her mother's faded chintz couch. One of Leo's jumpers was draped over the back and she pulled it around her, snuggling into the soft wool. She sat sipping the tea, wondering why everything kept going so wrong.

9

The department store bustled with shoppers. Crowded escalators moved between floors while grim-faced staff served the throng milling around the sales tables.

'I've had enough,' Annie complained to Lucy as they stepped on one of the escalators. 'Can't we do this some other time?'

'We'd miss the sales.'

'So what? I don't need anything new.'

Lucy shook her head and sighed. 'Let's at least check the shoes before we go. We're here now so we may as well see if there's anything you like.'

Below them on the next floor, the shoe department was packed with bargain hunters rifling through the old summer stock. When the escalator reached ground level, they pushed their way to rows of tables stacked with shoes.

Annie tugged Lucy's sleeve. 'Have you ever seen anything so ridiculous? They look like they'll die if they don't find something.'

'You need to get out more. When was the last time you bought shoes?'

'I don't know, maybe a few years ago. I get mine repaired when they need it and they always come up good as new.'

Lucy looked down at her mother's yellow loafers. 'You can't go to Paris in those; they're gross.'

'No, they're not. They're comfortable and anyway, I like the colour.'

'Stop putting up objections; you need new shoes.'

'I'm not wearing heels like yours; I'd go over on my head in a minute.'

'Okay, flats.' Lucy pursed her lips. 'At least they're still fashionable. What about a classic ballet flat? They come in bright colours.'

'If they're in colours I might look,' Annie smiled.

Lucy grabbed her arm, steering her towards a seat near the bargain tables. 'Sit there and I'll go round up some designs and a bit of help. Don't move.'

'Stop talking to me like I'm a child.'

'Stop being so touchy,' Lucy called out as she headed across to a display stand.

An hour later they left with several carry bags slung over their arms. Annie chose two pairs of flats. The red ones were tight around her toes, but the shop assistant had convinced her they would loosen up. Although she'd initially rejected a second pair in black, she agreed to take them only to stop Lucy's constant needling.

'You didn't have to buy them for me, I'm not a charity case, you know,' Annie said as they walked back to the car park.

'Consider them an early birthday gift.'

'What, eight months early?'

'Whatever; just accept them, will you?'

'Thanks; I'll think of you every time I wear them.'

Lucy put her arm around her mother. 'Let's go get something to eat before we both faint,' she grinned. 'By the way, how did it go getting your passport sorted?'

'I had to pay an extra fee to have it fast-tracked. The woman in the post office wouldn't let me smile. I felt like a criminal getting a mugshot.'

Annie's leg jiggled under the table as she strained to hear a distorted announcement blaring somewhere in the airport. The sun had set more than an hour before and floodlights bounced off the wide-bodied planes lined up on the tarmac. Men in yellow fluorescent vests were loading baggage on board two of the planes. As she peered at all the action on the other side of the plate glass, Mia reached over her and put a paper cup on the table. Annie flinched, nearly knocking it over.

'Oh, Mum, you're not nervous, are you?'

'I just didn't see you coming,' she croaked, pulling off the plastic lid. 'But I have to admit I'm feeling a bit jittery.'

'You're probably excited,' Mia said, sitting across from her. 'You know, like a kid on Christmas Eve.'

Annie studied her daughter's hopeful face, deciding not to disappoint her. 'That must be it, that Christmas feeling,' she said, sipping her coffee.

'Lucy texted. She's on her way. She's only now found somewhere to park.'

Annie looked at the sea of people milling around them. 'I'm not surprised; look at the crowds. How can they all afford to travel?'

'They're probably maxing out their credit cards.'

'How crazy; can you imagine having a holiday on credit?' Annie stared at Mia rubbing the back of her neck. 'Is something wrong?'

'No, I'm fine,' Mia said. 'I hope you have a good book. It's a long trip and you'll probably get tired of the movies.'

'Never mind books and movies, I only hope there's not a repeat of what happened last time I flew.'

'Poor Dad.'

'What about me? I was so embarrassed,' Annie laughed.

'Hey, here comes Lucy.' Mia stood and waved at her sister as she sprinted across the concourse towards them, her long legs accentuated by her black stockings and short skirt. She looked like a crane about to take flight.

'What's the joke?' she asked when she reached them.

Mia grinned at Annie. 'Mum's telling me about the last time she flew.'

'And chucked all over Dad,' Lucy smirked, sliding on a chair and pushing a small package across the table.

'I did not,' Annie protested. 'I used a bag.'

'I heard a different story. A reliable source once told me you brought up your lunch all over his shoes before you found that bag.'

Mia waved her hands. 'Can we change the subject? Go on, Mum, open your gift.'

'This is too much,' Annie smiled at Lucy. 'Your sister surprised me with a lovely pashmina to match the red shoes you bought me. I feel so spoilt. I don't know why you both think I need anything new. I'm only an invisible woman of a certain age. No one will even notice me.'

Lucy rolled her eyes. 'That's a hell of a way to think.'

'Wait until *you're* over fifty.' She looked up at Lucy with a lop-sided smile, wrestling with the wrapping paper. 'Sorry, I'll get it in a minute.'

'What's wrong?' Lucy asked.

'She's excited,' Mia offered. 'Aren't you, Mum?'

'I guess so.' She tore the yellow paper and pulled out a map the size of a small envelope. When she unfolded it, she stared down at the streets of Paris. 'Now I won't get lost.'

'I bought it in one of those travel shops in the city since I knew that old phone of yours could never help you get around. There seemed no point to get one for just a weekend in London.' Lucy leant over the map. 'Let's see if we can find that little island in the river where you'll be staying.'

10

An hour later, Lucy could see their mother still standing near the sliding doors in front of international departures. They had already said their goodbyes a few minutes before.

Lucy put her hand on her hip. 'Why doesn't she go in?' As she and Mia stared across the teeming concourse, Annie turned and began walking away.

'Poor Mum, she looks upset,' Mia said, shaking her head. 'She must have forgotten something.'

'No, she hasn't,' Lucy snapped. 'I knew it, I just knew it, she's doing a runner. Hold this while I try to stop her.' She threw her handbag at Mia and bolted into the crowd. 'You'll miss your flight!' she shouted, her stilettos clicking on the tiles as Mia ran behind her. Annie heard her and hurried towards the exit. Lucy caught up, grabbing her mother's arm. 'This is mad; stop and talk to me.'

'Leave me alone,' Annie hissed, pulling away. 'I'm going home.'

'You can't; it's too late,' Lucy pleaded. They were beginning to attract attention.

Mia was out of breath when she reached them. 'Mum, where're you going?' she asked, gulping her words.

Lucy answered for her. 'Home, can you believe it?'

Mia took a step back. 'What? You can't. If you go home now, you'll never get over this.'

'Get over what?' Annie's face was pale.

'You know what I'm talking about. Do I have to spell it out here in front of half of Melbourne?'

People were gawking as Annie raised her voice. 'Why won't either of you listen to me? I never asked for this. You both assumed I would be thrilled, but I'm not. I've tried; God knows I've tried. No trip will ever fix what happened. It will be with me for the rest of my life. I can't go overseas; it's too much. And I'm not about to be dodging bullets from some terrorist in Paris.'

'That's no excuse. Cancer would be more likely to knock you off than a terrorist in Paris,' Lucy spat, her hands on her hips. 'Look at poor Dad; he knew all about it. You're like Alice down the rabbit hole. If you do this, you'll never crawl out again and we'll have blown a lot of money for nothing. The travel insurance will never cover it because you've changed your mind. So, go home, but don't expect me to drive you. I'm over it!' she shrieked. 'Over it. Do you hear me?'

Mia stomped her foot, shouting at them. 'Stop it! I can't take any more. No more.' She staggered sideways, and Lucy put an arm around her shoulders.

'What's wrong?'

'I need to find a seat.' She handed back Lucy's bag, lurching into the crowd.

'See what you've done?' Lucy glared at her mother. 'We give you Paris and you throw it in our faces.'

She turned away and Annie followed her. They found Mia curled over on a metal seat. Annie sat beside her, touching her long hair while Lucy stood with her arms crossed.

'I'm so sorry.'

Mia looked up, her cheeks wet with tears. 'The trip was all my idea. I got it wrong.'

'I hate seeing you like this. I'll go and won't make any more trouble. I've had stage fright, that's all,' Annie joked, smiling tremulously. 'I'm going to Paris and will run away with the first Frenchman who even looks sideways at me. You may never see me again.' She leant across and hugged Mia. 'I'll say *au revoir* now and see you both in three weeks if I don't find that Frenchman.'

'I love you,' Mia said as she held on to her mother. Annie nodded, kissing her cheek before she stood to face Lucy.

'Come on,' she croaked, pushing back her shoulders, 'you can give me an escort to customs.' She picked up her tote bag and started to run with Lucy trailing behind her. Two middle-aged women witnessing their argument smiled as they passed them. One of them started to clap, but her companion stopped her.

'Shit, you can move it when you want to,' Lucy panted, stopping to take off her stilettos to keep up. When they reached international departures, she hugged her mother. 'Safe trip. I'll see you in three weeks.'

'I can't believe what happened,' Annie wheezed, patting her chest. 'I'm so ashamed.'

'There's no time to talk. Keep going or you'll never clear customs in time.'

Annie tried to smile at her and walked towards the sliding doors. As they opened, she turned and waved, her chin quivering. Lucy put on her shoes as she watched her go.

<h1 style="text-align:center">11</h1>

Annie hesitated at the end of the boarding bridge, touching the fuselage before stepping inside the plane. It seemed she was going to Paris whether she liked it or not. A flight attendant standing at the door smiled across to her.

'Good evening,' she said, glancing at her boarding pass and passport. 'Turn right and you'll find your seat halfway down in the middle section of the cabin.'

The plane was a bustling microcosm as passengers filed down the aisles while music droned in the background. Annie held out her tote bag in front of her, trying to decipher the seat numbers in the dim light. Across the rows of seats, she could see the terminal lit up in the darkness. She looked out at people standing at the expanse of windows like fish in an aquarium as she kept searching for her seat. Inside a niggling voice tried to be heard.

She could still turn around and go home. No one would know if she hid in the house for three weeks. If she circled back around the next aisle, she could tell the flight attendant she'd forgotten something. The fantasy faded when she found her seat. She glanced at the seat number and back to the man sitting in front of her. He looked away, ignoring her.

'I'm sorry, I think this is my seat,' she squeaked.

He pursed his lips and hesitated before pulling out a briefcase from under the seat in front of him. Passengers waited behind her in the congested aisle as he stalled for time. When he eventually stood, he shrugged before moving down the row to a seat near a woman with a screaming toddler. She checked the number on her boarding pass again before easing herself into the aisle seat, unsure of what to do next.

She looked up at a tall young man rearranging bags in the locker across the aisle. 'There's still some room over here,' he smiled down at her. 'Would you like me to squeeze in your bag?'

'Thanks; it's a bit bulky to put under the seat.' She pulled out her pashmina and a paperback before handing it to him. 'Will my jacket fit in?'

He reached out and took it from her. 'I think that's about it. If you need anything during the flight, let me know and I'll get it down for you. I'm sitting over there.' He pointed to his seat as he banged the locker shut. 'I better sit down now before your neighbour gets any more ideas.' He nodded towards the man still clutching his briefcase as he scanned the cabin for an empty seat.

'I'd hurry if I were you,' she smiled before he turned away.

The young man reminded her of a grasshopper when he sat down, folding his long legs under the cramped economy seat. She sighed as she peeled off her shoulder bag. It seemed she'd reached the in-between age of either being invisible or looking like she needed rescuing like a little old lady. Fifty-six and fading fast, she thought. The girls would be organising aged care next.

* * *

The floral fabric of her skirt snapped around her body while she plummeted towards the roses. Peppercorn tree branches waved at her as she fell, her screams for forgiveness blown away on the wind.

'Madam, may I help you? Madam?'

Annie jumped, knocking her paperback off her lap. Her damp blouse stuck to her back as she leant forward, disorientated in the dark cabin. She twisted in her seat, trying to get her bearings. The flight attendant stooped down beside her, touching her arm.

'I think you may have been dreaming. You screamed.'

'I'm sorry. I hope I didn't disturb anyone.' Annie glanced sideways at the man who had tried to take her seat. He scowled back at her under his reading light. 'Where is the woman who was sitting next to me?'

'She's walking off a leg cramp. She'll be back soon. Would you like a hot hand towel and some tea?'

'That would be lovely.'

'I'll bring something sweet with the tea,' she said before turning into the darkness.

Annie leant on the armrest, covering her face with her hand. She peeked through her fingers at the young man across the aisle. He wore headphones as he watched a movie, clearly having missed the commotion. She picked up her paperback from the floor, fanning her face with it while she sat looking at the blank screen in front of her.

The flight attendant returned with a tray. 'Let me know if you need anything else.'

She started to ask for help with the controls of the entertainment system in her armrest, but changed her mind as the attendant smiled down at her. She was too tired to think straight, wiping her face instead with the hot towel. As she sipped her tea she thought of the argument in the airport. It seemed she couldn't get anything right.

The woman with the cramp limped by, grabbing the back of the headrests while she did another circuit of the cabin. Annie had no idea how much further it was to London, but she knew no matter what, she couldn't close her eyes again. She wriggled in her seat; it was going to be a long journey.

12

Flight attendants collected breakfast trays as dawn broke over England. Annie squinted across the aisle to a patch of grey sky in the tiny window. She pulled out a toiletries bag from the seat pocket, manoeuvred herself into the aisle and hobbled to a queue outside the toilets.

The young man from across the aisle stood at the end looking as dishevelled as she felt. A long coffee stain on the front of his denim jacket was testimony to the storm they had flown through after leaving Singapore.

'How did you go in the wild weather?' he asked when she stood behind him.

'I thought it would never end,' she rolled her eyes, 'but it wasn't as bad as I expected when they first announced it.' She couldn't tell him she rode out the storm wishing the plane would go down. She'd held on to the armrests of her seat with each violent shudder, hoping her miserable life would soon be over. When the plane stopped pitching, she felt disappointed.

He interrupted her morbid thoughts. 'Have you been to London before?'

'I've never been any further than Tasmania,' she said, shaking her head. He smiled down at her and she could see a fine sprinkling of freckles on his unshaven face.

'London's a great city; you'll like it. I have an annual gig there and this is a bit like catching a bus for me.'

'What do you do?'

'I'm an art lecturer. The uni where I work has a guest lecturing arrangement with one in London and I'm part of it.'

'How fascinating. I always wanted to study art history, but it never happened.'

'Why not?'

She grabbed the headrest of the seat next to her as the plane banked to the right. 'I did a short course at a local TAFE college, but then life got in the way. I guess I'm too old now.'

'Rubbish, you're never too old to learn. You should enrol in a university course.' They were now at the head of the queue. The toilet door opened and a woman brushed by them as they both moved forward. He stood aside as Annie looked up at him. 'You go in, I can wait,' he said.

'Old ladies first?'

'Hardly; not with your flaming red hair,' he laughed, putting out his arm and bowing. 'After you, Madam.'

His small gesture surprised her and she was still grinning as she closed the folding door. She put the toiletries bag on the stainless-steel sink, wincing at her reflection under the harsh light.

* * *

It took longer to get off the plane than she expected. Her feet were throbbing as she stood in the aisle, the seediness from the long-haul flight overwhelming. She hesitated when she stepped on the boarding bridge to the airport, sucking in cool air spiked with fumes of jet fuel. The other passengers hurried by her like they were in a marathon. She stood against the flimsy wall of the bridge to get out of their way while she put on her jacket.

When she trudged into the arrivals lounge, she could see them sprinting ahead of her towards customs with the young man in the denim jacket at the head of the pack. She kept squinting into the distance as she walked, the occasional straggler from her flight nodding as they went by.

With no end in sight, she slumped on a seat, light-headed with exhaustion. By now she was alone in the empty space facing an expanse of plate glass overlooking the overcast morning. She was still checking for any sign of life when she saw some of the crew from her flight walking towards her. A flight attendant peeled away from them when she saw her. Annie recognised her from the night before.

'Is something wrong?'

'That seems to be the story of my life. I'm lost.'

'You have to claim your bag and go through customs first, so you can't be lost. There's no other way out. You have to keep walking in that direction.' She pointed to the end of a long corridor. 'If you hop on the travelator over there it will be quicker. It's not much further. Would you like to come with me?'

'No thanks, I'll sit here a minute. My feet are killing me.'

'Sitting is the worst thing you can do. Try to keep moving and drink lots of water. You'll be right in no time.'

She smiled again and Annie watched her walk away, marvelling at her energy after such a long flight. She glanced at a large arrivals monitor as she stood. It was seven in the morning, but her body was telling her otherwise.

The black cabs waiting outside the terminal looked like old friends when she walked out into the cool morning. The well-known British icons were so familiar, she felt better as soon as she saw them. She walked to the front cab and a balding man with a grey goatee stepped out when he saw her.

'Good morning, Madam; where're you going?'

'I'm booked into a hotel in Knightsbridge.' She pulled out her itinerary and showed him the name of the hotel. He nodded, taking her suitcase. The cab's wide door made it easy for her to pile in with her bulging tote bag, while the driver slid her suitcase in next to her.

'It's so good to finally be here,' she said as she fastened her seat belt.

He slammed his door, turning on the ignition. 'Where're you from?'

'Australia. I've been travelling for about thirty hours, but it feels like I haven't slept for a week.'

He nodded without comment as he pulled out from the kerb, gliding along the side of the terminal. When they reached the main entrance of Heathrow, she was already asleep.

* * *

'Madam. Madam, we're here.'

Annie blinked at the driver staring down at her from the open door of the cab. Exhaustion had disabled her, and she couldn't comprehend what he said.

'I'm sorry, I can't seem to focus.'

He reached for her suitcase. 'It's quite common. You should move about and try to stay awake.'

'Someone already told me that, but I don't know how I'm going to do it.' She scrambled out of her seat as the driver got back in the cab.

'You need to pay me over here,' he said through his open window.

'Why?'

'That's how we do it in Britain.' He sounded annoyed and she slammed the passenger door, pulling out her wallet.

'How much?'

'Sixty-five pounds.'

She didn't try to calculate the amount in Australian dollars, handing over several notes. He counted out change for her and she looked down at the strange coins in her hand, unsure of what he gave her.

'It's correct,' he said, turning on the ignition.

'Yes, I'm sure it is. Thank you.' She slipped the coins in her pocket as a doorman appeared, taking her suitcase while she followed him into the hotel.

Annie's breath was a frosted patch on the window as she looked out at the view that resembled a film set. White terraces lined the street and several displayed the Union Jack, the vibrant colours contrasting against the façades. Each terrace had a black door and brass knocker with topiary shrubs on the front steps.

It was all so British. She was still smiling as she turned away to ring Mia. When she answered, Annie could hear her excitement on the other side of the world.

'Are you in the hotel yet?'

'I just arrived. It's lovely.'

'How did you go on the flight?'

She cringed, thinking of her death wish as the plane rolled through the clouds. It seemed Muriel was right; her perspective was too self-centred. 'No sick bags needed this time. It was a bit rough once, but I kept thinking of other things.'

'Well done, I'll let Lucy know. Text us when you get to Paris; it'll save money.'

'I'm not very good at it. It takes me ages.'

'You'll be an expert by the time you get back. Everything will be cool. Don't worry.'

'It's only nine in the morning here. Everyone keeps telling me to walk and stay awake. You should see the size of my feet. They look like they belong to an elephant. I don't know how I'm going to do it.'

'Get on one of those open-top tourist buses. I did that when I was there. Somehow, I managed to stay awake all day. Hotel reception will tell you where to find one.'

'Thanks for the tip.' She sat on the edge of the bed. 'Before I go, I want to apologise for what happened at the airport.'

'Don't worry about it.'

'I don't know what came over me. Maybe the fear of flying.'

'Forget it and enjoy yourself.'

'You're very understanding.' The image of herself on the hospital balcony came out of nowhere as she listened to Mia's voice. An urgent need to tell her dark secret washed over her as she clutched her phone.

'Mum, are you still there?'

Annie blinked, dragging her thoughts back from the balcony. 'Sorry, must be the jet lag. I'm a bit out of it. I think I'll have a shower now before I go find one of those buses. Give Lucy and David my love.'

'Will do. Talk soon. Love you. Bye.'

She threw the phone on the bed, shaking her head. Mia sounded like she was already texting. She went back to the window, looking down at the foreign streetscape, but her thoughts were still at home.

13

The open-top bus swayed along Oxford Street while lunchtime crowds swarmed through the city, a sea of dark colours with the odd renegade in orange or red. As Annie looked down at them from the top deck, it seemed incredible to her she'd only left Melbourne the day before. She smiled when she thought of sitting on her suitcase trying to get it to close while Mia and Lucy waited in the lounge room. Now the dilemma of her bulging luggage seemed silly.

She listened to a running commentary through a pair of earphones while the bus crawled through the traffic. Many of the street names were the same ones from a board game her daughters played when they were young and she smiled, recognising the famous landmarks passing by.

She felt disjointed, like she was watching herself sitting on the bus while the backdrop of London slid by. The small part of her that could still focus fought to stay alert, but her body kept rebelling. The map of London she was given with the bus ticket blurred while she tried to follow the route. She eventually surrendered to the fatigue, too tired to care about where the bus was going. All she could do was keep her eyes open while it did laps of the city.

'Is anyone sitting here?'

She looked up at an old man in a baggy pinstriped suit gesturing towards the empty space next to her. He gripped the back of the seat as the bus lurched forward, almost stumbling before regaining his balance. She smiled and he eased down beside her.

'What a view from up here,' he wheezed, taking off his felt hat and smoothing his thick crop of white hair. 'It's worth the climb.'

She pulled out her earphones. 'Pardon?'

'I said it's worth the climb,' he shouted.

'Sorry, I couldn't hear you properly with these in,' she apologised, holding up the earphones. 'I'm not hard of hearing, I was listening to the commentary.'

'Oh, is that what these little gadgets are for? The lad selling tickets gave them to me.' He held up a small plastic bag.

'You can plug them in to hear information about what you're seeing.'

He fumbled with the bag, picking at the plastic with his arthritic fingers.

She pursed her lips as she watched him. 'Would you like me to unwrap them for you?'

'Thanks, lass, this is a bit fiddly for me,' he said, handing her the bag.

She slid the earphones out of the plastic, plugging the cord into a socket at the side of his seat. 'Now all you have to do is stick them in your ears,' she said, handing them back to him.

'What about my hearing aids?'

She tried to reply, her jet-lagged brain screaming for sleep. He looked at her, waiting for an answer.

'I guess you could either take them out or not use the earphones,' she eventually said. 'But to tell the truth, it's all too much information anyway. You're probably better off sitting back and enjoying the view. That's what I'm going to do now.'

'Sounds like a good idea to me.' He unplugged the earphones and dangled them in front of her. 'Here, you keep them.'

She laughed as she took them from him. 'I don't think I'll be needing two pairs.' She wrapped the tangle of cords around her own, shoving them down the side of the seat. The old man coughed and she could hear him wheezing. He smelled like tobacco and talcum powder.

'I'm not from around these parts,' he said, fidgeting with his hat. 'Don't like this city much, but my son and his family live here.'

'Where're you from?'

'A long way from here; you've probably never heard of it.'

She smiled at his broad accent. 'I may have. I'm an Australian, too.'

He grinned across at her and she could see laugh lines crinkle around his watery blue eyes. 'Go on, I didn't pick up your accent at all. Must be the jet lag. If you ask me, it doesn't need a fancy name. It's plain old lack of sleep.'

'It seems we're both in the same boat,' she grinned. 'I haven't slept much since I left Melbourne yesterday.'

'You better get some shut eye before you fall over.'

'I'm trying to last until the sun goes down.'

'Still a bit of time to go,' he said, glancing at his watch.

She smiled at him. 'So, where're you from?'

'Me? Oh, I'm from Horsham,' he wheezed.

'In the Wimmera.'

'That's right, lass. I arrived a few days ago, but I'm still knocked from the trip. I don't think I'll be coming back again.'

'Did you travel alone?'

'Yeah, my daughter put me on the plane and my son met me at this end. I'm here to see the grandkids, but the trip's too long. They're all teenagers now and old enough to come see me next time. Don't know how they would go in the bush, though; they're real Poms now.'

'Weren't they born here?'

He shook his head. 'They were very young when my son and his wife came to London for work. They don't remember Australia and I doubt if any of them will be coming home again. At least not in my lifetime.' He looked down at his hat and Annie could see fatigue etched across his face.

She draped her pashmina around her shoulders as the bus swayed past Hyde Park, the trees a picture postcard with their spring leaves. She had never believed the European light could be so different from the harsh glare she was used to. Now she could see for herself how diffuse the sun was, hanging in the hazy sky like a lantern that had been dimmed.

'It's all so lovely; look at the beautiful shades of green.' She glanced back at the old man when he didn't answer. He'd dozed off and she smiled, fighting her own fatigue as she listened to him quietly snoring with his chin on his chest.

A passing parade of tourists scrambled on and off the bus while it trundled between stops. Many of the passengers sitting near her hung over the side taking photos and as soon as they left, more tourists doing the same thing took their place.

She was now numb with exhaustion, lulled into a trance-like state from the swaying movement of the bus. Her throbbing feet looked like they were about to explode out of the confines of her new shoes, bulging over the red leather. She moved her legs to get comfortable, but no amount of flexing seemed to help.

The old man woke up when they passed Trafalgar Square. He snorted, blinked and cleared his throat. 'Did I snore?' he asked, fingering the hat on his lap. She laughed and he looked sheepish. 'I did. Sorry.'

'No, honestly, I didn't hear you. I think I may have fallen asleep myself. We're a fine pair.'

'What's your name, lass?'

'Annie Green.'

'I'm Bill Jenkins.' He put out a gnarled hand and shook hers before looking at his watch. 'I have to meet my son soon. He told me to get off near Big Ben. Did I miss the stop?'

'No, I don't think so. Let's have a look.' She unfolded the map on her lap, tracing the route with her finger. 'According to this, it's not much further.'

'Well, it's been good meeting someone from home. How long will you be here?'

'Only for the weekend, I'm leaving Monday for Paris.'

'Hope you like rich food.'

'You've been there?'

'No, but my wife went once with our daughter. She didn't like the food much.'

'Why didn't you go with them?'

'Couldn't leave the farm then, but by gee I wish I had. It's too late now.'

He took out his handkerchief and blew his nose. When he looked back at her there were tears in his eyes. Annie impulsively patted his hand.

'I understand; me too.'

'Yeah?'

She looked down at the street and nodded.

'How long ago?'

'Only a year.'

'It's six months for me,' he said, running his fingers around the rim of his hat. 'We were supposed to make this trip together. Mary was looking forward to seeing the grandkids.'

'I'm so sorry.'

'That's the way it is,' he whispered, shaking his head. 'You can't change anything.'

They sat in silence until she glanced back at the map. 'Bill, I think your stop is next.'

He blew his nose again and tucked the handkerchief in the top pocket of his jacket before putting on his hat. 'Enjoy Paris, lass, and try not to look back.' He struggled to his feet, hanging on to the seat as the bus shuddered to a stop.

'And you enjoy your family,' she said, her voice unexpectedly catching with emotion. 'Be careful with those steps.'

He turned down the aisle and she could see a collection of threads hanging from his ill-fitting jacket. She watched him make his way along the top deck, hanging on to the seats before disappearing down a spiral staircase to the street. When he reached the footpath, he looked up and she waved over the side of the bus. He lifted his hat to her, waving it above his head until the bus drove off.

A door banging in the hall outside her room brought Annie back from the hospital balcony and the rose garden rushing towards her. The nightmare had followed her to London and she was powerless to stop it. She sat bolt upright, her heart thumping. She swung her legs over the side of the bed, listening to her own ragged breathing in the shadows.

The glow from city lights filtered through the sheer curtains while she hovered between the confused state of the dream and her awareness of the hotel room. She turned on the bedside lamp and the rose garden evaporated in a pool of yellow light. When her pulse stopped racing, she limped across to the bathroom, the cold tiles soothing on her still swollen feet. She turned on the shower and sat on the toilet while the room filled with steam, trying to focus on what was coming later.

Although the alarm on her travel clock was set for seven, she was dressed and repacked by five o'clock. The clock had been used on all the family camping trips, still keeping perfect time even though its black leather case was now worn. She plumped up the pillows and flopped back on the bed, folding her arms across her chest. It was too early to go downstairs for breakfast and too dark to walk across to Hyde Park. Paris was only hours away and it felt like she was about to catch a train from Melbourne to Bendigo. But this wasn't going to be Bendigo; this was Paris, and she didn't know how she would ever survive it.

She stared at the ceiling thinking of how Leo had faced the unknown. Even though he'd been so ill, he'd insisted on building a small picket fence for their vegetable patch. It had taken him two months, although under normal circumstances it would have been a weekend project. Most days he could only nail up one picket and other days he'd been too sick to even go into the garden. They had celebrated when the fence was finished, drinking sweet tea in the sunshine, buoyed by his triumph. After that, the idea of one picket a day became their mantra to get through the ordeal facing them.

Not long after he'd died, she found his diary with notations about the fence along with dates of his medical appointments. She'd sat crying as she read about the progress of the fence along with his gruelling schedule of medical treatments and procedures. Afterwards, she'd picked an armful of flowers from the garden, propping them against the fence that was a symbol of his bravery in the midst of such hopelessness.

The muffled sounds of London outside the window drew her back from the lesson of the fence to her hotel room. Facing three weeks in Paris would never be like what Leo confronted. She closed her eyes and didn't wake up until the alarm clock buzzed two hours later.

14

An announcement blared in the busy train station. 'Attention, the eleven o'clock train to Paris is now boarding on platform five.' Even before it was repeated again in French, a large group of passengers seemed to rise off their seats as one, hurrying towards the escalators. Annie followed them, struggling with her heavy suitcase and the tote bag she now wished she'd left at home.

She teetered on the edge of one of the metal steps trying to balance her bags as she was propelled upwards. Behind her, the departures area of St Pancras International still thronged with travellers. From her position high on the escalator, she could see the enormity of the renovated heritage station with its brick walls, polished floors, and steel beams. It resembled an industrial style art gallery, and she couldn't help comparing it with shabby Flinders Street Station back home in Melbourne. The image of two old ladies, one with a facelift and gleaming veneers, the other with a sagging face and discoloured smile crossed her mind as she looked over her shoulder.

The speeding escalator spat her out on a long platform where the train was already a hub of activity. When she found her carriage, she assumed a porter would be there to lift her heavy suitcase. After several passengers brushed past her with their luggage, it was obvious there would be no one to help her.

She heaved the suitcase on board, silently cursing Lucy for talking her into taking so many clothes. As she wrestled with it, her tote bag toppled over scattering its contents in the doorway of the carriage and spilling out on the platform. A framed photo of Leo skidded across the cement along with her paperback and several sample toiletries from the hotel. A woman walking by retrieved the photo and book, handing them back to her as she stepped down on the platform.

'Thanks so much, I'm not too good at juggling.'

The woman nodded and said something in French before turning away.

Annie shook her head, the encounter a preview of how Paris would be, her smiling like an idiot not understanding what anyone said. The muscles in her shoulders began to knot as she picked up the toiletries and climbed back on the train. She scooped up her upended tote bag still in the doorway, dragging her suitcase to the baggage compartment near the door.

A shelf above her head was the only storage space left. Her heart raced as she looked up at it, her face prickling with heat. A pimply teenager with an overnight bag walked in on her growing anxiety. He towered over her and although they were nearly touching in the confined space, he ignored her as he searched for somewhere to put his bag.

'Excuse me,' she said, 'I need some help.' He seemed annoyed, but she persisted. 'I have to put my case up there. Could you please help me?' She pointed to the top shelf and when he didn't respond, she tried again. 'Do you speak English?'

He glared down at her through his long fringe. 'Of course,' he snapped.

'Well, can you give me a hand?' She could hear her own quivering voice. He silently grabbed her suitcase and lifted it on to the shelf, not bothering to push it in place. 'Thank you,' she croaked, as he wedged his own bag next to hers. He didn't answer, flipping his long fringe to one side with a toss of his head before disappearing through a sliding door into the carriage.

She stood willing herself not to run from the train, knowing there would be nowhere to go if she left. No taxi would be waiting at the front to whisk her back to the safety of her home. She blinked away tears thinking of the angry scene at Melbourne Airport. A man wearing a blue uniform smiled at her as she reached in her pocket for a tissue. She could smell a hint of aftershave as he came closer.

'Good morning, Madame; may I help you find your seat?' he asked with a thick French accent.

She tried to smile, handing him her ticket. He glanced at her seat number before motioning towards the sliding door with an outstretched arm. She picked up her tote bag and followed him into the carriage, her knees weak from stress.

She sat back in the roomy seat, glancing down the long aisle of the carriage. Double seats were on one side and singles on her side, most facing in the same direction. The double seats facing each other seemed to be occupied by people travelling together. She could hear their animated conversations as they pulled out books and laptops. Some passengers were still finding their seats while the attendant bustled up and down the aisle. He stopped and leant over when he noticed her.

'We'll be serving lunch soon, so relax while we get underway.' He turned to leave before hesitating, looking back at her again. 'Are you better now?' he whispered.

She nodded up at him before he hurried away, staring down at her hands when he left. It seemed she'd become so pathetic, complete strangers were always asking after her welfare.

The train began to move and she looked out at the station gliding by her window. As it picked up speed, her phone rang and the man across the aisle sat forward, glaring at her.

'I'm not putting up with this,' he barked, his voice booming above the noise of the train. 'It should be compulsory for all phones to be turned off on this service.'

She crouched down in her seat when she heard Lucy's voice, turning away from the aisle. 'You'll be happy to know I'm on my way to Paris.' She could hear Lucy laughing as she looked up into the flushed face of the man from across the aisle now standing by her seat. His eyes were slits of anger under his bushy eyebrows.

'Do you mind?' he asked in a clipped British accent.

'Pardon?'

He pointed to her phone. 'You're disturbing me and my son.' He snapped his fingers at her. 'Turn it off.'

'Lucy, there's terrible coverage here,' she whispered into the phone, her cheeks on fire as she backed into the corner of her seat. 'I'll ring back later.' The man was now swaying over her while he tried to keep his balance in the rocking carriage. She clicked off the phone and dropped it in her shoulder bag. 'That was my daughter in Australia,' she offered.

'Australia,' he sniffed, making it sound like something distasteful. The carriage pitched to the side and he almost lost his footing before staggering back across the aisle, collapsing on his seat. 'She's an Australian,' he sneered to his son. 'Typical.' He pulled out a newspaper from the side of his seat, unfolding it with a flourish to make his point.

Annie leant forward, pretending to reach in her tote bag so she could steal a second look at him. She recognised his son, smirking at her through his long fringe. She sat back in her seat, trying to hide from his line of vision. As the train clattered through the outskirts of London, she closed her eyes, longing for the pungent scent of the gum tree in the back corner of her garden.

The train was at full throttle, the green fields of Kent a blur as she leant on the armrest looking out the window. She'd finished a salad and cold roast beef, the meal surprisingly tasty compared to the food on the plane. Her red wine jiggled in a glass on the pull-down tray in front of her.

She tried not to look at the man across from her, but it was impossible to ignore him. He complained to his son about the food, the quality of service and the size of the seats, making sure everyone around him knew how he felt. His accent reminded her of a toff from a British film.

Four rows up, two small children wriggled in their seats, kicking their legs and banging on their window. She could see their mother trying to distract them with books while their father read a newspaper, oblivious to their rowdy behaviour. As she reached for her wine, a bread roll came flying over the seats landing in the aisle followed by a piece of cheese. The children were now in their element, laughing as they threw food at each other. Their mother tried to stop them as they pelted bread rolls into the aisle. Annie smiled while she sipped her wine, glancing at the man across the aisle. He looked like he was about to explode.

'This is intolerable. The CEO will be hearing from me about this,' he bellowed. He threw his napkin on his tray while his son lounged down in his seat staring out the window, looking bored with his father's latest outburst.

She had a clear view of the young family. Food littered the floor under their seats, along with an assortment of toys and games. The little girl began stripping off her clothes and as quickly as something came off, her mother put it back on again. Finally, she stood, herding the children down the aisle.

Their amusing antics were more interesting than the Channel Tunnel they were now passing through and by the time the train emerged into France, the mother and her children had returned to the carriage. The little girl ran down the aisle wearing only her pink knickers, while her brother pretended to be a lion. The man across the aisle slammed down his wine glass when the little boy roared in his ear. Annie smiled; if ever there was swift justice, this was it.

'I give up,' the mother muttered on the way back to their seats. 'Only another hour to go.'

The French countryside flashed by as the train sped on to Paris. Annie could see old farmhouses with patchwork fields of yellows and greens. Quaint villages flew past, their stone buildings and gothic church spires like nothing she'd ever seen in Australia.

'Madame, would you like some coffee?'

She looked up at the attendant holding a silver pot. 'Thanks for your help today,' she smiled. Before he could answer her, the man across the aisle made his presence felt.

'I want tea. English tea, none of that French rubbish.'

The attendant grimaced before he turned around. 'Certainly, Sir. If you don't mind waiting a moment, one of my colleagues will be here to serve you. She'll be able to offer you several varieties of tea.'

The man gave an exaggerated sigh, reminding Annie of a balloon deflating. 'If she doesn't hurry up, we'll be in Paris before I get it.'

The attendant turned back to her and smiled, filling her empty cup. 'Thank you, Madame, it's been a pleasure to help you.'

A few seats away, the frazzled mother was still trying to tame her children. Annie stifled a giggle; the whole journey was like a farce, reminding her she hadn't seen the funny side of anything for a long time. She pulled out her phone, leaning across the aisle.

'Excuse me, I'm ringing back my daughter now. The one in Australia.' The man puffed out his cheeks and she sat back in her seat before he could answer her. A young woman carrying a teapot walked up the aisle, distracting him.

'May I offer you some tea, Sir?'

'Is it English?'

'Of course,' she smiled broadly. 'We always have English tea on board.'

Annie heard him grunt as she rang Lucy.

15

Passengers from Annie's train marched across Gare du Nord platform, a chorus of luggage wheels humming in the bustling station. She didn't know where they were leading her as she tried to keep up with them. Her suitcase kept tilting and she stopped several times to realign it, all the while checking where the crowd ahead of her was going. Behind her she could hear the children from her carriage chattering above the noise of the station. She smiled when she heard the little boy's roars.

Not far ahead were the man and his son powering through the crowd with no regard for anyone else's personal space. She saw the man clip a woman with his briefcase, oblivious to what he'd done. When they reached the end of the platform, a man in a grey uniform and matching peaked cap took their bags as they followed him out of the station.

The majority of the other passengers turned right at the end of the platform. She hurried to catch up, following them through a bank of doors at the side of the station. Outside, a man in a black uniform was directing a convoy of taxis picking up passengers.

A long queue stretched under a white awning and although there seemed to be at least fifty people in front of her, it moved at a steady pace. When she took her place under the awning, she stood behind an American woman complaining about Paris to a young man in the queue.

'I can't wait to get on that plane today,' she whined.

'So why are you waiting for a taxi here?' he asked, his soft American accent a contrast to her grating voice.

'I tried to call one from my hotel, but they kept jabbering in French and I gave up. I didn't even try asking the stuck-up concierge for help. I knew there were plenty of taxis here. I've seen them picking up all the poor suckers getting off the train from London. Like it's so crazy, hardly anyone speaks English,' she told him. 'This place is a joke.'

Annie glanced across to the young man. A canvas bag was draped over his shoulder with a small logo of an American flag embroidered on the strap. She tried to ignore the conversation as she watched the stream of taxis, but it was impossible not to overhear them.

The young man shifted his bag to his other shoulder. 'I've only arrived, but I think I got ripped off buying a coffee. It was pretty pricey,' he offered, rubbing the stubble on his face.

His comment set the woman off again. 'Take it from me, this place will fleece you. And let me warn you,' she said, leaning closer to him, 'they drive like maniacs and everything is very expensive, not just the coffee. The food's awful. I was served raw hamburger meat one night. It was disgusting. Be very careful what you order.'

'Isn't French food the best in the world?'

She put her hand on her hip, jutting out her chin. 'Where'd you hear that?'

'I read it in a travel book.'

'Don't believe everything you read.'

A black taxi slid next to the kerb and the man directing the convoy waved at the American woman now at the head of the queue. He pointed to the car and she pulled up the expanding handle of her pink suitcase, smiling across to the young man.

'Good luck; you'll need it.' She didn't wait for an answer, flouncing off to the taxi wheeling her suitcase beside her.

The young American shoved his hands in the pockets of his jacket and turned to Annie. 'She isn't happy. Oh sorry, do you speak English?'

She nodded.

'I'm one of those suckers from the train,' he laughed. 'What about you?'

'I was on the same train, so I suppose I'm one, too.'

'Where're you from?'

'Australia.'

'You're an Aussie.'

'I guess I am,' she grinned.

'Long way to Europe, isn't it? I'm glad I took a break in London.'

'Where did you come from?'

'New York. It took me almost eight hours.'

'Is that all?'

'How long was it from Australia?'

'Almost twenty-three hours in the air plus the time waiting around between flights. I guess about thirty hours.'

'Are you kidding?'

She laughed at the expression on his face. 'Absolutely not.'

The man directing taxis waved and pointed at a silver car stopped in front of them.

'I guess this is mine.'

'Don't believe everything you hear,' she smiled. 'I'm sure Paris will be lovely.'

He waved before turning away.

The next taxi was for Annie. A man as tall as a basketball player climbed out of a small sedan and walked towards her.

'*Quel hôtel?*'

Annie's light-hearted mood vanished. She fished in her shoulder bag and pulled out her small phrase book, reading the words she'd scrawled on the back flap. '*Excusez-moi, je ne parle pas Francais, je suis Australienne.*' The foreign words sounded wrong and the driver looked amused as she stumbled over them.

'Ah, *Australie*,' he grinned. 'What hotel are you staying at?' he asked in perfect English.

She swallowed her rising panic. 'It's on one of the small islands in the Seine River.'

'*Île Saint-Louis?*'

She nodded, handing him the name of the hotel with a map Mia had downloaded from the internet.

He glanced at the name of the hotel. 'No need for the map,' he said, giving it back and opening the taxi door for her. 'I know where it's at.'

'You're a lot better than the taxi drivers where I come from. They can't move without a GPS,' she said, sliding across the backseat while he put her suitcase in the boot. She dumped her tote bag on the floor between her ankles, fastening her seatbelt as he steered into the traffic and noise of Paris.

When they turned the corner and stopped at a red light, she could see the American woman from the station in the back of a taxi. A frown pinched her face as she stared out the window. After the light blinked to green, the woman's taxi disappeared into the next lane while Annie was propelled in the opposite direction into a foreign world.

Annie stood on the kerb in front of the hotel as her taxi drove away. She watched it turn the corner at the end of the narrow street, battling an irrational sense of abandonment. She looked up at the hotel's distinctive red awnings and opened the glass door with her trembling hand. Inside, she could smell gardenias as she wheeled her suitcase across the foyer. They were in black ceramic pots positioned in a row on a polished table, their blooms so perfect they looked artificial. The heady fragrance reminded her of the gardenias growing in the shade of her back verandah.

The hotel foyer overlooked a courtyard with a mosaic fountain lit by a light well. It gave the space a distinctly Portuguese style, although the furnishings on the other side of the glass wall were unmistakably French. Ancient beams stretched across the high ceiling and a stone staircase with a wrought-iron banister spiralled upwards from a corner near the courtyard.

A young woman in a black suit looked up from her desk when Annie closed the glass door. '*Bonjour Madame, bienvenue à Paris, avez-vous une réservation?*' Annie opened the flap of her shoulder bag, rifling through the contents. 'I'm sorry, I don't speak French and I can't find my phrase book.'

The young woman walked across to her. 'I speak English, can I help you?'

'I … I have a reservation from a travel agency in Australia,' she stammered, blinking back tears. 'I'm here for three weeks.'

The young woman went back to the desk and checked her computer. 'Are you Madame Green from Melbourne?'

'Yes, that's me.' Annie's knees began to buckle, the roller coaster ride of the past five weeks now taking its toll. She flopped on the chair beside the desk, trying to steady her trembling hands. A look of concern flashed across the French woman's face.

'It's been a long trip,' Annie whispered.

'We have you here until April 16 in a single room. Do you want to have breakfast at the hotel?' Annie shook her head, unable to understand the woman's thick French accent.

'Sorry, I'm not quite myself. What did you say?'

'The young woman repeated her question, slowly enunciating each word while Annie nodded.

'I guess I'll have to eat somewhere.'

'It's fourteen euros and not included with the cost of your room.'

Annie tried to calculate the amount in Australian dollars while the woman waited for an answer. 'That sounds good,' she finally said.

'Fine, I'll organise it for you. Armand will help you with your luggage. Please return the key each time you leave the hotel.' The woman smiled, handing her a key on a brass knob. 'If you need any assistance, let me know. My name is Colette.'

Annie stood, her legs still wobbly as a man in a black uniform walked across the foyer and picked up her suitcase. He smiled at her and she followed him to a lift. When its decorative wire doors opened, they stepped inside, standing side by side in the cramped space. Their reflections in a three-sided mirror were distorted under the harsh spotlights. Armand stared down at her suitcase in silence while Annie fidgeted with the buttons on her cardigan as the lift creaked its way up.

It was obvious to her that Armand couldn't speak English. After they reached the third-floor landing, he pointed to her room and opened the door before putting her suitcase on a small bench by the window. She didn't have any coins, realising too late she couldn't give him a tip.

'I'm sorry; no euros,' she said, throwing her tote bag on a chair and holding out her hand. Armand nodded as he backed out of the room, quietly closing the door and she wasn't sure if he understood what she meant.

The room was small, but stylish. Oak beams arched high above her and a tall window with a decorative wrought-iron railing overlooked the street. When she turned the window's metal handle, two glass panels opened inwards and she could see tourists shopping in the narrow street below. Somewhere a siren wailed with a distinctive European sing-song sound.

She turned from the window, digging in her tote bag for Leo's favourite jumper. She tucked it under the pillow before standing his photo on the bedside table along with her travel clock. The room now seemed more like hers. She sat on the bed, tugging off her shoes and wiggling her toes.

The white lace curtains fluttered in the open window, the movement of air cool on her face. She fell back on the toile bedspread looking up at the oak beams while she listened to the sounds drifting up from the street. There could be no turning back now.

* * *

The Notre-Dame bells were ringing. The sound was mournful and uplifting all at the same time. Annie stood on one of the bridges near her hotel watching the Seine drift by. The river was dark green in the brilliant sunshine. She pulled out Lucy's map of Paris and spread it out on the stone balustrade in front of her, tracing the grand boulevards with her index finger. According to the map, the bridge she was standing on was called Pont Marie. She repeated the name aloud, trying to sound French without any success.

After three days in Paris, she still hadn't ventured from the island. Each time she tried to cross one of the bridges linking Île Saint-Louis to the left or right banks, she froze, unable to make the final step to the city she now longed to explore. She'd walked around the island's narrow streets looking in shop windows, but never found the courage to go inside any of them.

She passed cafés and restaurants, savouring the tantalising aromas wafting from the open doors, wishing she could be as carefree as the other tourists around her. She would stand in front of the art galleries, studying the work from her position on the footpath, sometimes cupping her hands to get a better view through the shiny glass. Several patisseries were across from the hotel and she often admired the artistic pastry displays in the windows.

She'd been existing on the hotel breakfasts and a handful of fruit bought from a small supermarket near the bridge. Hunger had forced her into the supermarket the day she'd arrived. She wandered around the aisles looking at the assortment of food, some products familiar, but branded with French labels.

She smiled when she saw her favourite breakfast cereal with a French name, making it look glamorous. After several laps of the supermarket, she picked up a few apples and bananas, cradling the fruit in her arms while she waited her turn in a long queue snaking along the shelves of wine.

An old man in a white duster coat sat behind a cash register near the entrance. He spoke with machine gun speed and she was sure even if she could speak French, he would still be hard to understand. When it had been her turn at the counter, she slid a note across to him before he could say anything to her. He handed her a paper bag and she dropped the fruit inside, scurrying out the door without waiting for her change.

She'd rationed her stash for the evenings when she would try to decipher the world news on French television. It was impossible to comprehend what the presenters were saying, giving her a new appreciation for non-English speaking migrants in Australia.

Now three days later, she tried to ignore her gnawing stomach while she looked down at a boat gliding on the water below her. Its wake rippled out across the river before splashing against the banks on either side. The ripples reminded her of Muriel's story about grief as she listened to the bells that were still chiming.

She walked along the bridge thinking about what had happened on her verandah that afternoon. The next day she'd wanted to ring Muriel to apologise, but she couldn't find the courage and as time went by, it became harder to pick up the phone. Eventually she'd given up, knowing she could never take back her angry words.

She looked down at the river; it was time. She dug out her phone, pressing a key to bring up her contacts. She scrolled through the list of friends gone from her life, asking herself if they had ever been real friends at all. Muriel was the only one always there for her and now she couldn't imagine life without her.

She bit the side of her lip, unsure what Muriel's reaction would be to a phone call. As another boat glided under the bridge, she tapped out a text message instead, sending an apology before she could change her mind. Music drifted up from the river as she slid the phone back in her bag. She was still thinking about Muriel when she reached the end of Pont Marie and walked off the island.

16

Annie turned into a street lined with trees. Green bookstalls stretched along the river for as far as she could see. Cars and bicycles streamed by while she soaked in the beauty of Paris.

The Seine bustled with boats. Tourists waved from the decks as if it all were choreographed only for her. She could hear snippets of lively music drifting across the water as they went by, the colour and movement exhilarating. The sensation surprised her. She took a deep breath, all the disturbing news images about the terror attacks in Paris fading as she gazed across the river. It didn't seem like the same place she'd seen on her television.

She glanced down at the list of tourist attractions on the back of her map. The bookstalls in front of her were known as *bouquinistes* and had been part of the city for centuries. Old postcards piled on a table at one of them caught her attention. She stopped, examining the faded script while she tried to read the dates on the postage stamps. Leather-bound books embossed with gold titles were stacked next to the postcards along with baskets of gaudy souvenirs.

She smiled down at a glittery Eiffel Tower key ring propped against a basket of fridge magnets depicting the French flag.

The bookseller perched on a stool looked up from the magazine on his lap and said something to her as he pointed to the postcards. She couldn't understand him and turned away, blending in with the tourists milling around her.

When she reached the corner of the next bridge, she stood on the kerb beside two soldiers with guns in animated conversation while they waited at the pedestrian lights. She imagined herself no different than an alien from Mars, dropped down from the heavens as she listened to their meaningless words. When the lights changed, they left her standing there, sprinting across the street still talking non-stop. As she stepped out to follow them a motorcycle roared into the crossing, steering around her. The driver was so close she could see him frowning at her behind his helmet visor.

Her Martian analogy evaporated in a cloud of exhaust fumes. She froze, dizzy with terror as two other cars manoeuvred around her. Everything seemed to be happening in slow motion with her still paralysed in the middle of the crossing while the drivers gestured for her to get out of their way.

The pedestrian lights turned red while she stood there and cars from the opposite direction began to bear down on her. Slow motion switched to fast forward. She ran out of their way, lurching across to a streetlight on the corner. The footpath seemed to sway under her feet as she hung on, trying to catch her breath. She wasn't sure if she were about to faint or drop dead on the kerb.

She didn't know what went wrong; something was lost in translation. The lights changed several times while she leant against the streetlight trying to decide what to do. If she went back to the hotel, she would be like a prisoner on the island for the next few weeks, but if she kept walking, there was every chance she might never make it back in one piece.

She looked out to the Seine, fighting her scattered thoughts as a tourist boat slid towards a landing on the riverbank. On impulse, more to escape the traffic than anything else, she shuffled across the bridge, still light-headed from her close encounter. The metal railings near the stairs were covered with padlocks gleaming in the sun. Young couples posing for photos giggled and kissed while she skirted around them, desperate to pull herself together.

She'd never intended to go on a river cruise, but it seemed the only option. Her feet throbbed from her tight shoes, each step like walking on hot coals. She lumbered down stone stairs to the river, hobbling to the end of a queue in front of a ticket booth.

She didn't consider how she would ask for a ticket until the family standing in front of her stepped aside, leaving her to face a young woman in the booth. Annie stood mute with embarrassment while the woman waited for her to say something. '*Combien de billets, Madame?*' she finally asked.

Annie blinked. '*Billets?*'

'How many tickets, Madame?'

'One,' she squeaked.

'*Treize euros.*'

'I beg your pardon?'

The woman pointed to a list of prices displayed at the front of the booth. 'Thirteen euros.'

She pushed a note across the counter and the woman pursed her lips as she counted out change, handing over a ticket. Annie nodded her thanks before turning towards a seat under a tree.

She pulled off her shoes and wiggled her toes, grimacing when she touched several blisters oozing blood. So much for fashion, she thought; she shouldn't have gone shopping with Lucy. She squeezed back in the shoes, steadying herself on the arm of the seat before limping across cobblestones to a refreshment van by the river. This time she was too thirsty to worry about what she would say to the man behind the counter.

'One water, please,' she said, holding up her index finger before pointing to a glass-fronted refrigerator behind him. She reached in her pocket for the change from her ticket.

'*Merci, Madame,*' he said, handing her a bottle as he took the coins. He smiled broadly, flashing a gold tooth and she felt a spark of confidence.

'*Merci,*' she answered.

She picked her way back over the cobblestones, collapsing on the seat again while traffic rumbled on the bridge above her. As she sat gulping water, passengers were already boarding the boat. She stood, wincing with pain as she tossed the empty bottle in a bin.

When she reached the landing, she could hear conversations in different languages. Two young German women in front of her skipped up the gangplank like children, showing their tickets to a man in a white uniform standing on the deck.

Annie followed them, taking several tentative steps before she stopped. She looked down from the gangplank at the green water slapping against the side of the boat, her knuckles white on the handrail. She turned, facing several people close behind her. She was trapped; there was no choice, she had to keep going.

The man in a uniform smiled at her, putting out his hand. '*Attention à la marche.*' She shook her head and he spoke again with a thick French accent. 'Watch your step, Madame,' he repeated, glancing at her ticket as he helped her on board.

She tottered across the deck to a seat inside near a window, easing herself on the hard vinyl. The crowd sitting outside on the open bow was already enjoying the spring sunshine while other tourists streamed on board, their excitement palpable. As the last passengers took their seats, engines purred into life and she could feel the deck vibrating as the boat glided out to the middle of the river.

A woman in a red uniform made an announcement in English, pulling out a stack of brochures from a box. She handed them out while she continued her spiel in two other languages. Music blared from a sound system when she finished. Annie couldn't understand the words of the mournful tune, but she soon got the message. This wasn't the kind of lively music she'd heard from the shore.

A middle-aged couple next to her smiled at each other, the man kissing the woman's forehead. Annie looked away as a wave of longing for what she once had threatened to engulf her. She clenched her hands, willing herself to ignore the intense feeling. Death had stripped away her status, leaving her unsure of where she belonged, her old life now nothing more than a mirage.

Passengers took photos and waved at people on the shore while Paris floated by. She gazed across at them, trying to detach herself from the music. If she tried really hard, the romance of the City of Light wouldn't overwhelm her. She needed to concentrate.

When the Eiffel Tower appeared, a collective gasp rippled through the crowd. The tower was like a giant on the horizon, dwarfing the streetscape around it. Several passengers jumped from their seats and ran to the already crowded bow to photograph the star attraction of the cruise. They hung over the side, their experience of Paris only enjoyed through the cameras on their phones.

Edith Piaf began to warble over the sound system while Annie tried to recall where she'd heard the sad song before. Tears stung her eyes as she listened. She didn't know if the tears were for herself, for Leo or for what their lives could have been.

As the music seemed to get louder, she began to sob. The couple beside her turned away, adding to her embarrassment as she tried to ignore the music. When she couldn't stop her heaving chest, she did what had now become a regular reaction; she took flight. She climbed over the other passengers, apologising as she squeezed down the row of seats, her head bowed with shame. When she broke free, she limped down the aisle to the rear of the boat. To her surprise, it was as crowded as the front; there was nowhere to hide.

She stood in the aisle, unnoticed by the crowd fixated on the Eiffel Tower while a hot flush spread over her. When she spotted a vacant seat, she crawled over another row of passengers and flopped down. She rummaged in her bag for a tissue, finally giving up and dabbing her hot face with the back of her hand. Her sobbing had stopped with the distraction of finding a seat, but she couldn't control the tears. Her nose and eyes were still streaming.

She sat with her head bowed until the woman in the next seat touched her arm, speaking in French. She looked across to the bluest eyes she'd ever seen, unable to answer her.

'Would you like some tissues?' The woman asked again in English with a British accent. 'I have plenty and I promise they're all clean.'

'Yes, that would help,' she mumbled, wiping her wet cheeks with her hand.

The woman handed over a wad and she nodded her thanks. 'I seem to be doing a lot of this lately, I'm sorry.'

'Sorry for Edith pushing all the right buttons? Don't be.'

Annie blew her nose before crumpling the tissue into a ball. She looked down at remnants of red lipstick smeared across the tissue. Now she was not only a blubbering idiot, but also looked a mess. The sad French music continued and she could still feel tears spilling down her hot cheeks.

'You've got it bad. I'd ask them to turn off the music, but I wouldn't get very far,' the woman nodded. 'It's supposed to be part of the experience. They think the tourists need to be serenaded.'

'The scenery is enough,' Annie sniffed into the tissues.

They sat in silence looking out to the moving shoreline until the woman turned to her again. 'It's more than the music, isn't it?'

Annie closed her eyes. Maybe Jess had been right all along; she needed help. She felt a hand on her arm and opened her eyes.

'If you're in trouble,' the woman said, leaning towards her, 'you know, here in Paris, I'd be happy to help you. I understand how beautiful yet overwhelming this city can be.'

'Really?'

'I know my way around now,' she said, 'but the first time I came here years ago it was difficult. They wouldn't speak much English to tourists in those days and I hardly knew any French.' The woman's eyes danced. 'It's all changed now. Some restaurants even have English subtitles on their menus. With the Channel Tunnel and cheap air fares it's almost part of Britain, but I wouldn't say that in front of a local.'

'I thought you were British,' Annie said, her tears now almost gone.

'It sounds so proper, doesn't it?' she laughed. Fine lines around her eyes crinkled as she pulled at a striped scarf draped across her shoulders in a very French way.

Annie looked at the woman's hands. She wore one large silver ring on her middle finger. 'I stayed in London for a few days before I came here,' she offered. 'For some reason, I felt different there. It seemed strangely familiar.'

'Maybe you lived there in another life.'

'You never know,' she sniffed, 'but it's clear I never lived in Paris.'

'You sound like an Australian.'

'Is it that obvious?'

'With everyone travelling these days, it's easy to pick up accents.'

'I don't travel much, although I sometimes watch foreign films.'

'Did you see any on the plane?'

'No, I wanted to catch up on some reading. Maybe I will on the way home.' She didn't mention she was too embarrassed to ask how to use the passenger entertainment system, enduring the long flight with a boring paperback and a catnap topped off by her usual nightmare. She was still thinking about it when the boat docked at one of its scheduled stops. The woman stood and looked down at her.

'I'm getting off here, are you sure you'll be okay?'

Annie smiled up at her. 'Yes, I'll be fine. I'm only a bit homesick. Thanks for rescuing me with the tissues.'

The woman was petite with spiky grey hair and although her delicate features were etched with fine lines, she seemed much younger. She wore a cropped black jacket and tight jeans tucked into a pair of red high-heeled boots, accentuating her still youthful figure. Coils of silver bracelets jangled on her wrist when she scooped up a leather bag from under her seat and smiled at Annie.

'I see you like red too.'

'Pardon?'

'Your shoes, they're red.'

Annie stuck out her feet. 'They were a gift from one of my daughters.'

'They suit you,' the woman nodded, looping the bag over her arm. 'Enjoy the rest of the cruise and try not to listen to the music.' She turned away, waiting to file off the boat.

Annie watched her with a flash of envy. If only she had such style and confidence. She gazed out to the riverbank; if only. Someone calling out interrupted her thoughts.

'Yoo-hoo. Yoo-hoo.'

She looked back at the crowd leaving the boat. The woman in the red boots waved at her.

'I'm going to the Musée de l'Orangerie tomorrow morning,' she shouted. 'Why don't you join me?'

'I'll do my best to find it,' Annie shouted back, her heart beginning to race.

The woman put up her thumb. 'I'll be at the main entrance at ten,' she called out before she stepped ashore. Annie waved to her as the boat pulled away from the riverbank, realising she didn't even know her name. She could still smell the woman's sweet perfume as she stuffed the damp tissues in her pocket and reached for her map of Paris.

17

Georgina checked the time again on her phone; it was clear the woman from the river cruise wasn't coming. She turned towards the main entrance of Musée de l'Orangerie, joining the ticket queue spilling out across a forecourt.

She hadn't visited the gallery for decades. In those days there were never such large crowds or the need to have her bag checked by security. When it was her turn to buy a ticket, she glanced around one last time. She saw a woman with red hair, but it wasn't the Australian.

Before she went into the first room of the gallery, she stood in the vestibule thinking of how Claude Monet helped design it to create what he called a decompression space between the outside world and his art. The concept was still relevant in the twenty-first century and she thought modern architects could learn a thing or two from the old master.

The silence of the gallery seemed charged with an unseen force reminding her of a cathedral. The white rooms glowed with Monet's water lilies that wrapped around curved walls, engulfing her in their subtle colours. She sat on a seat in the middle of the gallery, concentrating on one painting at a time as she was drawn into the canvases. When she closed her eyes, she felt immersed in the beauty of the art, imagining herself swimming in cool water as the petals of the lilies touched her skin. The feeling reminded her of a photo she'd once seen of a child in a pond smiling among water lilies.

A school group broke Monet's spell. She stood, unsure of how long she'd been sitting there. The children gathered to one side of the room, whispering to each other as their teacher counted heads. They were a stark contrast to their rowdy British counterparts on school excursions she'd often seen in galleries all over London. When the teacher began to speak, she moved to the next room.

Nothing had changed; the paintings were as powerful now as when she'd first seen them all those years ago with Alain. They felt like old friends waiting for her return, only this time she was alone.

Georgina took a sip of coffee, watching the pigeons foraging under the trees in the Tuileries Garden. She was still thinking about the Monet paintings and who introduced them to her the first time she came to Paris. It was ridiculous to get sentimental, she lectured herself; it was all so long ago. She shouldn't have gone to see them; they were stirring up too many memories.

She pulled a brochure from her bag, studying the information about the cooking classes she'd booked weeks ago. It would be three days of pure bliss with no time to dwell on the past.

She took another sip of coffee as a waiter weaved around the tables of the outdoor café, bustling across to her. He placed a plate of steaming crêpes in front of her, positioning it like an art installation. She sighed as a forkful of buttery crêpe melted in her mouth. She needed to stop thinking of Alain; it was ruining her day.

18

Two kilometres from the Tuileries Garden, Annie waited in the hotel foyer for the tour bus taking her to Giverny. This was supposed to be the highlight of her trip, the *pièce de résistance* of the whole European exercise. She loved Monet's paintings and now she was about to see where he once lived. She would walk through rooms where he walked, smell the roses in the garden he designed. Today she would be as close to Claude Monet as she could ever be.

'The bus will be here soon,' Colette said from behind her desk, interrupting the daydream. 'I'm sure you'll enjoy Monet's home.' The artist's name rolled off her tongue, her accent making Annie shiver as she smiled across to her.

'I've always wanted to see where he lived. I have quite a few books about him.'

'It sounds like you're a fan.'

'Oh yes, very much,' she said, her eyes shining. 'I adore his paintings.'

A minibus pulled up to the entrance and Colette nodded towards it. 'They're here; have a good time.'

The driver hurried in as Annie walked across the foyer towards him.

'Madame Green?'

'Hello,' she nodded, handing him her tour voucher.

He ticked her name on a list and smiled down at her. 'I'm Luc. You can sit in front with me or at the back.'

She hesitated, the thought of having to make conversation all the way to Giverny seemed too hard. 'I'll sit at the back if you don't mind.'

'Not at all, Madame. I'm picking up only one other passenger so there'll be plenty of room for you there.'

She followed him into the chilly morning, glancing back to the hotel while he opened the sliding door of the minibus. Colette waved to her from the front window. She waved back before stepping up into the bus, squeezing by a young couple in the middle row of seats. Her floral skirt tangled as she plopped down on the cramped back seat.

The young man in front of her looked over his shoulder, beaming as Luc closed the door. 'Hi, I'm Emilio and this is my wife, Rachael.'

The brunette sitting next to him turned around. 'We're from Boston and we've been visiting family in Italy. We flew in yesterday,' she recited like a contestant in a television game show. 'And you are?'

'I'm Annie.'

Emilio smiled broadly, flashing his dazzling white teeth. 'Where're you from?'

'Melbourne in Australia. I've been here for a few days.'

Luc slid behind the steering wheel and looked in the rear-view mirror. 'Are we all set back there?'

'Yes,' the young couple chorused as the bus turned towards Pont Marie.

'What about you, Madame, are you comfortable in the back?'

'Yes,' Annie mumbled.

'Can't hear you,' he called out.

'Fine, I'm fine,' she answered, wishing she could disappear. She crouched down in her seat, grateful she was in the back even though she felt like a sardine in a tin.

The minibus rattled across the bridge, passing the pedestrian crossing where she was nearly flattened the day before. The crossing now looked benign as she gazed down on it from the safety of the back seat. She flexed her blistered toes plastered with dressings, grateful for remembering to pack her first aid kit.

She would have missed the tour if Colette hadn't mentioned it when she limped through the hotel foyer after the cruise. Her simple observation about the expected weather in Giverny the next day jogged Annie's memory and she'd gone upstairs to check her tour voucher.

She'd pulled out all of her travel documents from the small metal safe in the wardrobe, rummaging through them until she found the voucher under her airline ticket. Colette had been right about the tour to Giverny. She'd glanced at the airline ticket still in its white envelope, asking herself what if she hadn't come to Paris. She'd stared out the window to the apartments across the street as if seeing them for the first time. Lucy's comparison of her to the fictional Alice had started to make sense, the realisation dawning on her as she sat at the end of the bed with the documents spread around her.

She'd walked over to the window and looked out at wrought-iron balconies with pots of red geraniums, her eyes still sore from crying on the river cruise. Her heart had fluttered with excitement as she'd stood there thinking about the tour. Below her in the narrow street, local residents had been walking their dogs and tourists strolling along the cobblestones. Her only regret had been that she would miss visiting the gallery with the woman from the cruise.

Annie was still thinking about the cruise and the kindness of a stranger as the bus drove along the Seine. It was too late now; she would never see her again. She looked out to the river sparkling in the morning sun. In the distance, she could see a white boat gliding through the water. Tourists were hanging over the bow taking photos, the scene a re-run of the day before. The minibus slowed and Luc started his commentary.

'On our right is the Musée de l'Orangerie where Monet's famous water lily paintings are displayed,' he said, his French accent sounding romantic as he spoke.

The coincidence surprised her and she leant forward looking for the woman with red boots, but there was no sign of her in front of the gallery. She was still thinking about her as Luc pointed out the landmarks they were passing. Paris seemed like a dream and this one wasn't a nightmare.

* * *

They had two hours before they were to return to the minibus. 'You'll need to be back here by three,' Luc said, handing out tickets. 'The traffic gets heavy in the afternoon so try to be on time.'

Annie took her ticket from him as they walked along a high fence at the side of Monet's garden. The young couple walked behind her while the man they had picked up at a hotel near the Palais-Royal walked ahead. They went through an underpass to the main entrance and when they emerged into the garden, she didn't know where to start, doubting if two hours would ever be enough time to see it all.

She followed the others along a bank of lush bamboo to the misty lily ponds depicted in Monet's paintings. She gazed down at the lilies that were beginning to open, showing their delicate colours in the shadows. When she came to the famous Japanese bridge she stopped, admiring the spectacular show of spring wisteria.

As she stood there, she was aware she was in one of the most famous gardens in the world without a camera. She thought of Lucy pressuring her to upgrade her phone and how she'd resisted, insisting her old one was still serviceable. She hadn't told her the phone was a birthday present from Leo and she couldn't part with it.

She knew it would die one day like he had, but until then she wanted to take it with her on the trip. It was like an old friend and she'd secretly given it a name. She couldn't explain why having Betty tucked in the bottom of her bag gave her some sense of security, even though it wasn't a smartphone.

Lucy would have laughed at her like she did when she named her car, but now as she stood looking at the beauty all around her, she wished she'd listened to her daughter. She was still lost in thought when Emilio tapped her arm. She flinched and he stepped back.

'Hey, I didn't mean to scare you. I only thought you might want to have your picture taken on the bridge. Where's your camera?'

She could feel her cheeks flushing while she tried to think of an excuse.

Emilio shook his head. 'Don't tell me you've come to France without a camera?'

'I … I left it at the hotel,' she stammered.

'What about your cell phone?'

She ignored his question. 'I don't want any distractions today. I plan to do some sketching.'

He looked as surprised as she was by her own answer. 'You're an artist?'

She was cornered. 'Well, it's certainly not my day job, but I like to paint and sketch.'

'Wait till I tell Rachael; we've never met a real artist before,' he smiled with his super white teeth. 'Since you can't sketch yourself on the bridge, do you want a picture? I can take one for you and email it.'

Annie began to back away; she hadn't turned on her computer since she'd cancelled the internet. Life had passed her by while she scrabbled around in a void. She was an oddity in a modern world: no email address or smartphone. Emilio cut across her thoughts.

'Come on, stop being shy. Rachael's already up there and I'll take one of you both.' He touched her elbow, steering her towards the bridge.

'My computer isn't working at the moment,' she gulped, her web of lies almost choking her. 'Give me your email address and I'll be in touch when it's fixed. You can send the photo later.'

'Only if you scan one of your sketches for us; we would really like to see your work.'

'Sure,' she whispered, wishing she could run away.

'Rachael,' he called out, 'Annie's having her picture taken with you.' She waved and Annie cringed when the other people on the bridge looked around at them. Rachael greeted her like a long-lost friend.

'Come over here with me.' She put her arm around Annie's shoulders and they smiled for a series of photos before Emilio ran up beside them.

'Will you take a few of us?' he asked, handing Annie his phone.

She'd never handled a smartphone before, but mimicked all the other tourists, extending her arm and touching the icon on the screen.

'I better go now,' she said, handing it back.

Emilio looked at his wife. 'Annie's an artist; isn't that cool? She's going to sketch while she's here.'

'Wow, are you for real?'

She nodded at them, turning from the bridge.

She hurried alongside the lily ponds until she could see Monet's house in the distance. Time was running out and she'd hardly seen anything. She stopped when she came to a series of metal arches covered with climbing roses. A border of spring bulbs swayed in the breeze in a kaleidoscope of colour. The arches created a tunnel through the garden, framing the house at the other end. She marvelled at Monet's genius; the view was a perfect composition.

She hadn't picked up a pen to sketch since Leo's cancer had changed her life, but now she needed to get down on paper what she was seeing. She searched her shoulder bag looking for a piece of paper. All she could find was her phrase book and a few paper napkins she'd picked up at the café where they had stopped for lunch. She pulled out her pen and looked up to the house, cradling the bag in her arm with one of the napkins spread out on top of it.

She thought of Jess in the supermarket as she arranged the makeshift sketch pad. When she'd told her she planned to sketch at Giverny, she'd never thought she actually would. The significance of the moment wasn't lost on her and she was grinning when she began to sketch.

Her hands flew across the paper, the lines on the napkin creating a true likeness of the house at the end of the floral tunnel. As she stood in the spring sunshine, she wasn't aware of the tears streaming down her cheeks, settling in the creases of her smile.

19

Annie gazed at the blue and white Rouen wall tiles, trying to commit every detail to memory. The self-guided tour of Monet's house ended with the kitchen and there would be no time to go through again. She took one last look at the copper pots on the wood fire stove before turning towards the door.

Outside, she could see another group of tourists filing through the entrance at the far end of the house. She wondered what Monet would have thought about his home being turned into a museum with strangers looking at his personal possessions, thumping up and down his stairs and staring out the same bedroom window he stood at each morning.

She followed a gravel path to one of his studios, walking around a chicken pen on the way. Two hens scratched in the dirt, ignoring a rooster flapping its wings. She could hear its raucous crowing as she read the information board near the entrance. It noted the studio was where Monet painted the large paintings now at the Musée de l'Orangerie. She shook her head while she read; it seemed she was meant to visit that gallery.

Although the studio had been converted to a gift shop, she could still feel Monet's presence as she looked up to the high windows. Light flooded down into the room while she tried to imagine how it once was. If only she could stand there longer soaking up the history, but it was almost time to leave.

Across from her she could see the other man from the tour studying a display of maps. She didn't know his name and was reluctant to approach him. He'd rejected attempts at conversation from anyone after he was picked up at his hotel in Paris and when they had stopped for lunch, he took his meal to a table outside to eat alone. Luc had told her he was from Canada, but she didn't know anything else about him. He was tanned with a buzz cut, his face always expressionless. She hadn't seen him smile once since he'd joined the tour. He made it clear he wasn't enjoying anything, as if they were all to blame.

She recognised something of herself in him as she kept glancing across the shop, certain now she also appeared withdrawn and angry. It was no one's fault Leo had died, leaving her alone to reinvent herself. Maybe she needed to make an effort.

She thought of Muriel as she went across to a display of books, looking through the titles until she found a glossy publication about Monet's house. It could be her peace offering when she returned home, but she doubted if she would ever have the nerve to actually give it to her. Muriel hadn't answered her text and it seemed their friendship had ended that terrible afternoon on her verandah.

Art supplies were stacked on shelves near the books and she chose a selection of pencils and a sketch pad branded with Monet's initials. As she walked towards the cash registers, she saw a shelf of miniature ceramic cats similar to the Japanese one Monet had kept on a cushion in his dining room. It was still curled up in the house looking like it was waiting for him to return home. She chose a pale blue one, tucking it on top of the other souvenirs.

The woman behind the counter said something she couldn't understand as she handed over her purchases. Annie smiled at her, aware it was the first time she wasn't panicking when she was spoken to in French. As the woman scanned the barcodes, she kept thinking of the ceramic cat. She could clean out one of the spare bedrooms and make it into a new studio. The ceramic figurine would take pride of place on a cushion like Monet's cat at Giverny.

She'd abandoned her studio behind the garage when Leo's health had failed, her creativity disappearing as the life drained from him. It was now full of junk, a constant reminder of how her life had changed and she knew it would be easier to start afresh than to clean it out. She thought of her conversation with Lucy in the back garden on Leo's anniversary. Her old bedroom being turned into an art studio probably wasn't what she'd had in mind about moving on.

Luc was leaning against the bus when she walked up the unmade road to the car park.

'How was it?' he asked.

'Fabulous. Much better than I ever imagined.'

'You look different.' He smiled, tilting his head to one side. 'Really different.'

'I do?'

'*Oui, magnifique,*' he said, kissing one of his fingers in a gesture of appreciation.

'I loved it all,' she blushed. 'I guess it shows.' He laughed as he unlocked the minibus. 'Can I sit up front this time?' she asked when he opened the door.

'Of course; here let me help you.' He held her hand while she balanced on a low step before sliding across the front seat. As she put her carry bag on the floor, she could see the Canadian walking across the car park. He nodded to Luc before climbing into his seat behind her. She turned around when he clicked on his seat belt.

'What did you think of it all?'

He glanced out the window, avoiding any eye contact. 'The garden was interesting, but the house was claustrophobic. I didn't like all the junk like those kitsch Japanese prints.'

'I thought they were beautiful,' she offered while he reached in his carry bag from the shop, unfolding a map and ignoring her. She turned around, relieved to see Emilio and Rachael running up the road laden with carry bags.

'We've been shopping,' Rachael giggled as she bounded on the minibus.

'My credit card melted,' Emilio called out behind her. 'I've got third degree burns on my fingers.' He laughed at his own joke and Rachael affectionately elbowed him. 'Hey Annie, how was the sketching?' he asked, loading their bags on an empty seat.

She could have kissed him. 'Great, I made real progress.'

'Progress?'

'Yes, with the sketches.' She smiled; if he only knew.

Rachael leant towards the Canadian in front of her. 'Did you enjoy it?'

'Not much,' he mumbled.

She looked at Annie and they both raised their eyebrows as Luc climbed into his seat, slamming his door.

'Thanks for being on time; we should be back in Paris by five.'

'How often do you make this trip?' Annie asked.

'Twice a week.'

'What a wonderful job.'

'Not always,' he said, steering out of the car park.

She stared out at the stone houses while they drove through the village of Giverny, wondering if she would ever return. She tried to push the irrational thought away, but as she looked out at the beautiful countryside, she couldn't imagine not ever seeing it all again.

The minibus inched its way through the centre of Paris. Luc's commentary had petered out, leaving everyone subdued as he negotiated the heavy traffic. The slow trip gave Annie a chance to get a different perspective of the city, many of the wide boulevards reminding her of home. The Canadian called out when they drove by the Louvre.

'Driver, I need some air. You can drop me off at the next corner.'

Luc glanced back at him. 'Are you sure? We're on the way to your hotel now.'

'Yep,' he snapped, picking up his carry bag ready for a hasty exit. They turned out of the traffic and Luc unfastened his seat belt. The man tapped him on the shoulder. 'Don't bother, I'm quite capable of opening a door without you.'

Luc put up both hands in resignation as the man slid the passenger door open and scrambled out. He slammed it behind him, turning away without a backward glance. Annie looked at Luc and he shrugged.

'It happens often,' he said, steering back into the traffic.

'So that's why your job isn't always wonderful.'

'Exactly.'

She shook her head and they drove in silence until Emilio called out to her.

'Hey Annie, we're going to have an early dinner before we go back to our hotel. Will you join us?'

Her heart skipped a beat. 'Thanks, but I've got a terrible sense of direction. I'd never find the way back to my hotel.'

'We'll walk you back. We're in the Latin Quarter about ten minutes from you.'

'Really?'

'Yeah. Come on, you can show us your sketches.'

'I'm not dressed for dinner.'

'Look at us; we're hardly fashion material,' Rachael giggled.

'Sounds like an offer too good to refuse,' Luc grinned across to her.

'Drop us at one of the bridges near Île Saint-Louis and we'll make it up from there,' Emilio called out.

'I guess I'm going,' Annie laughed, but inside she was beginning to panic.

The hot flush radiated from her chest, swamping her. She wiped her moist hands on her skirt, trying to ignore her thumping heart. Luc helped her out of the minibus, retrieving her carry bag with Giverny stamped on the front.

'Enjoy yourself,' he smiled, handing over the bag as Emilio and Rachael joined her on the footpath.

She shook his hand, trying to hide her emotions. 'Thanks for making this such a special day.'

'We'll book a tour with you next time,' Rachael smiled while he slid back behind the steering wheel. They all waved as he pulled out into the traffic. 'He was nice,' she said when the minibus swung around the corner. 'I wanted to slap that man for being so horrible to him.'

Annie dabbed her hot face with the back of her hand. 'He told me it happens a lot, poor bugger.'

'Come on, ladies,' Emilio interrupted them, juggling an assortment of carry bags. 'Paris awaits us and we can't stand here forever.'

Annie took several deep breaths as they walked across Pont Marie. The world was shifting under her feet.

20

A waiter greeted them at the door of the crowded restaurant, asking a question in French. Emilio glanced around at Rachael and Annie before nodding at him as they were led to a table in the corner overlooking the street. His smile seemed permanently plastered on his face as the waiter handed them each a menu. Annie fumbled with hers, a sea of French words swimming in front of her as she looked for the English subtitles the woman in the red boots had told her about.

Emilio leant towards her. 'Do you speak French?'

She shook her head. 'I thought you did. What do you think the waiter just said?

'Beats me; I only pretended I knew.'

The waiter overheard them. 'I speak English if you need help with the menu,' he offered.

'That's cool because we can't read a word of French,' Emilio said, handing the menus back to him. 'Sorry.'

The waiter tucked them under his arm and patted his chest. 'I'll be your menu.'

'That's so funny,' Rachael giggled as he smiled down at them, rattling off the names of various dishes.

'Why don't you recommend something,' Emilio interrupted. 'We've been out all day and we're starved. We love French food and we'll eat anything.'

'Except snails,' Rachael added. 'And frog legs.'

'Very well; may I suggest the duck? It's served with vegetables. Cassoulet's also delicious and filling.'

Emilio looked back and forth to Annie and Rachael. 'How does duck sound?'

They both nodded.

'And what about wine?' The waiter showed him the wine list, pointing to several selections. 'What do you drink down under, Annie?' Emilio asked as he studied the list.

'Red, but if you both like white wine, I'm happy to have that,' she gulped, wringing her hands under the table.

'We drink any ol' colour,' Rachael drawled, patting Emilio's hand.

He grinned at her as he handed back the list. 'Could we try some red wine from the Burgundy region? Only three glasses for now, thanks.'

When the waiter turned away, Annie sat back, her mouth dry as she battled her anxiety.

'What restaurants have you tried since you've been here?' Rachael asked.

In that split second Annie decided to be honest. 'This is my first one.' The sheer exhaustion from trying to stay upbeat all day had chipped away her brave veneer and she blinked away tears. 'I've mainly been having breakfast in the hotel and a bit of fruit in the evenings,' she said, forcing a smile. 'Although I did stop for a baguette in the street yesterday after a cruise.'

'How long did you say you've been here?' Rachael asked.

'Four days.'

Emilio shook his head. 'Why?'

'I've felt like such an idiot since I can't speak French. I've been too embarrassed to go in anywhere.'

She could see them exchanging uncomfortable looks, but she rushed on. Emilio played with the cutlery in front of him and Rachael picked at a stray thread on the cuff of her blouse while she listened. 'I'm only here because my daughters organised this trip. They thought it would help me get over the death of their father last year.' She pushed a stray curl back from her forehead. 'It was so generous, but I didn't want to come here. I wasn't ready for France until today. Today was different.'

Annie knew she'd said too much. She'd been through this before and shutting herself off from everyone seemed easier. No one wanted to hear the truth; she should have lied.

Rachael patted her arm. 'How sad. You're very brave.'

Her pitying tone annoyed Annie, but she tried to ignore it. She wouldn't be sitting in a restaurant if it weren't for this young couple and she needed to turn the conversation around before she ruined such a perfect day.

'Not brave at all. Like I said, France wasn't my idea, but now I'm here I'm trying to make a go of it.' She glanced out the window to the busy street. In the distance a jazz trio played to a crowd on the footbridge connecting the island to Île de la Cité. She forced another smile and looked back at them. 'That's enough about me; tell me about your trip. How was Italy?'

The sombre mood lifted as Emilio told her about visiting Naples where his great-grandfather was born. 'He migrated to America when he was a young man. I was named after him and have always felt a real connection between us although he died long before I was born.'

Annie smiled across the table. 'There's a large Italian community in Melbourne, so I've heard your name before. What's your surname?'

'Oh, we didn't get that far, did we? Back home we call it our last name. Mine is Lanza.'

'Wasn't there a famous singer with the same name?'

'Yeah, Mario, but he was no relation and apparently it was his stage name. So, what's yours?'

'Green. It sounds so plain compared to yours. My maiden name was Mathews.'

'I think your name is pretty,' Rachael said. 'Green is my favourite colour. My name used to be Jones. A lot of my friends have kept their own last names after they married, but I now love having a name sounding more European.'

Annie smiled at her as Emilio continued his story, one elbow on the table.

'Anyway, I always wanted to see where the first Emilio came from.'

'Do you speak Italian?' Annie asked.

Rachael's eyes danced. 'Go on, tell her,' she laughed, nudging his arm. He ruffled his dark hair.

'I thought I would be okay, but when we got there no one could understand me. My grandmother used to speak Italian when she took care of me,' he explained. 'Since I was named after her father, she wanted me to learn his language. I was a little kid and never knew the Italian she taught me was mainly baby talk.'

'A tour guide told us,' Rachael laughed. 'You should've seen Emilio's face.'

The waiter returned to their table with the wine on a silver tray, interrupting his story. Emilio raised his glass. 'Cheers,' he toasted. 'Here's to good times.'

'You'll have to take Italian lessons before you go back again,' Annie offered, sipping her wine.

'I never thought of that. What a good idea.' They clinked glasses and Annie grinned, finally relaxing.

The duck arrived on large white plates accompanied by green beans and potatoes. Annie hadn't realised how hungry she was until she started eating. Her meal disappeared in minutes while she washed it down with the tangy wine. When she finished, she patted her mouth with a linen napkin, sitting back while Rachael picked at her food.

'Don't you like it?' she asked.

'She always does this,' Emilio said, taking another piece of bread from a basket on the table. 'Eats like a bird.'

'You know I'm a slow eater. I can't wolf it down like you can.' She shook her head. 'I've really had enough.'

Annie glanced down at her own empty plate, draping her napkin over the gleaming porcelain that looked like it had been licked clean.

'I guess you won't have room for dessert.' Emilio observed, his face deadpan.

'Stop teasing me, where's the waiter?'

'Over there,' Annie pointed. 'Should I wave?'

'Whistle; it's easier,' Emilio laughed, putting two fingers to his mouth.

'No,' Annie and Rachael shouted together, outstretching their arms to stop him. The waiter saw their antics and rushed across the restaurant.

'Finished already?' They all nodded and grinned up at him.

'We loved it all,' Annie said. 'Could you recommend a dessert?

'Our crème brûlée or chocolate mousse would be perfect after the duck.'

'Definitely chocolate mousse for me,' Annie smiled, unconsciously licking her lips.

'We love crème brûlée,' Rachael squealed, clapping her hands like a little girl at a birthday party.

'For two?' the waiter asked, writing in a small notebook.

'Yes, please and we'll all want coffee.'

He tucked the notebook in the pocket of his black vest and began to clear the table. '*Café noir?*'

Rachael and Emilio looked at Annie. 'That's black coffee,' she whispered.

'Three of those,' Emilio nodded. When the waiter left, he leant across the table. 'What's this about not understanding French? I think you're a complete fraud, Annie Green.'

For a moment she thought he was serious until she saw his grin, realising she'd lost the art of conversation during her year of self-imposed isolation. 'I'm actually fluent in five languages,' she whispered, cupping one hand around her mouth. 'I'm working undercover to write a book about the perils of travelling alone in foreign countries. Shush, don't tell anyone.'

Emilio laughed at her. 'Now, undercover agent, when do we see those sketches?'

'Artists never show their work until it's finished,' she grinned.

'So, where're you hiding them?' He pulled up the linen tablecloth and looked underneath, making her laugh.

'In my bag, I'll send you one when they're all done. And just to keep the record straight, I really can't speak French. I've only picked up a few words from a phrase book I bought at my local post office.'

'Don't believe a word this woman says,' Emilio whispered to Rachael. She giggled and took out a pen and paper from her handbag.

'Emilio, that's enough.' She looked at Annie. 'He gets carried away sometimes. I'll give you our contact details so we can keep in touch.'

Annie smiled, buoyed by their banter. Here she was having dinner with two strangers and she couldn't remember when she'd last felt so happy. She watched Rachael writing, remembering earlier how she'd nearly ruined the evening by telling the truth. No one wanted to hear her sad story. It appeared from now on, lies were the way to go.

The street near Annie's hotel glowed under amber streetlights as they looked in the windows of the shops that were still open.

'Could I buy you a souvenir?' she asked when they stopped at a homewares shop. 'You wouldn't let me pay for anything and it's the least I can do.'

'No, we've already bought too many.' Emilio smiled down at her. 'It's all cool, really.'

She could see Rachael peering at something. 'What have you spotted?'

'There's this teeny-weeny knife in the corner,' she giggled, tapping the window. 'It's so cute. See, it's pink. I've never seen anything like it before.'

Annie looked to where she was pointing. All the products in the window were made from resin in a rainbow of bright colours. The pink knife had a small Eiffel Tower suspended in its handle. 'I've never seen anything like it, either. Let's go in and have a closer look.'

The shop was like an Aladdin's cave of brightly coloured gadgets. Annie had walked by it many times, but never found the courage to go inside. This night was full of surprises, she thought, as she glanced around the shelves. A shop assistant behind the counter smiled at them.

'Hello,' Rachael said. 'Sorry we don't speak French. We want to look at something in the window.' She pointed to the pink knife.

The shop assistant plucked it out, handing it to her. 'For *fromage*,' she said.

'That's cheese,' Annie said, and Emilio laughed.

'The undercover agent has spoken.'

'How much?' Annie asked, stifling a giggle.

'Five euros.'

'Is that all?'

'Yes, Madame, will you take it?'

Annie nodded and Rachael grabbed her arm. 'No, I can't let you buy it. I was only looking.'

'Please, I want to,' she smiled, pulling away as she reached for her wallet. She pointed back to the window. 'I'd also like the little board it was sitting on.'

They waited while the shop assistant wrapped the knife and cheese board in tissue paper. 'Twenty euros, Madame,' she said, and Annie handed her several notes. As they walked out into the cool evening, she shook her head. It was so easy; what a fool she'd been.

The hotel was lit up when they reached the main entrance. They could see a couple inside posing for a photo in front of the Portuguese fountain.

'I can't thank you enough for taking me out to dinner,' Annie smiled.

'Tomorrow's our last day,' Rachael said. 'It's a shame we're leaving so soon; we could've done something else together.'

'Maybe next time; remember you promised Luc you'd be back.' Annie tried to sound upbeat, but inside she was fighting her emotions again. Any goodbye now had taken on a new layer of meaning. Emilio seemed to sense how she was feeling and hugged her.

'Goodbye,' he whispered. 'Take care of yourself. We'll be waiting for your sketch of Giverny.'

Rachael grabbed her hand when he stood back. 'Come see us in Boston. We'd love to show you our city.'

'I'd really like that,' she smiled as Rachael hugged her.

'We'll break out the *fromage*,' Emilio laughed, pulling Rachael away. 'It's now time to pack our loot,' he said, holding up their carry bags. 'I don't know how we'll squash it all in.'

'Sit on your suitcases; it really works,' she called after them.

'I'll be in touch soon.' They waved before disappearing into the evening crowd of shoppers while she turned back to the hotel, knowing she'd never see them again.

Colette looked up from her desk when she walked in. 'Are you still here?' Annie asked. 'It's such a long day for you.'

'I only work four days a week and they're longer hours. Tomorrow is my day off. How was Giverny?'

'The best,' she grinned, taking her room key. 'I think you say *magnifique.*'

'See, you're already learning French,' Colette grinned.

Annie put the key in her pocket. 'I'm trying. Enjoy your day off.'

When she stepped in the lift she glanced at her reflection in the three-sided mirror. Luc was right, she looked different.

21

The breeze drifting through the open window ruffled Annie's hair, waking her from a deep sleep. She opened her eyes, listening to Paris pulsing outside. People laughed on the street below and somewhere a dog barked. She could smell bread baking at the *boulangerie* across the street as she smiled up at the oak beams towering above her. Almost a week had gone by without a nightmare, the luxury of enough sleep a small miracle.

She stretched across the bed, thinking of Monet's garden and the other miracle that had happened there. It had seemed she would never pick up a brush or pen again and now she had a series of sketches. Perhaps her life really could start over. Images of Giverny danced around her. She could still see the colours of the garden with mist hanging low over the lily ponds, the house like a jewel in the middle of it all.

The alarm buzzed on her travel clock, interrupting the potent memory. As she groped to turn it off, she was face to face with Leo's photo on the bedside table. She squinted at it, her smile melting. Here she was after a day out in the French countryside and there was

Leo, dead. She studied his image, trying to decipher the unfamiliar emotion overwhelming her. Guilt had never been part of her grief before and she grabbed the photo, burrowing under the blankets while she held it to her heart.

She wasn't sure how long she'd hidden under the blankets, but eventually her aching body forced her out of bed. She put the photo back on the bedside table, moving her head from side to side to loosen the tight muscles in her neck. Across from her, the carry bag from Giverny sat crumpled on the floor. She reached inside, unwinding a small wad of tissue paper. The ceramic cat rolled out into the palm of her hand and as she looked down at it, the idea of a new studio in Lucy's old bedroom now seemed impossible. The tears she'd fought under the blankets were sliding down her face. She put the souvenir in front of Leo's photo, turning towards the bathroom.

When she stepped into the shower, her pent-up emotions exploded under the hot water. She began to howl, the mournful sound like a wounded animal as she slid to the bottom of the shower recess. The toxic cocktail of guilt and grief catapulted her with lightning speed to the edge of hysteria. She leant against the tiles, remembering when she'd collapsed at the hospital after Leo's cancer operation, her emotions disabling her now like they had then. She sobbed into her hands, trying to muffle the sound of her despair while the memory washed over her with the cascading water.

She was transported back to that time when Leo's surgeon had invited her into a family lounge outside the theatre suite. Every detail of the lounge was still clear: the outdated curtains with geometric swirls, the worn couch, stains on the coffee table. He'd sat across from her analysing the surgery, the medical jargon like a foreign language.

She thought of his guarded eyes and the fleeting glances to the wall clock, making it clear she'd only been allocated a certain amount of his precious time. As he'd talked, she tried to second-guess what he was getting at, but she'd been unprepared for what came next even though they had already been warned about the probable prognosis.

After he'd finished his medical report, the main function of the family lounge had been revealed to her, the lesson administered with clinical precision as he confirmed Leo's terminal prognosis. She'd cried out at the death sentence as if he'd punched her, jumping up from the couch and backing into a corner of the room. He'd stood to face her without a trace of emotion, asking if she had any questions.

His voice had sounded distorted to her like he was talking under water. Mute with shock and unable to utter a single word, her legs had given way as she slid down the wall. From her vantage point on the floor, she'd seen his mismatched socks, a small detail in the eye of the storm.

The image was still so vivid, she was sure she could see him now looking down at her through the steam in the shower. The vision fuelled her distress as she remembered him coaxing her back to the couch. He'd sat looking down at the scuffed floor tiles, his arms folded tight across his chest while he'd waited for her to pull herself together. By then it felt like she was hovering on the ceiling looking down at her other self, broken and battered as if he'd beaten her.

Eventually he'd cleared his throat, handing her a box of tissues branded with the hospital logo. She'd glimpsed his socks again as he'd hurried out the door, leaving her still slumped on the couch while he went to find a nurse to clean up the pieces of her shattered world.

That night played out like a film in her head while she huddled in the shower. She could see Leo still unconscious in the recovery room as she'd sat beside him, unsure of how to tell him the grim news. They had always hoped his prognosis would be proven wrong. Even when he'd been taken to theatre, both of them had been sure everything would be okay.

Annie thought of the devastation during the rest of that year as the cancer devoured him and the life they had once known. The film was now on fast forward, all the images spinning out of control. Water from the shower pummelled the top of her head while she hugged her knees trying to stop what she was feeling, but she was powerless.

She could see herself flushing all of Leo's medication down the toilet the day after he'd died. The empty packets littered the bathroom tiles as she'd punched the silver button on the cistern again and again, the pills a colourful whirlpool in the toilet bowl. When they finally disappeared, she'd gone into the kitchen, empty-ing the refrigerator shelf of morphine that hadn't been collected yet by the palliative care nurses.

She'd grabbed a box of matches and a bag of syringes, running outside with the morphine stuffed in her pockets. She'd dumped it all on the lawn under the clothesline and lit a match with her trembling hand. When the fire had taken hold, the vials in the boxes had exploded like fireworks, sending her staggering back to the verandah where she'd crawled up the steps, crumpling at the top.

She'd cried out at each explosion, her heart racing while she watched the spectacle. When it had ended, she'd curled into a ball, wanting to die. She'd been too exhausted to move, eventually falling asleep where she'd collapsed while the remains of the fire smouldered under the clothesline. The scorched grass had taken months to fade, but the scar that day left in her mind couldn't be erased no matter how hard she tried.

Annie tilted her face towards the shower rose to wash away the mucus and the terrible memories choking her. She braced her back against the tiles trying to control her scattered thoughts. When the water began to cool, she reached up and pushed off the mixer tap with the tips of her fingers. The noise of the gushing water gave way to the sound of the gurgling drain. She sat with her chest still heaving from the outburst, unsure how she could reach such depths after what she'd felt at Giverny. She needed to think of something else.

The tiles were cold on her back as she closed her eyes, trying to focus on the breakfast room in the hotel cellar. It would be open now, all the pastries, cheeses, fruit, and cold meats displayed on platters while little tubs of yoghurt would be sitting on ice in a silver bucket. Downstairs everything was normal, but at the bottom of the shower recess, her world was threatening to fall apart again.

She arched her back, looking around for something to grip, but there was only the mixer tap high above her. If she didn't crawl, she would be trapped. She glanced down at her ample curves, silently cursing for gaining weight. Pain stabbed at her knees as she crept out of the shower recess on all fours. When she reached the sink, she grabbed the white porcelain while she pulled herself to her feet.

Water dripped from her wet curls as she wrapped a towel around her body. She wiped her hand across the fogged mirror, gasping at the stranger looking back at her through the smear. She touched the puffy skin around her swollen eyes, knowing she couldn't face the other hotel guests at breakfast.

After she dressed, she scooped up her shoulder bag from the bedside table and tucked the ceramic cat into the drawer. Her makeup case was in the bathroom, but she was too exhausted to fix her face. Why bother, she thought; she was only a nobody in a big city.

She put on her sunglasses and looked around one last time. If she didn't hurry, Armand would soon be knocking on her door to clean her room and she didn't have the energy to play happy tourist. When she went into the hall, she could see him through the open door of the next room. He was making a bed and didn't notice her as she hurried to the lift, hiding behind her over-sized sunglasses.

She had no idea where she was going. When she reached the corner, two cafés were already open. She walked across to the one overlooking the river, choosing a table in the sun. As she scraped back a chair, a waiter appeared out of nowhere, startling her.

'*Bonjour, Madame.*'

There was no time to pull out her phrase book, but some of the right words rolled off her tongue. '*Café crème*, please.'

He slipped into English. 'Would you like something else with your coffee?' She stared at him through the blue tint of her sunglasses, flopping on the chair. He was an older man with grey hair and looked tired. Behind him inside the café, she could see a glass stand of pastries on a counter.

'Could I please have a plain croissant?'

'Yes, Madame; it won't be long.'

She watched him shuffle back into the café, his shoulders slightly stooped. It seemed unfair he was waiting on tables at his age, but life wasn't always fair, even in the City of Light. She looked out to the river. Five days ago, she'd been on the train giggling at the wild children throwing bread rolls down the aisle.

Her phone rang while she watched a stream of tourists passing the café. She answered without checking the incoming number, blinking when she heard Muriel's voice.

'I got your text.'

'I'd given up ever hearing back from you.'

'Sorry,' Muriel apologised, 'but there's been a lot of stuff going on here. Paul's away on a business trip and Jason moved out yesterday to live with his girlfriend. It's been a hectic few days getting them both launched.'

Annie listened to her trying to find excuses. She knew her well enough to recognise she was nervous.

'I don't know where to start,' Muriel rushed on. 'If I could change a few things in my life, one of them would be the last time I saw you. I'm so sorry for what happened.'

'It was all my fault. I think I went mad.'

'No, I said all the wrong things and it's bothered me ever since. I'm the one who should be apologising, and I should've done it sooner than now.'

'I don't know what to say,' Annie gulped. There was a silence and she squirmed in her seat.

'So how do you like Paris?' Muriel asked, her voice strained.

'It's been difficult, but I'm trying. Yesterday I went to Giverny to see Monet's house and garden. It was beautiful. Other than that, I haven't seen much. I'm taking one day at a time.'

'Maybe it will get better.'

'I hope so.'

Their stilted conversation petered out and there was another silence.

'Well, take care of yourself. I might ring again another time to see how you're going.'

'That would be nice.' Annie put her phone on the table, biting the side of her lip. The call had been like talking to a stranger.

22

Georgina finished her tea and looked out at the rooftops. Decorative wrought iron wrapped around the balcony outside the apartment window. Across the square she could see the Pompidou Centre with its famous exposed pipes. The modern gallery always reminded her of a spaceship that had just landed in the middle of Paris. She sat at the small table by the window smiling at the crowds streaming through the entrance. No matter how many times she came back, she could never get enough of this city.

She was enjoying the leisurely start to the day and stretched, thinking of Patrick as she walked to the door. His first birthday was coming up in a few weeks and she wanted to buy him something, but she wasn't quite sure what. She'd seen a toyshop at Île Saint-Louis on her last trip to Paris and decided to start her search there. Grabbing her keys from the hall table, she smiled as she went out the door. Somewhere out there a special toy was waiting for her darling grandson.

The cafés in Rue de Rivoli were busy with locals gulping down their first coffee of the day. Tourists were emerging from their hotels in casual clothes, looking like they were all stamped with the same brand. Georgina shivered; please, God, never let her want to wear cargo shorts.

When she reached Île Saint-Louis, most of the shops weren't open yet and only two cafés on the corner were serving customers. She walked by several closed restaurants before she saw the little toyshop with fairy lights twinkling in the window. Its front door was open. She stopped to admire a display of pink dollhouses before walking around the aisles while she waited to be served. Fairy dresses hung from a rack in an aisle devoted to dolls. She smiled as she listened to a young shop assistant helping a customer choose one of the dresses.

'They're so cute,' the customer said with an Irish accent, holding up a frilly confection of pink tulle and lace. 'I'll take this one and the purple one, too. I can't wait to see my little granddaughter's face when I show her these.'

Georgina waited until the dresses were packed into a carry bag before she walked to the counter. The Irish customer glanced across to her. 'I love being a grandmother,' she giggled on her way out the door.

Georgina smiled at the shop assistant behind the counter. 'I'm another grandmother.'

'You're the third one this morning.'

23

The corner café on Île Saint-Louis buzzed with conversations. Annie sat thinking of Muriel's awkward phone call, doubting if she would ever ring back. It seemed their fractured friendship was beyond repair. As she began to count out euros to pay her bill, a blaring horn interrupted her calculations. She looked up at a car stalled in the middle of the narrow street. The driver of a delivery van behind the car leant on his horn, shouting out the window.

A petite woman on the corner watching the altercation caught her eye. Her skirt billowed in the breeze around her red boots. Annie acted on pure instinct, leaving the money on the table and running out to the street.

'Excuse me, excuse me!' she called out as she ran towards the woman.

The woman turned and Annie laughed. 'I can't believe it's you. I recognised your boots.' The woman stepped back and Annie realised she might have done the wrong thing, but it was too late. 'You gave me the tissues on the boat,' she blurted.

'Yes, of course; you're the Australian.'

Annie fidgeted with the top button of her cardigan. 'I'm Annie Green.'

'And I'm Georgina Hasluck.' She put out her hand and Annie smiled as she shook it.

'I'm sorry if I startled you,' she said, and Georgina's expression softened.

'I wondered whatever happened to you.'

'There's a simple explanation. Would you like to join me for a coffee?'

'Perfect, I've been shopping and could kill for an espresso.'

Georgina followed her back to the café. Annie touched her sunglasses, conscious now of how dishevelled she looked. 'I'll leave these on if you don't mind; the glare is hurting my eyes. It must be jet lag.'

'That's fine,' she nodded, sitting down. 'How have you been?'

Annie thought about the lesson in the restaurant. Lies, she must stick to lies. 'I'm having a great time.' She smoothed her still damp curls, looking at the glamorous woman across the table. Her blue eyes were penetrating. Annie shifted in her seat. 'I'm really sorry I didn't show up yesterday. I forgot about a tour booked for Giverny.'

'I did wait for a while.'

'I had no way of contacting you.'

'It doesn't matter now,' Georgina said, waving her hand. 'Did you like Giverny?'

'I loved it. I love Monet full stop.'

'That makes two of us.'

Annie forgot about her appearance as she became animated, recounting her day trip. She eventually took off her sunglasses and if Georgina noticed her swollen eyes, she didn't mention it as they discussed their favourite artist. Two coffees later, they stood to leave.

'Shall we try again?' Georgina asked, slinging the toyshop carry bag over her arm.

'I'd like that, but maybe we'd better exchange phone numbers this time.' Annie pulled out one of the napkins from the wad still in her bag. She tore off a corner and as she jotted down her number, Georgina saw the sketch.

'You're an artist.'

She looked up, surprised. 'I used to be.'

'You still are; this sketch is exquisite. Do you have any more?'

'Only these,' she said, pulling out the other napkins. 'I haven't done anything for ages and never thought to bring a sketchbook to Giverny. The napkins left over from a lunch were all I had on me.'

Georgina examined each drawing. 'They really are lovely. You'll get some proper paper while you're here, won't you?'

'I already have. I'll be doing more sketching today.'

'Would you be free on Saturday afternoon?'

'I'm free most afternoons for the next two weeks,' Annie smiled, taking back the napkins.

'Why don't we meet at the Louvre? I could be there at one o'clock if it suits you.' She pulled out a black-and-white business card from her bag. 'Here's my number if you get lost. I'll be in front of the glass pyramid.'

'Thanks, Georgina, I'll definitely be there this time.'

Georgina ruffled her spiky hair, the silver bracelets coiled around her wrist sparkling in the sun. 'I've never liked my name, it's so old school. Call me George; all my friends do.'

24

Lucy threw her keys on the hall table and turned on the lamp, kicking her stilettos in the corner. Her legs ached from standing all day. New autumn stock was now hanging in her shop after days of unpacking and she was exhausted from running a one-woman show.

She padded into the kitchen, thinking of her mother. She wasn't prone to sentimentality, but a niggling emptiness haunted her when she thought of that night at the airport. Her mother had been a forlorn figure in front of international departures, clutching her shabby tote bag like her life depended on it. She'd almost cried watching her. But if she'd offered any words of comfort, she knew Annie would never have boarded the plane.

Now here in the sterile kitchen of her South Yarra apartment, all she wanted was her mother. Lucy smiled as she thought of her on the other side of the world and couldn't wait any longer to hear her voice again.

* * *

The phone rang several times before Annie answered.

'Hi, it's Lucy.'

'What a lovely surprise; it's so nice to actually talk to you. I hate this texting business.'

Lucy smiled; her mother was so anti-technology. 'I know you do, but it saves money.'

'If you want to save money, why are you ringing me?'

'I don't think a couple of calls will matter. Anyway, we didn't have much time to talk when you rang from the train. So, what's new?'

'Well, let me think.' Her voice trailed off and Lucy could hear traffic noise.

'You're in Paris for God's sake. What have you been doing?'

'Trying to get used to it all.'

'Your last text said you were on your way to Giverny. How was it?'

'Beautiful.'

Lucy tilted her head; something wasn't quite right, but she wasn't sure what it was. 'Tell me how you really are.'

'It's been hard; I wish your father was here.'

'Can't you try to enjoy yourself without him?'

'You'll never understand how I feel, so I won't waste your time and money trying to explain.'

Lucy ruffled her hair. 'Of course I know you miss Dad, but I want you to have this special time to grab some happiness while you can.' She could hear her mother laughing.

'What's with your generation? You always have to grab something or tick a box or make it happen. You're in such a hurry, rushing through life without really seeing it.'

Lucy paced around the kitchen as she listened. Fuck, where was this coming from? She eventually got a word in. 'All I want you to do is enjoy yourself.'

Annie talked over her. 'You make happiness sound like it's a tangible thing you can take off a shelf and buy. What a ridiculous concept.'

'Right, I won't ask how you are,' Lucy snapped.

'Don't get huffy; I was only giving you my opinion. But to finish answering your question about Giverny, I loved it. I'll always be grateful for what you and Mia have done for me. I've even started sketching again.'

'That's fantastic. Are you going to keep at it?'

Annie's voice became lighter. 'I hope to. I'm going out to sketch by the river today and on Saturday I'm going to the Louvre. The art here is amazing. The whole city feels like one big gallery. I'm meeting George there.'

'George? Who's George?' Lucy leant against the kitchen bench, stunned.

'Not that Frenchman I've been looking for,' Annie giggled.

'Mum, who in the hell is he?' Annie's phone cut out. 'Shit, why do you always forget to use your charger?' she shouted, stomping out of the kitchen.

Lucy paused the vacuum cleaner and looked out from the Victorian weatherboard. Rampant groundcover wrapped around the trunk of a weeping cherry tree while leaves covered the verandah. Weeds choked the flowerbeds, spilling out over the edge of the driveway and brick border near the steps. Two rubbish bags on the verandah had tilted sideways, blocking the screen door.

She started the vacuum cleaner again. Its drone competed with the whine of the lawn mower in the back garden. Lucy moved all the furniture in the lounge room as she vacuumed her mother's house, throwing anything in her way on the couch. The growing pile included yellowed newspapers, two worn paperbacks, a shrivelled apple core and several odd socks. She'd just found one of her father's slippers under the leather recliner in the corner.

The state of the house had surprised her. She was so busy with her own life, she hadn't noticed how much her mother had let things go. The vacuum cleaner was caked with dust and smelled like a wet dog. She wrinkled her nose while she worked, trying to reach all the neglected corners of the room. As she pushed the vacuum under the coffee table, it sucked up something solid, sounding like metal crunching while it tried to digest the offending object. She flicked the switch with her foot and it ground to a stop.

'Hey, what's going on in there?' Mia called out from the kitchen. 'It sounds like you've just murdered the vac.'

'I ran over something, but don't ask me what it was,' she shouted back. 'This room is a tip.'

'You should see the pantry if you think that's bad.' Mia's voice was muffled. 'Come have a look.'

Lucy unplugged the vacuum cleaner and walked into the kitchen. It looked ransacked. Mia was down on her knees with her head in the cupboard under the kitchen sink. 'What are you doing?'

'We decided to clean the house, so I'm cleaning. I've already put a few bags of rubbish out the front.'

'We only agreed on a tidy-up to surprise Mum, not to go through all the cupboards.'

'Well, I might as well,' Mia said, brushing the knees of her jeans as she stood to face her sister. 'Did you know there's an infestation of bugs in the pantry? I don't know where they're coming from.'

Lucy went into the walk-in pantry with Mia behind her, swatting a tea towel at the insects scurrying across the floor. 'Maybe they're coming from those bags of flour,' she pointed to the corner. 'There, near the baskets on the floor.'

Mia pulled out the bags and the floor looked like it was moving as the insects swarmed towards them. 'Oh no, what are they?'

'Weevils.' Lucy pushed a bag with the toe of her shoe. 'Mum has weevils.'

'Why hasn't she got rid of them?'

'She might not come in here anymore.'

Mia pulled a tin of soup off the shelf and checked the label. 'This is out of date. Probably everything in here is. It's a bit like a time capsule. Everything has been left since Dad went.'

Lucy turned her around by the shoulders. 'Out; I can't stand to look at it anymore.' She flicked off the light, closing the door behind them. 'Let's have a coffee. Check if David wants one.'

She filled the kettle and looked out the window. She could see him mowing the back corner of the lawn near the vegetable patch. His jumper was hanging on the picket fence her father built before he died.

'I moved the mugs to the cupboard near the sink,' Mia called out as she went into the garden. She waved at David to get his attention. 'Lucy's making coffee. Do you want one?' she shouted across to him.

He turned off the mower, wiping his forehead. 'What?'

'Coffee?'

'Not now, I still have to load up the junk from the shed.'

'Let us know when you're going and we'll pack up, too.'

He waved and turned on the mower again, the whine deafening as she went back to the kitchen. 'He's too busy to stop,' she said, taking a mug of coffee from Lucy. 'Anyway, I think he's over it. He probably can't wait to get out of here.'

'Can you blame him?'

'Not really,' Mia said, sitting on the stool by the sink. 'This is all terrible. It feels like the house has lost its spirit. A bit like Mum.'

Lucy sipped her coffee. 'It's not as if she's a frail old lady unable to fend for herself. I can't understand how she could let things slip like this.'

'I think what's worse is we let her.'

'That's bullshit.'

'It's true. She's been going down the gurgler and we should've stepped in.'

'So, what are you suggesting?'

'For a start it'll take another go to clean up this mess,' Mia said, looking around the kitchen. 'And then we should organise some counselling for her when she gets back.'

Lucy crossed her arms, glaring at her sister. 'Weevils in the flour hardly means she needs a shrink.'

'It's more than the weevils. You know how house-proud she used to be. And she used to love her garden. All this is a reflection of what's going on in her mind. It's obvious she's given up on life. And now I'm really starting to wonder what was happening on that balcony at the hospital.'

'She sounded pretty good last night.'

'You only told me a little while ago you thought she sounded odd.'

'Yeah, she did, ranting about our generation. It was so unlike her. But I have to admit she actually sounded happy about getting back to her art. I would just like to know who this guy is.'

'Why is that bothering you?'

'You know she's not streetwise. Anyone could take advantage of her.'

'That sounds Victorian,' Mia laughed. 'You've been watching too many of those historical films.'

Lucy shrugged, draining her mug. 'So, when is our next cleaning gig?'

'What about Wednesday night?'

'Suits me. The shop won't be open.'

'We should just about finish it, but we'll have to attack those weevils before we go today.'

'What about Dad's stuff? His clothes are all over the house.'

'That's a no-go area,' Mia said, putting her mug in the sink. 'It's something Mum has to do herself. If she comes back and finds his things gone, she'll be really upset.'

'It doesn't seem normal to me. It's all a reminder sitting here every day. We should at least pack it away out of sight in the garage. I could get some boxes from the shop.'

'You can't erase Dad to heal her. It all takes time. His clothes are obviously giving her some sort of comfort. I saw her squeezing one of his jumpers into her tote bag before we went to the airport. It was the blue one he loved so much. I didn't have the heart to say anything.'

'Now you sound Victorian. She's like Queen Victoria making a fucking science of grieving and you're encouraging her.'

'You're getting hard. You need a man in your life.'

Lucy felt her face flush. 'Yeah, sure and end up like Mum. No thank you.'

'You're always pushing the boundaries, aren't you? I don't want to hear any more. Just leave it.'

'Okay, Saint Mia; I'm going. You can deal with the weevils.' Lucy banged her mug on the bench and flounced across the kitchen, snatching her handbag from the table. 'See you on Wednesday night.'

'About seven o'clock; I'll bring a pizza,' Mia called after her, as Lucy slammed the front door.

Lucy finished wiping the top of the vanity, looking around her mother's bathroom. Every surface sparkled under the fluorescent lights. She could smell the faint odour of insect repellent that still permeated the whole house, evidence of Mia's killing spree in the pantry on the weekend.

'How are you going?' Mia called out from the kitchen.

'Just finished,' Lucy shouted back. 'I'll need a drink after this. Two cleaning gigs in a week are too much. You owe me big time.'

'You're no domestic goddess,' Mia laughed, adjusting the blind over the kitchen sink.

Lucy came out of the bathroom peeling off a pair of disposable gloves. 'I heard that.'

'I thought you would've taken it as a compliment.'

Lucy's broad smile faded as she surveyed the kitchen, sorrow clouding her face. She ran her hand over the benchtops, blinking back tears as the dishwasher whirred in the background. 'This place looks totally different.'

'It's how it was before Dad got sick,' Mia said, hanging a tea towel on the side of the sink.

'The cancer ruined everything.'

Mia nodded, the look exchanged between them transcending the transformed kitchen. 'I'll wait until this load of dishes is finished. You go and I'll lock up when it's done.'

Lucy started to say something, but didn't finish, adjusting the pots of African violets on the windowsill over the sink. She stood with her back to Mia, taking a deep breath. 'You're a star,' she chirped when she turned around, her cheerful tone at odds with her sad expression. She picked up the empty pizza box from the kitchen table. 'I'll bin this on my way out. What about a drink soon?'

'Sounds good. Anyway, as you said, I owe you one.'

Lucy looked back at her before she went out the door. 'This was one of our better ideas, kiddo; the house looks awesome.'

25

The cobblestone street snaked up the hill from the river. Georgina walked along a narrow footpath, wondering why the conversation with the Australian woman had made her long to see these streets again. She'd avoided the Latin Quarter for years, but the chance meeting the day before had changed her mind.

They hadn't discussed anything more than Monet, but even as she asked herself the question, she already knew the answer. When she looked at Annie, she saw herself after that first trip to Paris all those years ago. It was easy to spot a wounded soul; she was an expert on the subject.

As she walked the familiar street, she thought about the first time she'd seen the Latin Quarter. Her hair had been long and blonde, her skirt thigh-high. She had been wearing her favourite cropped leather jacket and a pair of ill-fitting platform shoes that had nearly crippled her on the cobblestones.

She had been with a group of university friends, her last-minute decision to join them fuelled by both peer pressure and the desire to conquer her fear of the sea. The rough English Channel crossing was endured out on the deck of a small ferry. She'd sat gazing at the grey horizon trying to overcome the nausea that had started as soon as they left Dover.

When she'd wobbled down the gangplank in Calais, she'd thought she would never recover, but she did and a few days later they had all been invited to a student party somewhere near the Sorbonne. By then she had felt such a connection with France, she'd been sure she'd inherited some memory gene from an unknown French relative.

It had been no surprise she'd been attracted to Alain when he'd started talking to her at the crowded party, charming her with his accent and brooding, brown eyes. He hadn't been like anyone she'd ever met before and at the end of the party she left with him, walking the dark streets of the Latin Quarter near the university.

The sky had been turning a soft pink over the rooftops of Paris when she climbed the steep stairs to his tiny attic bedsit feeling like she'd known him all her life. She didn't go back to London with her friends at the end of the week and it wasn't until winter the following year that she had returned home. By then she'd been fluent in French, but there had been no language to describe a broken heart.

She tried to ignore the memory that still had the power to torture her. A young Alain wasn't going to appear around the next corner on his motorcycle and whisk her away to a happy ever after. She needed to stop thinking of the past. He'd been the shooting star in her life, lighting up her world for a brief time before disappearing on the horizon. But she had John to remember him by and now Patrick with those brown eyes like his grandfather.

She stopped at an antique shop, peering at a tall silver vase displayed in the window. The shopkeeper saw her, slipping his reading glasses into his shirt pocket before walking towards the door. She turned away, her vow to stop buying antiques wavering as she hesitated on the corner before continuing along the cobblestones. No more silver vases, she lectured herself; there were already five tarnishing in a cupboard at home.

26

The river was the colour of green olives. Annie sat with a sketch pad propped up on her knees as tourist boats glided by. Snippets of music drifted across the water while she worked quickly to capture the scene in front of her. As she sketched, she thought of what Georgina must think of her. Each time they had met she was either bawling her eyes out or trying to hide the evidence of another crying binge.

She would redeem herself at the Louvre on Saturday and there would be no sad stories, no tears, only a bland version of what Georgina wanted to hear. There could be no smeared lipstick this time. She would have to spruce herself up, maybe buy a new scarf.

She looked down at the sketch. It was nearly done now, a replica of what she was looking at. She finished the shading around one of the boats before holding out the drawing, smiling as she compared it to the view across the river. It seemed she still had it.

*　*　*

Gravel crunched under Annie's feet as she wandered through the garden. The paths were laid out in a pattern of long avenues with statues and wide terraces adding to the formality. She kept walking until she found somewhere to sit, propping her Giverny carry bag beside her as she eased down on a garden seat. A large pond in the distance was dotted with toy sailboats. She could hear children squealing with excitement as they raced the boats across the water.

The design of the garden was soothing and she felt herself relaxing while she soaked up the sun. She pulled out her tiny map, moving her finger across the page to find where she was. By tracing from the river, it seemed she was in the Luxembourg Garden.

The garden was a long walk from the river, but she'd been swept along by the crowds, using them as a buffer to cross the busy streets. The panic of those first few days was gone, but she was still wary of the traffic. She closed her eyes, tilting her head backwards. She couldn't waste the chance to sit in the sun on a warm Parisian day; it would never come again.

Her eyes flew open when she felt her body sliding sideways. She sat upright, hoping no one had seen her nod off. A man walking with a young child grinned across to her. She felt her cheeks flush as she realised she must have been snoring. She reached for the carry bag of sketches at her feet, trying to bend forward with her bulging shoulder bag still strapped across her chest.

She took several deep breaths before she stood, walking back along a gravel path. When she reached the busy street, she looked across to a restaurant on the corner. Her growling stomach told her it had been hours since breakfast. The traffic light changed and she followed the crowd in front of her to the other side, debating whether she could face a solo lunch. Her stomach growled again and she took a chance.

The restaurant hummed with the lunchtime crowd. Annie stood on the threshold looking for a vacant table. A waiter hurried across to her.

'*Bonjour, Madame.*'

She tried to imitate Emilio's self-confidence. '*Bonjour,*' she smiled. 'A table, please.'

'There's one near the window,' the waiter answered in English, leading her to a small table overlooking the gated garden across the street.

'*Merci,*' she whispered as he pulled out the chair for her.

'Will you be having wine with your meal?'

Annie looked around at the other diners. 'Could you choose for me? I'd like a glass of red wine.'

He smiled and handed her a menu. She watched him walk away, silently thanking Emilio for being such a perfect role model. The menu was extensive. She took a deep breath, trying to decipher the words. If she took out her phrase book now it would take too long to try to translate. Don't panic, she told herself, it's only a menu. She would have to wing it. When the waiter returned with her wine she was still struggling.

'Do you need some help?'

'It's all in French.' As soon as the words slipped out, she laughed, looking up at the waiter's amused expression. 'What a ridiculous thing to say; I'm sorry,' she grinned. 'I'd really like some meat; is there any on the menu?'

He pointed to several dishes listed on the second page. 'If you like beef, steak tartare is always popular. It's prepared with spices and served with an egg and potatoes.'

'It sounds delicious. Yes, I'll have that.'

He took the menu, disappearing into the crowded restaurant. She picked up her glass, studying the light filtering through the ruby liquid before taking a sip. The fruity wine warmed her throat as she looked out to the garden. She was thankful she wasn't sitting in the middle of the restaurant with no one to talk to while the other diners chatted around her.

As she sat looking out at the busy street, the waiter returned with a basket of bread and a small bowl of nuts, carefully placing them in front of her. Annie touched the linen tablecloth; it was all so stylish. Her wine was nearly gone when he came back with a large white plate, placing it on the table with a flourish.

'*Bon appétit,*' he trilled before turning away.

Annie reeled back when she saw what was in front of her, remembering the American woman complaining about French food at Gare du Nord. She looked down at a patty of raw mince steak sprinkled with parsley and capers. A raw egg yolk like a yellow eye stared back at her from the top of the pink meat. It was nestled near a mound of thin chips on the side of the plate.

She didn't know what to do. If she sent it back, she would appear foolish and if she left money on the table before walking out, she would seem rude. She picked up her fork and toyed with her meal.

She slid the egg off the patty, dipping the bread into the runny yoke before eating all the chips. When she finished, she took a forkful of meat and squeezed her eyes shut before putting it in her mouth. It was surprisingly tasty as it slid down her throat, but the texture made her gag. She washed it down with the last of her wine knowing if she tried to eat any more there was every chance she would vomit.

She pulled out a wad of tissues from her shoulder bag, glancing around at the other diners. No one seemed to be looking in her direction as she scooped up a handful of mince with the tissues, shoving the small parcel inside her bag. She stared down at what was left, trying not to retch. There had to be a reward after this, she thought, and it had to be chocolate.

When the waiter returned, his lips pursed as he picked up her plate. 'The steak tartare wasn't to your liking?'

'It was lovely, but I want to leave room for dessert.' His face lit up and Annie sighed; she'd become a chronic liar. 'Would you have something chocolate on the menu? Anything will do.'

'We have chocolate soufflé. Would you like that?'

'It sounds divine,' she smiled up at him before he hurried back to the kitchen with her plate. She could still taste the raw meat as she opened her bag to search for a mint, careful not to disturb the bundle already leaking blood through the tissues.

27

Lucy felt someone watching her. The feeling was there before when she'd cleared her mother's letterbox, but she never saw anyone. She flipped back the lid of the wheelie bin, dropping in a pile of junk mail. A rustling noise made her spin around, trying to gauge where the sound was coming from. Jess was standing at the end of the driveway in a purple dressing gown and fluffy slippers with the morning paper jammed under her arm.

Lucy recoiled. 'Shit, you scared me. I didn't expect to see anyone so early in the morning.' She slammed the lid, pushing the bin back into place.

'And I could say the same. Why are you here at this time of the day? Is your mother sick or something?'

'She's on a holiday. Didn't she tell you she was going away?'

'We don't talk much these days,' Jess sneered, fidgeting with the newspaper. Her discoloured teeth reminded Lucy of the pet rat in Mia's classroom. She blinked to concentrate on what the old woman was saying. 'I did run into her at the supermarket about six weeks ago, though. She told me some story about going to Paris.'

'And you didn't believe her,' Lucy bristled.

'Well, I found it hard to imagine your mother going on a trip like that.'

'I can assure you she's in Paris. Don't you think she deserves a break after everything that's happened?'

'But she's been so emotional, especially with all that business about those nightmares. When she told me she was going overseas, I thought it was all wishful thinking. I mean really, how could I believe she was fit to go anywhere in her state?'

'What nightmares?' Lucy demanded.

Jess looked triumphant. 'It seems your mother has been keeping secrets from you.'

'What are you going on about?'

'Maybe you should ask your mother. It isn't my place to be telling tales,' she smirked.

'Since when?'

Pink blotches bloomed across Jess's neck as she clutched the collar of her dressing gown. 'You always were the cheeky one, even when you were a little girl. You're nothing like your sister.'

'What the fuck do you mean?'

'You have a foul mouth, young lady.' The blotches had now reached her face, droplets of saliva spraying as she spoke. 'Your mother will be hearing about your disrespectful language when she gets back.'

'Fine, and I won't forget to tell her what you've been saying about her. No doubt the entire neighbourhood knows by now.'

'How dare you.'

'Come on, Jess, it's too early for all this shit.'

'Stop swearing; you're a disgrace. And it's Mrs Walker to you, girlie.'

'Yeah, whatever,' Lucy said, brushing by her to the street. When she reached her car and looked back, Jess was still standing there. 'Go inside,' she called out, 'you'll be scaring the fucking neighbours in that little purple number.'

Jess lurched sideways into the fence, dropping the newspaper.

Lucy had to talk to someone, or she was sure she would explode. The clock on the dashboard displayed seven thirty as she parked in the next street and rang her sister. Mia sounded half asleep.

'Sorry it's so early,' Lucy apologised, 'but I need to talk for a minute.' She could hear Mia sigh.

'What's wrong?'

'I cleared Mum's letterbox a few minutes ago and ran into that bitch next door.'

'Mrs Walker?'

'Yeah, she cornered me in the driveway. And why do you always use her surname? You sound like you're still a kid.'

'Tell me why we're discussing this now? I'm trying to get ready for work.'

'The old girl told me something that's bothering me. She said Mum had been having nightmares and keeping it a secret. It sounds serious. Do you know anything about this?'

'Of course not; why would Mum tell me and not you? And if it's a secret, how does she know?'

'Don't fucking grill me; I don't know. I only needed to ask you.'

'Come on, Lucy, you're overreacting. It could have been a one-off nightmare Mum mentioned and now Mrs Walker is making it into a big deal. You know how malicious she is.'

'Would you ring Mum and ask? You're the diplomat.'

'I thought we were only going to text each other.'

'Stop being such a tight-arse.'

'I'll have to work out the time differences and ring her after school.'

'And ask about George.'

'I get it now,' Mia laughed. 'That's the real reason you want me to ring her.'

'I never said that.'

'So why do you mention him every time I talk to you?'

'I'm only worried about her state of mind now, not anything else, especially after what we saw when we cleaned the house. She's losing the plot. Ring me back after you've spoken to her.'

'Only if you promise to cool it.'

'Yeah, whatever.'

Lucy threw her phone on the passenger seat, staring at a man jogging by her car. When he reached the next corner a black-and-white Jack Russell on its morning walk nipped at his ankles while the owner pulled on its lead. Maybe she should get one of those for her mother. A mental image of a feisty Jack Russell chasing Jess down the driveway made her smile as she turned on the ignition.

28

David pulled his tie around his collar, walking into the kitchen behind Mia. 'I thought I heard your phone. Everything all right?'

'It was Lucy,' she said, turning towards him. 'She's worried about Mum.'

'That's a switch.'

She told him about their conversation as he made toast, smearing the sourdough with butter. He slid a plate across the bench, their breakfast ritual like a choreographed routine performed every morning as they stood in the kitchen before rushing out to work.

'That old woman's a real piece of work.'

'She's been like that forever,' Mia said, toying with her toast. 'Dad used to laugh at her, but she always got under Mum's skin. That's why I can't imagine her confiding anything to the local gossip. Anyway, I'm sure there was nothing to tell.'

David gulped his coffee. 'Stop speculating about it; just ring your Mum.' Mia dumped her untouched toast in the bin. 'No breakfast?'

'I'm still feeling queasy, the doctor said it will soon pass.'

He grinned and reached out his arms. 'Give me a kiss.'

* * *

Mia smiled when Annie answered her phone. 'It's great to hear your voice. I thought you'd want a break from texting.'

'How thoughtful of you.'

'So how's Paris?'

'Amazing. I'm in a beautiful garden behind Notre-Dame right now. I just had breakfast.'

'I won't keep you, but I want you to know Lucy ran into Mrs Walker this morning while she was clearing your letterbox. She said you're having nightmares and keeping it a secret from us. She made it sound pretty bad. Lucy's all worked up about it.'

'It's a long story,' Annie whispered.

'So, it's true?'

'She caught me off guard one day and I made the mistake of telling her. I blame it on the weather. It was stinking hot and I wasn't thinking straight. I've regretted it ever since.'

'Why haven't you told us about them?'

'It would only worry you both.'

'Are they that bad?'

'They were pretty regular and driving me nuts. I haven't had one for a while now.'

'That's a relief. What were they about?' Mia could hear her mother take a deep breath.

'I could never remember afterwards, but they used to wake me up all the time. I think being away from home has helped. Maybe Paris has something to do with it. I'm finally getting some sleep.'

'David's mother says the City of Light mends broken hearts. It might also banish nightmares.'

'Maybe it does.'

'I'm so proud of you.'

'Thanks, darling. I couldn't have done all this without your help. Please tell Lucy not to worry about me. And tell her I feel safe.'

'Any message for Mrs Walker?'

'Tell her to fuck off.'

'Mum,' she laughed. 'I can't believe you said that.'

'Neither can I. I guess I'm reinventing myself.'

'Before I go, I want to tell you something.'

'What is it?'

As Mia tried to answer, bells started ringing in the background.

'Tell me later, I can't hear you,' Annie shouted. 'I'm still near the cathedral. Love to everyone.'

29

The bells were deafening as Annie walked along the side of the cathedral. Ever since that first day in Paris, she'd heard them in the background, sometimes making her sad with their mournful notes, other times lifting her spirits. Today they would have made her happy if she hadn't heard what Jess said. As she walked, she thought of her neighbour. She should have known better than to confide anything to her and now she'd been forced to lie to Mia. The truth about the nightmares would have reminded her of that day at the hospital and she couldn't risk Mia figuring out what really happened. It had to stay a secret.

She went through a wrought-iron gate to a square crowded with pilgrims, tourists, and beggars. Two old women by the gate were on their knees, one holding out a paper cup, the other one saying the rosary. The woman with the rosary had her eyes shut, oblivious to the crowd around her as her lips moved in silent prayer. The woman begging called out to people as they went by, raising her cup in their direction.

Annie dropped a few coins in the cup. The woman bowed her head in thanks and she felt a twinge of sadness as she looked down at her. Colette told her not all beggars were genuine, but as she looked at the old woman's weathered face, she found it impossible to believe she was only acting. There could be nothing easy about kneeling all day while tourists walked by without a second glance. Annie smiled at her before turning away into the square, her own misfortune diminished. She would never be forced to beg in front of St Patrick's Cathedral in Melbourne.

Although it was only mid-morning, a queue of tourists was already waiting to go into the cathedral. She looked up, shielding her eyes from the sun with her hand. Workmen renovating the spire were on scaffolding like small stick figures against the backdrop of the cloudless sky. While she stood watching them, two young women ran across to her holding out clipboards with forms attached, gesturing for her to sign them.

'You sign, you sign,' they chorused.

She backed away before weaving across the square with the young women chasing after her. They were persistent and when they wouldn't stop following her, she turned and confronted them.

'I don't want to sign something I know nothing about. What's it for anyway?'

They shrugged and ran off, pestering another woman taking photos of the cathedral. Annie glared across at them, shaking her head. She'd seen them earlier in the week chasing a group of young Asian tourists. Today they were hitting on middle-aged women. She turned away, her face hot from the sprint across the square. When she reached the corner, the pedestrian lights changed and she was swept along with the crowd to the other side.

She skirted around a tour group, smiling at their broad British accents. As she kept walking, a large yellow sign in the distance caught her attention. It was partially hidden behind a row of trees in full bloom. When she was closer, the heady scent of the pink blossoms made her stop, reminding her of the trees in her own garden.

The distinctive sign stretched across the facade of a bookshop with a courtyard. Several people were hunched over reading on a weathered wooden pew near the entrance, the courtyard a quiet oasis in the middle of the bustling city. Paperbacks were displayed on tables nearby and she could see a crowd inside browsing for books. She stood smiling at a cat curled up on a windowsill. It all looked too inviting to pass by.

The smell of new books was unmistakable when she stepped inside. All the titles were in English. She stood in the corner near a rickety staircase listening to the ancient boards creaking as a flow of customers climbed to the next floor. Across from her a young woman stamped books piled on a counter, the sound exaggerated in the quiet bookshop.

Floor-to-ceiling shelves wrapped around the walls. Serious readers studied the book titles, while browsing customers circled the shop in the same direction. Annie squeezed between two women on a mission for a particular book, following them until she came to the art books. As she was trying to read the titles on a top shelf a loud voice boomed in the silence, making her flinch.

'Hey, Aussie.'

She turned around along with every other customer in the bookshop.

'Aussie, over here.'

A young man waved his arms in the air as if he were at a football match. She recognised him from the taxi queue outside Gare du Nord. When she waved back, he said something to the woman behind the counter before threading his way through the crowd towards her.

'I thought it was you,' he smiled.

'I can't believe what a small world it is,' she said, fluffing her curls.

'Yeah, I'm finding that out every day. By the way, I'm Ed Lewis.'

'I'm Annie Green,' she smiled up at him, unsure how this stranger could seem like a friend.

'So, Annie from Australia, how's Paris treating you?'

'Really good. What about you?'

'It's been awesome.'

She bit the side of her lip, not sure what else to say. Ed interrupted her thoughts. 'Do you feel like a coffee? I'm on a break and the café next door makes a good brew.'

'A break?'

'Yeah, I'm doing some work upstairs. If you have time, I'll fill you in on what I'm doing.'

Annie kept laughing as Ed described his blunders and triumphs in Paris. His face became animated when he told her about the first time he'd ventured into a Paris Métro Station. She leant across the table listening to the born storyteller in front of her.

'I was feeling pretty proud of myself,' he said, patting his chest. 'I managed to buy a ticket from a vending machine, checked the map on my phone and even counted all the stops to where I wanted to go. When I squeezed in a carriage everyone was packed in like sardines, but they kept joking around. You wouldn't see that where I come from. It was Sunday and I guess they were all feeling pretty mellow after their long lunches. I could smell a lot of garlic and wine.'

He took another gulp of coffee, grinning at the memory. 'When I got out, I looked up and saw this sign with the word *sortie* printed in big letters. I thought I'd missed my goddamn stop. I'd never heard of that place.'

'What did you do?' Annie grinned.

'I wandered around these white tiled tunnels trying to get out. It was crazy, I kept going in circles. Have you been in the Métro yet?'

She shook her head.

'Well, it can be confusing the first time. That day a jazz group was playing somewhere in the station and I could hear all this cool music. I finally went back to the platform and waited until another train came in so I could follow the crowd out to the street.'

Annie put down her cup. 'Did you find out where you were?'

He laughed, banging his hand on the table. 'As it turns out, *sortie* isn't a place, it's the French word for exit.' They both howled with laughter as people around them kept glancing in their direction, smiling at their noisy outburst. 'Man, I'll never forget that word,' Ed laughed, wiping his eyes. 'I see it everywhere now. And you know what, it turned out to be the right station. The name was displayed, but I didn't see it. The *sortie* sign was bigger.'

When Annie's fits of laughter subsided, she told him about the steak tartare. 'I kept thinking of the woman complaining about it to you outside the station.'

'Yeah, it really freaked her out. Did you eat yours?'

Annie wrinkled her nose. 'Only one mouthful. I put the rest in some tissues while no one was looking, although it made a real mess in my bag. I hate to think what happened when that woman was served hers.'

'She was something else. I feel sorry for the locals being invaded by so many tourists who can't speak their lingo. It must drive them nuts.'

Annie studied his face as he talked. Faint laugh lines were around his brown eyes and he had a wide smile. 'What work are you doing here?' she asked. He ordered more coffee and told her about the travel book he was writing.

'The bookshop has a library upstairs and they've let me use a desk if I do a few shifts in the shop. Someone in the States told me about the bookshop last year and I contacted the owner when I decided to come over. I'm lucky to be here; the place is famous.'

'I didn't know. I'm glad I stumbled across it.' She sat back in her chair. 'So, how long are you staying here?

'Until the end of the month. I want to try Italy next. What about you?'

'I still have a few weeks. My daughters gave me this trip as a special gift.'

'That's some gift. It must have been quite an occasion.'

Annie looked down at her hands. 'They thought I needed a holiday and wouldn't take no for an answer. How could I refuse?' It was clear they were running out of things to say. 'I better let you get back or you'll lose your spot in the library.' She stood and he joined her.

'Do you want to buy a book before you go?' he asked, putting a few coins on the table by their empty cups.

'I was looking for one about Monet. I love his work.'

'Let's go see if they have anything.'

It didn't take long to find what Annie wanted on one of the top shelves. Ed climbed a library ladder to retrieve it for her. 'Don't forget to have it stamped,' he said when he handed the book to her. 'They have this cool stamp that says where the book is from.'

'I was wondering what the shop assistant was doing when I came in.' She reached for her wallet, a faint whiff of dried blood making her nostrils twitch.

Ed was waiting for her by the door after she paid for the book and had it stamped. 'There's a reading here tomorrow night by an Irish author. Why don't you come? It starts at six upstairs in the library where I've been writing. There's no obligation to buy a book, but it's always interesting to meet the person behind the words.'

Annie hesitated, looking up at Ed's hopeful face. He seemed to read her mind. 'It's only for an hour and won't be a late night.'

'Okay, I'll be there,' she said on impulse. 'Thanks for asking me.' When she reached the kerb, she clutched the new book to her chest. She glanced back at the bookshop, wishing she'd said no.

The music grew louder as she climbed the worn stairs. Annie was gulping for air when she reached a small library where a young man was playing a piano. His back was to her and she could see his thin shoulders through his shirt while she tried to catch her breath.

A young woman standing next to him smiled, gesturing for Annie to take a seat. Her companion stopped playing and turned around. His face was flushed and a dark fringe flopped over his eyes.

Annie took a step back. 'I think … I think I'm in the wrong place,' she stammered. 'I came for a reading, not a recital.'

'You're in the right place,' he said in a thick Irish accent. He stood, pushing hair from his eyes. 'I'm just playing while they sell books downstairs before it starts.' He pulled across an old chair from the corner and she had no choice but to sit down. 'If you don't mind, I'll just finish this.' He continued playing while the young woman next to him turned the pages of sheet music. Her silver mini dress sparkled under the library spotlights.

Annie smiled at the young woman's boots that seemed like an odd choice for a warm spring evening, reminding her of her own slavish devotion to fashion when she was young. The weather had never dictated what she'd worn and she often froze or sweltered through the seasons. She glanced down at her puffy ankles, asking herself how that young woman from long ago could be her. It didn't seem possible as she sat there so far from home.

She squirmed on the chair, ready to bolt as someone tapped her on the shoulder. She looked around into Ed's smiling eyes. 'You brought me here under false pretences; I thought I was going to listen to an author,' she whispered, feigning annoyance.

'That's him – Rowan Finn.' He nodded towards the young man at the piano. 'He's hot property in publishing with four books out in the last few years.' She shook her head and he grinned. 'He's older than he looks.'

Annie fidgeted while she listened to the tedious reading. The young audience squeezed into the library was perched on every available chair while others stood with their backs against the bookshelves.

She kept glancing around trying to gauge if anyone else found the reading obscure, but the audience seemed enthralled with what they were listening to.

'The power of the force within is part of the wider world, the universe, the thing we call eternity.' The author stopped and looked up, gazing over his audience. When he looked directly at Annie, her cheeks burned. 'And eternity is the force within,' he said, closing the book he'd been reading from. The audience clapped and someone at the back whistled. He nodded to the woman who had introduced him before the reading and she joined him at the front of the room.

'Thank you, Rowan,' she said, touching his arm. 'I'm sure we'll all look at life differently now after your inspiring words.' She smiled across the sea of faces. 'If you want to have your books signed, Rowan will join you downstairs shortly.'

The applause started again and Annie stood, waving to Ed across the room. He followed her down to the bookshop.

'Did you enjoy it?' He seemed anxious to hear her opinion, his expression serious.

Annie thought it was safe to be honest. 'I didn't understand any of it. He was talking in riddles.'

'Why don't you buy his first book? I'm sure it would give you an insight into this latest one.'

'I'm not smart enough.'

'Don't say that about yourself.'

'It's true.' Hot tears stung her eyes as the old panic bubbled up from nowhere. She'd expected a pleasant night out, not a university lecture. She shouldn't have come.

He reached out and touched her elbow. 'What's wrong?'

'I'm not myself tonight, sorry.'

A young woman in a skin-tight dress with flowing black hair interrupted their conversation, tugging at Ed's shirtsleeve. 'We're waiting,' she whined, 'will you be much longer?'

'Give me a minute and I'll catch up,' he said over his shoulder.

She gave him a dazzling smile as she pranced out the door in her silver stilettos, ignoring Annie.

'She writes poetry,' he explained. 'We're going with a few other people to a jazz club in the Latin.'

Annie glanced at her own dowdy skirt and twinset reflected in the shop window, wishing she could disappear. 'You don't have to explain. I won't keep you.'

'Are you sure you'll be okay?'

'I'm a bit tired from this hay fever.' She rummaged through her bag for a tissue, pulling one out and blowing her nose to reinforce her lie. 'I get it every spring at home and it seems to be the same here.'

Ed glanced through the plate glass at the young woman and another couple waiting for him in the courtyard. When he looked back to Annie his forehead was furrowed. 'You don't happen to like jazz, do you?'

'You're very kind, but I don't think your friends would appreciate someone as old as their mothers tagging along,' she said, looking out to the courtyard. 'Thanks anyway.'

He shrugged, pulling at his collar. 'You'll have to come back again.' He opened the glass door, following her outside. 'I'll be upstairs most days. And if you change your mind about Rowan's book, you'll find it here. There's a display in the window.'

'I don't think I'll be buying any more books while I'm in Paris, but I'll definitely stop in before I leave for home. Enjoy yourself tonight.' She turned before he could answer her, blinking back tears as she hurried to the bridge on the corner.

While she walked, she tried to shake off the dark mood that had crept up on her without warning. The hip crowd had unsettled her, reducing her to nothing more than a middle-aged observer on the rim.

Everywhere couples were promenading along the streets arm in arm. She could hear laughter from the tables in front of cafés and music from buskers on the bridge. Lights were twinkling on all over the city as she stood looking down at the Seine. She could see people sitting on the banks of the river, the reflection of the lights on the water illuminating their silhouettes in the twilight.

She'd never felt so alone. Paris was no place for someone like her. When she dug in her bag for another tissue, she found Georgina's business card stuck under a bag of mints. She squinted at it in the half-light. Without thinking, she pulled out her phone and rang her. As she stood looking across to the shimmering Eiffel Tower on the horizon, Georgina answered, her posh British accent making Annie smile.

30

Annie stood searching the faces of the boisterous crowd. Lively French music pulsed in the background and she could smell the delicious aroma of something sweet. She wasn't sure what it was, but as she stood there, she had a fleeting memory of homemade apple pie in her mother's kitchen long ago. A waiter smiled when he saw her near the entrance.

'I'm here to meet a friend,' she told him as he smoothed his long apron, listening intently to what she was saying. 'But I can't see her anywhere.'

'I'll help you find her.' His English was halting and she felt a flash of remorse.

'I'm sorry I don't speak French.'

'It's okay, I need to practise my English,' he said, labouring over every word.

'For what it's worth, your accent is beautiful,' she offered and he grinned across to her.

The bistro reminded her of a film set with its wood panelled walls and chequerboard-tiled floor. Waiters rushed around them as they stood in front of the potted palms. When she saw Georgina waving from a back table, the waiter put out his arm to guide her, revealing a small star tattoo on his inner wrist. She blinked, thinking of the rude girl with the same design on her neck at the café in Melbourne. It seemed like a lifetime ago.

Georgina stood when they reached her. 'It's good to see you again. Did you have any trouble with my directions?' The waiter pulled out a chair and Annie slid on to it, stowing her bag under the table while Georgina sat down again.

'No, they were very clear, the striped awning was easy to spot.' She felt dishevelled from the brisk walk to the Marais, raking her fingers through her wild curls. 'I'm glad you could meet me at such short notice.'

The waiter leant towards her. 'Madame would like something to drink?'

She glanced across to Georgina's glass. 'A wine would be nice.'

'Do you like red?' Georgina asked.

'That's what I drink at home.'

Georgina looked up at the waiter, speaking in French as she held up her glass. He nodded and she smiled across the table to Annie. 'I hope you'll like the Bordeaux Rouge, it's a beautiful wine.'

'I'm sure I will. Just listening to you order it was beautiful. Where did you learn to speak French like that?' Georgina fingered the stem of her glass, multi-coloured bangles on her wrist jangling as she moved her arm.

'It's a long story.'

Annie glanced around at the buzzing bistro before looking back at her, now realising she expected an explanation for the phone call. She couldn't tell her she had been in tears again, desperate for company when she'd left the bookshop. The seconds were agonising as her mind raced. She shouldn't have made that call; she hardly knew this woman.

Georgina interrupted the awkward moment. 'You sounded a bit edgy on the phone.'

'Did I?'

'I must have been mistaken; you seem fine now.'

'I'd been to a reading in a bookshop. When I left, it seemed like everyone in Paris was out enjoying themselves.' She fidgeted with the top button of her twinset. 'I thought it would be nice to maybe have a coffee. Your card sort of popped out of my bag.'

'You don't have to explain,' Georgina said, putting up her hand. 'I only was surprised to hear from you tonight. Do you still want to meet at the Louvre on Saturday?'

Annie clenched her hands into tight fists on her lap. 'Of course; I'm really looking forward to it.' The waiter returned with the wine on a tray and put a glass in front of her. She took a sip. 'I see what you mean. Delicious.'

'Tell me about the reading.'

'I'm still trying to figure out what the author was talking about; it all went over my head.' Annie could hear her own voice quavering. 'Everyone else seemed to get it, which made me feel really dumb.' She took another gulp of wine while her leg jiggled under the table. 'Do you know anything about the force within and the universe?'

'Don't say another word.' Georgina waved her hand. 'I've heard it all before. Was the author about ten and you were surrounded by a bunch of literary groupies not much older?'

'I thought he looked more like twelve,' Annie grinned.

'I bet they all hung on every word and you felt like you were at least a hundred. When it ended, they went wild clapping before nearly trampling you as they rushed to get their books signed.'

'I left before the stampede,' Annie laughed. 'It sounds like you've been to a few of these before.'

'Oodles. I used to organise events for a PR firm, but like everything in my life now, it all happened years ago.'

'How interesting.'

'I still do a bit of consulting once in a while, but I try to avoid that precious literary stuff.'

Two wines later Annie was seeing double. 'I don't think I better have any more to drink on an empty stomach.'

'Same here,' Georgina giggled, her sophisticated persona beginning to dissolve. 'Why don't we order something to eat?'

'Are you sure?' Annie pulled at her curls. 'I don't want to take up too much of your time. I never expected you to have dinner with me.'

'You shouldn't do that,' Georgina lectured.

'What?'

'Be so apologetic, so …' Her voice trailed off as she tried to find the right word.

'Anxious?'

'That's it,' she agreed.

The wine had dulled Annie's inhibitions. 'I wasn't like this before. I've turned into another person and I can't seem to go back to the way I was.'

'Before what?'

The waiter with the tattoo returned to their table, interrupting them. He started speaking in French before hesitating, looking at Annie. English won out and she smiled up at him, nodding her approval as he spoke. 'Would you like more wine?'

'I think we need to see the menu first,' Georgina said, pushing her empty glass into the middle of the table. 'We'll have another wine, but only with a meal.' He grinned, handing them two vinyl-covered menus he'd brought to the table. 'He thinks we're drunk,' Georgina smirked as he walked away.

'Where I come from, we call it pissed.'

'We do, too,' Georgina said, pulling out a pair of red-rimmed reading glasses from her handbag. 'I was only trying to be polite.' She slipped them on, flipping through the pages of the menu. 'It's all in French so I better translate. What do you feel like?'

'Anything but steak tartare.'

'Don't tell me you've come across that?'

Annie made a face. 'I thought I ordered a grilled steak and eggs, but something got lost in translation. Didn't you tell me that day on the boat that the French were putting subtitles on their menus these days?'

'I did say that, didn't I?' Georgina took off her glasses, grinning across the table. 'Some restaurants and cafés are doing it now, but not all of them.'

'Maybe the ones doing it should advertise in their windows.'

'You have a lot to learn about the French,' Georgina nodded, putting her glasses back on and glancing down at the menu. 'What about duck? I can see it here at the top of the page.'

'I've already tried that. What else is there?'

'Snails, fish, cassoulet.'

'What's cassoulet? I've heard of it before.'

'A bean dish with meat. Sort of like a stew.'

'I'll have that; it'll soak up the wine,' she said, glancing over her shoulder.

Georgina read her mind. 'At the back on the right. I'll order cassoulet for both of us.'

The bistro tilted when Annie stood. She swayed, hanging on the back of her chair before picking her way around the tables. No one seemed to notice she was unsteady on her feet. She could hear different languages as she tottered to a queue outside the toilets. Two women in front of her were having an animated discussion in French. She smiled to herself; she was almost falling down drunk in Paris and it seemed like Melbourne didn't exist.

She leant against the wall listening to the upbeat music. As she stood there, she could see Georgina across the room ordering their meal. She wore a black jacket with a white shirt. A red scarf draped casually around her neck looked striking with her grey hair. Underneath the table, she could see a black ruffled skirt and Georgina's red boots. She thought of the girl in the library at the reading. It seemed she was completely out of touch with fashion. She glanced down at her multicoloured skirt and shook her head; she looked like an advertisement for fruit salad.

When she went back to the table Georgina poured water from a frosted bottle and pushed a glass across to her as she sat down. 'What did you mean before about how you've changed?'

Here it comes, Annie thought; she could lie or tell the truth. 'I guess it all comes down to what you want to hear. Truth or fiction.'

'Truth is always right in the end.'

'Not from my perspective; it's got me in a lot of trouble lately. Some people can't handle it.'

'Try me.'

The waiter brought more wine and a basket of bread. Annie drained her glass, taking a gamble she wasn't about to ruin the whole evening. Her words came out like a bullet-point list.

'My husband died in my arms from cancer last year. I've been a mess ever since. Nothing makes sense anymore. I'm not the person I used to be. I've been told I'm like Alice down the rabbit hole.' She couldn't believe she'd said that about herself, remembering Lucy's cruel words at the airport and the painful argument with Muriel.

'There was no warning anything was wrong until he collapsed and was rushed to hospital.' She looked down, blinking back tears. 'After they operated a few days later a surgeon told me Leo was dying. He never offered any hope to soften the blow. He was such a cold bastard.'

'Most of them are. I guess they have to be, or they would burn out,' Georgina offered.

Annie shrugged. 'After that it was like a beast came into our lives. It ate him alive and there was nothing I could do about it except pretend to be positive even though it was tearing me apart. He was sick for a year, then he was gone. A lot of people have expected me to pick up the pieces like nothing happened. They call it moving on.'

She took a deep breath, trying to contain her raw emotions while the bistro hummed in the background. 'How can I forget such a beautiful, brave man who never deserved what life dished out to him?' She looked down at her empty glass. 'How can I forget the love of my life? I've tried to move on, but I can't do it. It's been easier to hide away from the world.'

'So that's what was wrong with you on the boat.' Georgina reached across and touched Annie's arm. 'I knew it had to be something more than beautiful scenery and sentimental music to make you cry like that.'

'I felt like such a fool. The sad music triggered everything. I'd only arrived in Paris and was feeling completely overwhelmed. I thought I'd die that day.'

'It took a lot of guts to come here on your own. Don't be so hard on yourself.'

Annie's eyes brimmed with tears. 'My daughters gave me this trip so there was no bravery on my part. To tell the truth I felt bullied into coming, but I can see now they were only trying to pull me out of a very dark place.'

'And has it?'

'All I know is being here means there isn't a memory around every corner.'

A flash of pain crossed Georgina's face. 'I've been in a dark place too, but for different reasons. It happened right here.'

'In Paris?'

She nodded. 'It was a long time ago, but even now there still are a few memories around the odd corner for me.'

'What happened?'

'I was young; there was a university student, and he was French. When it ended, I was left with a baby and my life in tatters.' She twirled the silver ring on her finger. 'I lived with him here for almost a year. When I fell pregnant, he encouraged me to go home to have the baby. The morning sickness was relentless and he thought

I should be with my parents. The plan was he would join me as soon as he deferred his studies and we would marry. I was broken-hearted having to leave, but he convinced me it was the right thing for our baby.' She shook her head, looking down at her hands. 'I never heard from him again.'

'Not even a letter?'

'Nothing; it was terrible. There wasn't a phone where we were living, so I couldn't ring him. If only there had been mobiles in those days. I wrote to him for months, even after our son was born, but never had an answer.' She looked up at Annie, sadness etched on her face. 'I had his sister's address in Provence and in desperation wrote a few letters to her when I didn't hear from Alain. We had met several times and I liked her. I even went to her wedding. My written French was pretty basic in those days, but she would've known the letters were from me. She never wrote back either. That's when I knew I'd been dumped.'

'How did you ever recover?'

'Time fixed it, but it took years. After I pulled myself together, it was hard to ever trust anyone again. Eventually I married some-one else.' She played with the bangles on her wrist. 'William was older, but it wasn't much of a marriage. It was a relief when it was over.'

'Did you ever remarry?'

Georgina shook her head. 'It seems easier to be alone. I'm lucky to have my son, John, and I'm close to his wife. In many ways, I feel blessed. Now I have a little grandson. I was shopping for his first birthday the day we ran into each other again. The thing is, John has his own life, and I can't expect him to prop me up.'

Annie gulped her wine. She'd found a kindred spirit.

* * *

The lights of Paris sped by. Annie rested her head against the window in the back seat of the taxi, listening to Georgina's bangles jingling next to her in the dark. 'How are you over there?' she asked, squinting at Georgina silhouetted against the backdrop of lights.

'Bloody awful. Why did we order cognac?' she moaned, her words slightly slurred. 'It isn't sitting well with the cassoulet. God, all those beans.'

'I guess the chocolate soufflés wouldn't have helped either,' Annie giggled.

Georgina sighed. 'Don't even mention soufflés. I'm taking some cooking classes while I'm here and they're on the program. The way I'm feeling now, I don't know how I'll face the first class in the morning.'

'I'm sure you'll be fine.'

'Do you want me to check if there are any places left in the other classes?'

'I should be dieting, not learning to cook rich French food,' Annie grinned, 'but it sounds great.' She stifled a burp, blowing cognac fumes across the back seat as the taxi stopped outside her hotel.

Georgina wouldn't accept any money towards the fare and Annie could see her waving from the taxi as it disappeared around the corner. When she turned back to the hotel, the lights outside the entrance were dimmed. She put her nose against the glass searching for any sign of life as she rattled the handle of the locked door. The foyer was almost in darkness.

She imagined herself sleeping on the front steps when something moved on the other side of the glass. A young man switched on a lamp in the foyer. He was dressed in black, looking like he'd stepped out of a fashion magazine. She tried to steady herself as he rushed to the door.

'Madame?'

'I'm a guest in this hotel,' she slurred. He opened the door wider and she could smell his heady aftershave as she wobbled by him. 'I'm in room twelve,' she whispered, concentrating on enunciating each word.

He went behind the desk, retrieving her key on its brass knob. 'Did you have a pleasant evening?' he asked, handing it over.

'Lovely, although I've had a little too much to drink.' She grimaced as soon as she said it. 'What time is it?'

'Almost midnight.'

'I'm sorry I disturbed you.'

'Not at all, Madame, I'm here to help our guests after hours.'

'*Merci.*'

She swayed in front of the desk before turning towards the lift, trying not to put a foot wrong. When the doors opened, she glanced back at his amused expression in the dim light. She couldn't avoid her reflection in the three-sided mirror, squinting under the bright spotlights at her unruly red curls and blotchy face. Chocolate was dribbled on her yellow twinset near the bulge of her waistline. She put her hand over her mouth as the lift shuddered to a stop on the third floor, the gas in her stomach dislodging with one loud burp.

She steadied herself against the wall in the hallway. Somewhere nearby a television blared as she tried to unlock the door of her room. It eventually opened with a reassuring click after several attempts. She stumbled inside, the memory of the reading lost in a haze of alcohol as she collapsed on the bed. A few minutes later the phone buried deep in her shoulder bag pinged with an incoming text message. Annie was already asleep, snoring as the lights of Paris glowed through the uncovered window.

31

Georgina sat by the window of the second-floor apartment sipping peppermint tea in the shadows. The sound of late-night traffic was muffled as she watched dots of light criss-crossing the streets below. She didn't know what had made her eat and drink so much; her stomach was on fire. She put down the cup, shuffling across to the couch. She thought of her confession as she stared into the darkness. The powerful emotions she'd buried long ago surfaced without warning, taking her by surprise. All she could do was keep drinking to dull the pain and hide how upset she felt.

Annie asked the question she'd avoided answering for years, even to herself. Why did she keep coming back to Paris? She managed to get around a straight answer, but now in the darkness she had to admit what she had always known in her heart. She was still looking for Alain, searching the face of every man in the street, trying to find the love she'd lost.

She thought of the small black-and-white photo in her desk drawer at home. The grainy image was all she had of him. He was leaning against his motorcycle with his hands shoved in the pockets of his leather jacket, a long scarf wound around his neck. She closed her eyes, thinking of the lean line of his jeans and how he'd kept fidgeting as she took the photo. They had been in Normandy with some friends for the weekend and she smiled, thinking of how happy she'd been.

Before consciousness gave way to sleep, she thought she could see him standing next to the couch, his dark hair curling over the collar of his leather jacket. A cigarette dangled from his full lips while he looked down at her. The vision seemed as real as if she were looking through a crack in time. When she blinked, he was gone.

Sun streamed through the uncovered window, waking Georgina. She was sprawled across the couch with all the cushions on the floor. The hazy details of her surroundings came into focus as she blinked into the sun, unsure why she was on the couch. She winced when she pushed herself up, grabbing at her lower back. Pain rocketed up her spine as the memory of the night before began to register.

The need to drink and the urge to pee were both so urgent she grabbed the cup of leftover tea and took it to the bathroom with her. She licked her dry lips, trying to erase the rancid taste in her mouth. This was a new low, she thought, as she sat on the toilet gulping the tea.

She stared at her reflection in the mirror on the opposite wall. What a difference a few decades made. She used to wake up bright-eyed after a night out drinking and dancing in Paris with Alain.

He would kiss her good morning, telling her she was his sexy little Londoner. She shook her head; not anymore.

This morning her short grey hair stood on end and her puffy eyes were circled with smeared mascara trailing down the fine creases on her cheeks. The porcelain skin, mane of fair hair and full lips were gone, etched away by the years. She put the cup on the edge of the sink and flushed the toilet, trying not to look at the mirror while she washed her hands and face.

The polished parquetry was cool under her bare feet as she padded out to the kitchen, grabbing her pashmina from the back of a chair and wrapping it around her shoulders. She made fresh tea and took a cup into the sitting room overlooking the balcony. Traffic noise drifted up from the street and somewhere in the distance she could hear a siren. The pain in her back had moved and was now jabbing at her forehead. She perched on a chair in front of a small table, trying not to move her throbbing head.

The alcohol-fuelled vision of Alain was still unsettling, even now in the light of day. It seemed as if the night had unlocked her subconscious mind, disgorging a disturbing stream of thoughts and emotions. It had never dawned on her that closure was an issue to be worked on. She understood how the concept upset Annie so soon after Leo's death, but it was different in her case. It was clear she needed to turn her back on Paris to let Alain go. He belonged in the past and she had to leave him there.

She sipped tea, contemplating her disastrous marriage to William and how she'd fled when it ended, spending so much time away from home John complained she was in Paris more than London. She looked down at her cup, remembering their argument.

At the time, he was at university and almost the same age she was when she'd met his father.

He'd shouted at her, telling her she'd been looking for someone who had abandoned them both without even a second thought. Even when they patched things up months later, she'd never really grasped what he'd been talking about because she hadn't been consciously looking for Alain.

Georgina glanced out the window. If her brother hadn't bought the apartment in the Marais twenty-five years ago, maybe it would have all been different. She wouldn't have been able to make so many trips, always convincing herself she was only in Paris to shop. He hardly used the apartment even though he originally bought it as a base for his business trips to Europe and over the years she was there more than he was.

She smiled thinking of Annie's observation that if she ever bumped into Alain now, she might not even recognise him. He could well be a fat Frenchman running a bookstall in a flea market somewhere in Paris. His dark hair would be white and his fingers stained from too many cigarettes. Her description had sent them into fits of laughter and once they had started, they couldn't stop, adding more to it.

She thought he may have a nagging wife while Annie said he could well have had a string of wives and was now broke from paying alimony. Their game had gone on until the waiter brought the soufflés and cognac they had ordered, keeping up the momentum of the unexpected evening that had buoyed their morale.

She finished her tea, thinking of Annie. There seemed to be some connection between them as their paths kept crossing all over Paris. She could still see her staggering out of the bistro in her printed skirt, yellow twinset and red shoes. Georgina smiled; she'd never met anyone quite like Annie with her wild red curls and broad Australian accent.

Two hours later, Georgina rushed into the cooking school in a pair of jeans and her trademark red boots, the ravages of too much alcohol repaired with a few clever makeup techniques. Alain was pushed to the back of her mind as she adjusted the lapels of her linen jacket and opened the glass door. A young woman with an American accent greeted her.

'Welcome to Délicieux Paris. I'm Sally.'

'And I'm Georgina Hasluck. Do you want to see my class voucher?'

Sally looked down at the laptop on her desk. 'No need; you're right here,' she said, handing her a brochure. 'We have you registered for three classes.'

Georgina glanced at the glossy leaflet. 'Would there be any places left in the other classes I'm taking? I have a friend here in Paris who could join me for one of them.'

'I'll check,' she said, scrolling down the screen of her laptop.

Georgina looked around the reception area while she waited. Shelves lined the walls of the small room, displaying cookbooks and kitchen utensils. A row of copper pots gleamed under overhead spotlights. Market baskets stacked in the corner added to the charming French ambience. Several women were leafing through a pile of cooking magazines on a long table while they waited for the next class.

'There are two places left in the soufflé class tomorrow,' Sally said, her eyes still on her laptop. 'Do you want me to put your friend's name on the list?'

'I better check first. Is there time for me to make a quick call?'

'The class starts in five minutes and we do like to be on time.'

'I won't be long,' Georgina said, turning towards the door.

Annie's voice was raspy when she answered her phone. Georgina smiled; she wasn't the only one with a hangover. 'I'm at the cooking school. Do you still want to do a class?'

'I'm not sure; I can't seem to think straight this morning. How are you after last night?'

Georgina touched her throbbing forehead. 'Not good, but I'm determined to go through with the class today.'

'I haven't had so much to drink in years,' Annie giggled.

'Me neither and I don't want to have a repeat performance. Listen, I don't have long to talk. There's a vacancy in the soufflé class tomorrow.'

'Weren't we meeting at the Louvre in the afternoon?'

'Definitely, but the class is in the morning. It starts at ten and only goes for two hours. There's no pressure, but whatever you decide, the gallery is still on.'

'It sounds like a lot of fun, but doing both in one day may be a bit rushed. I know the gallery takes hours to get around. I'm not leaving until next week, so I guess there's still plenty of time to see it.'

'You know, I've just thought of something,' Georgina chipped in. 'We could go see the Monet panels at the Musée de l'Orangerie after the class if you're going to the Louvre another day. It's much smaller and we could get through it in no time. I don't mind going again.'

'That sounds so special.'

'Brilliant. I have to fly; the class is about to start and I can see someone waving at me. I'll text the address later. The school is only around the corner from your hotel, so you won't have any trouble finding it.'

'George, wait. What about the payment?'

'I'll take care of the sixty euros now and you can fix me up tomorrow. Is that all right?'

'Of course, thanks a lot. This is very exciting. See you tomorrow morning.'

The small group was climbing the stairs when Georgina went back inside. Sally waited for her near the door. 'I was about to come out and get you. Can your friend come?'

'Yes, she's quite enthusiastic. She loves soufflés.' She smiled thinking of Annie licking the chocolate on her lips the night before. 'Can I finalise everything now?'

'See me after the class.'

'You're an American,' Georgina said as she followed her up the stairs.

'Yes, from California.'

'How long have you been in Paris?'

Sally grinned down at her. 'I came for a vacation five years ago and never left. I met a Frenchman.'

'Say no more,' Georgina nodded.

When they reached the kitchen, a young man in a white chef's tunic with black-and-white checked trousers was doling out plastic aprons to the small group.

'Philippe, this is Georgina,' Sally called out, beaming at him from the doorway. He winked at her and it was obvious he was her Frenchman.

'Welcome,' he said, handing Georgina an apron. He turned back to the group. 'Before we start, I'd like you all to wash your hands.'

She joined the queue at the sink while Philippe walked around a long stainless-steel table distributing recipe cards. 'I can't believe I'm at a cooking class in Paris,' a woman next to her giggled. Georgina winced as she lathered her hands. The last thing she needed was a roomful of over-excited Francophiles.

Philippe clapped his hands. 'Okay, we begin. Today we are making croissants. Recipe cards are on the table in front of you.'

Georgina walked over to the table in the middle of the kitchen, looking down the expanse of stainless steel at Philippe. Something about him reminded her of Alain. The other women at the table were hanging on his every word and she wondered what it was about Frenchmen. She'd asked herself the question for many years.

32

Rain pelted sideways along Toorak Road. Lucy flicked on her shop's security lights and went out into the deluge, locking the front door. There had been no customers all afternoon and she could see the clothes inside hanging untouched on their spindly racks. She pulled up the collar of her trench coat, peering through the plate glass at the leather couch in the corner. What a waste of money; four grand to impress the customers and no one ever looked twice at it.

Her stilettos skidded on the slick footpath as she hurried to the car park around the corner. She'd left her umbrella at home and was soaked when she dived into her hatchback, her hair plastered to her head. Peak hour was in full swing with no hope she could inch her car into Toorak Road. She sat listening to rain pounding on the roof, lost in the dilemma of whether to wait it out or run back to the shop. She was still trying to make a decision when her phone rang.

Mia's voice cut through the gloom. 'You up for a drink tonight?'

She wiped a small circle in the fogged windscreen, looking out at the traffic. 'Toorak Road's a car park and I'm still stuck outside the shop,' she shouted over the drumming rain.

'You sound a bit stressed.'

'You would be too if you were soaked to the skin and freezing cold. Melbourne is doing my head in. I wish I could run away.' She thought of the travel brochures in the shoebox under her bed as she watched sheets of rain illuminated under the streetlights. It was pointless to confess now she was sorry she'd opened the shop.

'Didn't you want to do that before?'

'Do what?'

'Run away. You know, before you decided to open a business.'

'Yeah, whatever; I can't remember any details now.' She pulled out a tissue from her pocket and blotted her damp forehead, trying to pull back from the regrets surfacing out of nowhere in the dark car.

'What about that drink? I could meet you at the Wellington in half an hour.'

'That might be pushing it.'

'I'll wait; there's something I want to tell you. See you soon.'

Lucy threw the phone back in her handbag. She would never make the Wellington in half an hour.

She could see Mia sitting at a corner booth when she hurried through the front door of the wine bar forty-five minutes later. 'Sorry I'm late, one drop of rain and Melbourne grinds to a standstill,' she complained, kissing her sister's cheek.

'Don't worry, I haven't been here long.' She patted the black vinyl, making room on the seat while Lucy pulled off her damp trench coat. 'Have a seat.'

'I'll go order something first. How's your drink going there?'

'I'm fine.' Mia pulled out her wallet and handed her a note. 'Take this for the drink I owe you. I couldn't have done all that cleaning without your help.'

Lucy waved the money away. 'Forget it; I was only joking.' When she came back with a glass of wine, she flopped down, sliding her handbag on the table. 'It's been a long day.'

'What happened?'

'Nothing. That's just it, no one comes in if it's hot or cold or raining. They all would rather sit at home in their pyjamas and shop online at midnight. It drives me insane.'

'Is that why you want to run away?'

Lucy shrugged, staring down at her wine. 'I'm just fed up.'

'You probably need a break. Why don't you go overseas? Don't you know someone in Italy?'

'Yeah, Prue.'

'Couldn't you visit her?'

'Don't start working on me; I'm still paying off my half of the Paris trip.'

Mia's eyes widened, searching her sister's face. 'Why didn't you tell me it would be a problem? I thought you had the spare cash to help out.'

'I didn't want to ruin your grand plan. Anyway, everything's cool now, I juggled a few things.' She ruffled her damp hair, trying to believe her own lie. 'You did the same thing, so what are you worried about?'

Mia looked across the room. 'David's still shitty about it, but I've started working in the after-school program which has helped. The money is good, and I'll have everything paid off soon.'

'You always have been a good organiser. Listen, I can't seem to warm up, I'm getting a brandy this time and then that will be my limit.' Lucy drained her glass and stood, scooping her handbag off the table. 'What do you want?

'Another juice.'

'No vodka with it?'

Mia shook her head, grinning up at her.

'Are you about to say what I'm thinking?' She nodded and Lucy grabbed her hand, sitting beside her again.

'I'm due in six months.'

'What great news. My little sister's having a baby; I can't believe it.'

'I can hardly believe it myself. When I missed my last two periods, I blamed it on the stress of worrying about Mum. But I knew it couldn't be that when I started getting morning sickness. I nearly fainted the night we were chasing her through the airport.'

'You should've said something.'

'How could I with all that drama going on? Anyhow, it wasn't confirmed then.'

'Does she know?'

Mia fiddled with a cardboard coaster on the table. 'I wanted to tell her when I rang to ask about those nightmares, but we were interrupted and I gave up. That's also why I didn't find out about George.'

'I assumed her phone had died again when you told me about your call. What was the interruption?'

'The Notre-Dame bells,' she laughed. 'She was in a garden near the cathedral. I'll wait now until she comes home. Please don't say anything if you're talking to her. We're really happy about this baby and I don't want to give her the impression we've forgotten everything that's happened.'

'Why worry? I think she's already forgotten what happened. It gives me the shits thinking of what we went through to get her on the plane and now she's cutting loose all over Paris.'

'It sounds like you're disappointed she's enjoying herself.'

Lucy sidestepped the statement, trying to hide her bitter feelings. What really was eating at her was how her father had been replaced by some guy her mother hooked up with on her first week in Paris. 'I'm just finding it hard to swallow after she's been the big martyr.'

'Don't be so tough on her.'

'Why not? She isolates herself from the world playing the poor widow, then one trip away and she's suddenly someone else. And if those nightmares were so bad, they couldn't just stop like that unless she exaggerated everything.'

'A few days ago, you were worried about her and now you're pissed off because she's happy. Stop being so cold-hearted. You know, this hotshot businesswoman image doesn't suit you.'

'I didn't come here for a lecture.'

'I'm not lecturing; I'm being honest. You need to get away and you need to stop picking on Mum. You're coming across like a bitch.'

'Yeah, yeah, I hear you. Let's drop it and talk about something else like nappies.' She picked up her handbag and looked at Mia. 'I'll go get those drinks.' By the time she reached the bar her face was pinched with pain from the tight knot in her stomach. It seemed everyone was getting on with their lives except her.

Lucy traipsed through the door of her cold apartment two hours later. She threw her trench coat across the island bench in the kitchen and filled a saucepan with water. She was beyond hunger. All she'd eaten that day was a salad roll topped off by a string of espressos and the drinks with her sister. She couldn't be bothered to go to the supermarket on the way home and the cupboards in the ultra-modern kitchen were bare except for a few packets of dried noodles.

Another fucking gourmet dinner in trendy South Yarra, she thought, pulling out a packet and tearing at the packaging with her teeth. The wrapper split, spewing noodles across the tiles.

'Shit, shit, shit,' she hissed, dumping the saucepan in the sink and stomping down to her bedroom. The blinds were up, and the room was bathed in amber from the city lights. Her umbrella was on the bed along with a pile of fashion magazines she'd intended to take to the shop that morning.

She scooped them aside before throwing herself across the faux-fur bedspread, trying not to cry. The shop was bleeding money and her love life was non-existent. She didn't need a holiday; she needed a new life. She stared at the ceiling, wondering if she was really a cold-hearted bitch.

The prickly relationship with her mother had hit another low and it seemed her attempts to hide it were a failure like everything else in her life. Maybe she should shut up shop and go to Europe;

it obviously agreed with her mother. She could visit Prue at that vineyard she was always rabbiting on about in her emails.

The fantasy took over her troubled thoughts as she listened to the rain tapping against the windows. She could rent a room somewhere in Italy and live on bread and cheese with lots of cheap wine. Geraniums would be growing in a pot on the windowsill. A handsome Italian would sweep her off her feet. They would make passionate love during the hot afternoons and eat bowls of steaming pasta in the local piazza every night.

She rolled over, thinking of Tuscany. It would be so easy to slip from the everyday world of Melbourne into the chaos of Italy with its beauty and history all rolled into one. Her new life would be like all those Italian films she always drooled over. She could go for a year or two. Maybe she would never come back.

An hour later the fantasy had morphed into a plan. She grabbed the bedspread and pulled herself up, thinking of what she was about to do. She would be labelled impulsive, but there was no one to talk it over with. It didn't matter anyway; in the end she would be a long time dead. If anyone doubted her logic, she would remind them of her father, cut off at the knees at fifty-seven before he even retired.

She flicked on the bedside lamp and looked under the bed. The shoebox was still there next to a deflated sports ball and pink barbells she never used. She pulled it out, wiping off the layer of dust on the lid with the back of her sleeve. It felt like she was holding a time capsule of all her secret dreams, everything she'd sacrificed to open her business. The contents of the box scattered across the bed when she turned it upside down.

Old postcards from Prue beckoned from the other side of the world. She smiled as she read her friend's familiar scrawl. All the messages ended with Prue inviting her to Italy. She blinked, trying to ignore the nagging restlessness as she sat surrounded by the treasures from the box. She looked down at a worn travel brochure with notations in the margins. A handwritten list of airline prices and a pasta menu from a Carlton restaurant were folded into a dog-eared Italian phrase book.

She picked up a small foldout map of Rome. It was from the same travel shop where she'd bought the map of Paris a few weeks ago. Her mother could never have guessed her new map was the same design as one hidden in a shoebox in South Yarra. She smiled, tucking it into her pocket as she went back to the kitchen, stepping over the noodles scattered on the floor. Tonight, she was ordering a pizza.

Almost twenty-four hours after making her decision, Lucy was still waiting for her mother to respond to the text message she'd sent that morning. She kept checking her phone for a missed call, but there was nothing. By seven o'clock she decided to try ringing, hoping her mother had charged her phone. It nearly rang out before she answered.

'Did you get my text?'

'Is that you, Lucy?'

'Of course it's me. What's wrong?'

'Sorry, I just got up not long ago. I slept in.'

'So, what did you think of the text?'

'I haven't read it yet. I've been on the phone to George.'

'Well, I hope you can spare me a minute of your time.' Lucy bit her lip, wishing she hadn't said that.

'Give me a break,' Annie snapped. 'Your text arrived in the middle of the night and I haven't even had breakfast yet. What time is it there?'

'Friday night. There weren't many customers, so I closed early. So, how are you?'

'I've got the worst hangover I've had in years. George and I were out last night and I'm afraid we drank too much.'

'Poor you.'

'You sound annoyed.'

'It's hard to imagine you getting pissed with some guy.' She could hear her mother sigh on the other side of the world.

'You need to know about George.'

After her mother's explanation, Lucy plonked on to a chair. 'We thought you were having a fling,' she whispered.

'I know you did, and I'm ashamed to admit I secretly enjoyed letting you both think that.'

'Why?'

'I'm sick of being dull old Mum.'

'I never thought of you like that.'

'That's how it's come across and it annoys me. These days fifty-six is hardly old. I'm a long way off a nursing home yet.'

Lucy screwed up her mouth. Shit, another tirade.

'It took a little while, but now I feel liberated,' Annie went on. 'I guess I can say this to you now since I'm so far away. The longer I stay here the more I can look back at my life as if I'm someone else watching a film about me.' When she hesitated, Lucy got a word in.

'You sound different.'

'I feel different, but I won't bore you with the details. Now, about your text I haven't read yet. What's going on?'

Lucy looked out at the city lights thinking of Mia's sobering words as she tried to make peace with her mother. 'I wanted you to be the first to know about a decision I've made, but I'll wait until another time.'

'Stop playing games,' Annie demanded, and Lucy felt ten again.

33

Annie decided not to wait for the lift and turned to the stone staircase at the end of the hall. The aroma of coffee drifted up from the breakfast room in the cellar as she gripped the curved wrought-iron banister, clomping down to the foyer. Her head throbbed with each step, but she was resolved to walk off the excesses of the night before.

The first wave of tourists had arrived when she stepped outside. Fine weather had brought them out earlier than usual and the island was crowded with mature couples window shopping, backpackers powering down the middle of the street and small groups clustered on corners listening to their tour guides. Thrown into the mix was the occasional local, like the man walking his terrier in front of her, trying to ignore the invasion.

She did two circuits of the island, weaving along crowded footpaths and lanes, occasionally stopping to look in a shop window. It seemed like she'd been in Paris for a long time and Île Saint-Louis was now almost as familiar as her own suburb back in Melbourne. As she walked, she tried to pinpoint when she'd changed to feeling like the other tourists were intruding on her home turf. She was still thinking about it when she turned the corner.

The café near Pont Marie was already crowded. The grey-haired waiter working tables out the front recognised her, nodding towards a spot almost hidden behind a large pot plant. She gestured she wanted coffee, pointing to the croissants displayed on a glass stand inside. He smiled, acknowledging her order without a word being spoken as she sat down, settling herself in the morning sun.

She rubbed her throbbing temples thinking of the sparring match with Lucy. It seemed the Toorak shop was another one of her whims, abandoned when the excitement wore off. She thought of how she and Leo had tried to talk her out of opening a shop in Toorak Road with its exorbitant overhead costs, but she accused them of always playing it safe. Now it seemed they were right all along. She didn't dare mention their advice or the money they had contributed to help her follow her dream.

Lucy had never said much about Italy before except for a vague reference to a friend living there. She couldn't understand why she'd waited to go until now if it were so important to her. Annie looked out to the river; this was another example of Lucy's unpredictable nature. She was always flighty, even as a little girl. None of it added up, but she had no say in the matter and that's what was so frustrating.

The waiter interrupted her thoughts as he slid her order across the table. She nodded her thanks, staring down at the croissant, conscious of her tight waistband. Another pastry didn't matter, she reasoned; Jess wasn't around to notice if she gained more weight.

A flotilla of tourist boats glided under Pont Marie while she lathered the croissant with apricot jam.

She gazed at the bridge with unexpected longing. This time next week she would be on the plane and Paris would be gone forever. Georgina's call from the cooking school had been a jolt, reminding her that time was running out. It seemed like Paris would never end and now in six days she would have to return to her old life. She had to go back to it all: her neglected house and garden, lost friendships, and memories around every corner.

She drained her cup, thinking of what she would lose at the end of the week. There would be no *boulangerie* across the street with her purchases carefully wrapped as if they were gifts, no more strolls at twilight watching the Seine sparkling with the city lights, no more Notre-Dame bells making her heart sing, no fruit shop on Rue de Rivoli with the man polishing apples, no more chocolate crêpes served hot in the street or onion soup crusted with cheese at the café near the bridge.

No more sculptured gardens or *bouquinistes* lining the river. No more streets washed clean every day or ancient cathedrals that smelled like roses and melted wax. No more cafés with waiters in black vests and long aprons or tables and chairs under colourful awnings facing the passing parade of a city that never seemed to sleep. There would be no more of any of it.

She'd never planned to like Paris, but now it seemed she loved it. It had taken every shred of courage she could muster to get on the plane for France and now it would take even more to actually leave it.

* * *

The open-top bus thrummed with languages from all over the world. Annie climbed to the upper deck and found a seat at the back, the excitement of the other passengers sparking around her. She thought of the last time she'd been on a tourist bus and what the old man had said to her. The poignant image of him standing on the footpath with his hat held high in her direction still made her eyes mist. As she sat waiting for the city tour to begin, his advice to never look back now seemed more pertinent than it had that first morning in London.

Like on the river cruise, the Eiffel Tower was the main attraction. When the bus stopped in front of it, most of the passengers hurried down the aisle as if drawn by a magnet. The tower had been visible in the distance for weeks, but now she needed to bend her head backwards to see the top.

She was still debating whether to get off and join one of the queues fanning out across the tower's forecourt when the driver revved the engine, making up her mind for her. Her hair stood on end as the bus lurched into the traffic and picked up speed. She grabbed at her curls, glancing back at the tower, determined to return before she went home.

Her heart raced as the bus trundled over a bridge, heading in the direction of the Arc de Triomphe. It drove along the Champs-Élysées before circling around the monument. She thought of how she'd told Jess she would have a coffee for her there, realising if the old woman hadn't been so rude, she probably wouldn't have gone anywhere.

The bus passed Place de la Concorde, driving around other major city attractions while a man sitting in front of her leant over the side taking photos with his phone. Just like at Giverny, she was caught out again with no camera. As she sat there, the idea that had been simmering in her subconscious since then became clear. She'd missed her chance this trip, but all those photos could wait until next time.

She not only wanted to come back, but it also felt like the most important thing in her uncertain life. She smiled, looking down at the traffic. Although she felt stateless, for now it seemed she belonged to Paris.

When the bus returned to its designated stop near Notre-Dame, she climbed down from her perch high above the street flushed with excitement. She was swept along with the crowd milling around her until she stood facing a flower market on the corner. She walked across the street, breathing in the heady scent from the pots of spring bulbs lining the entrance.

Inside, stalls were crammed with garden ornaments and indoor plants stretching out in long rows facing the river. The delicate chorus of wind chimes was soothing above the background noise of the city. As she stopped to admire a display of hyacinths, her phone rang. Muriel's voice was muffled when she answered.

'I have no idea what time it is in Paris; I hope you aren't in the middle of something.'

'I'm out walking. I actually didn't expect to hear from you again.'

'Don't you want to talk to me?'

'Of course I do,' Annie backtracked. It felt like she was in quicksand. 'I just didn't think you'd have time to ring so soon. Never mind, it's lovely that you have. Is everything all right?' There was a silence before Muriel answered.

'I'm a bit edgy with Paul still away. I don't know how you deal with the long nights. I can't sleep and keep hearing every little sound. I'm a big sook.'

She listened to Muriel's weary voice, remembering those first endless nights after Leo's funeral. 'Leaving on a light can help.'

'Any other tips?'

'If all else fails a few glasses of red can do the trick.'

'I'll let you know how I go. So, how's Paris now?'

'I think it's cast a spell on me.'

'It agrees with you?'

Annie looked down at the pots of hyacinths. 'It more than agrees with me. I love it.'

'What about the security situation? I've heard there's yellow vest protesting going on.'

'I haven't seen anything yet, although I know about it. There are police and soldiers everywhere with lots of security checks at the main attractions. It all makes me feel safe and I'm not worried like I was before. As you said, we can't let fear stop us from living our lives.'

'You sound a lot better.'

'I can hardly believe it myself. I honestly don't know how it happened or even when.'

'I'm so glad, but I still think I should've gone with you.'

Annie took a deep breath, trying to avoid the raw emotions still under the surface. 'I really needed to come here on my own without anyone propping me up. I can see now if I didn't, I probably would've had a complete meltdown. I want to come back here again, but I'll have to sell the house first. And I want to pay back the girls for this trip.'

'I can't believe you've decided.'

'I guess being so far away has helped. As you know I've been thinking about it for quite a while. Now the time seems right. There are too many memories between those walls and they'll always be a reminder of what I once had. I just can't spend the rest of my life crying.'

'We'll have a lot to talk about when you get back.'

'We sure will.' She looked behind her at a group of tourists with their guide. 'Muriel, I have to go. I'm at the flower market and it's really crowded. It's a bit hard to talk now. I hope you get some sleep.'

'Wish me luck.'

'Get out the merlot.' She could hear Muriel laughing as she clicked off her phone, standing to one side while the tourists squeezed around her in the narrow aisle of plants.

After several rounds of the market, she bought a bouquet of daffodils from a flower stall. A man wearing a leather apron wrapped them in white tissue paper, smiling as she paid him. When she refused to take any change, he plucked a long-stemmed rose from a metal bucket and nestled it into the daffodils, handing the bouquet to her with a flourish. His gesture made her heart race. It was a sign, she thought smiling across to him; everything would work out.

She was still thinking about her decision as she stopped at a café with a few spare tables out the front. Waiters raced around as if they were on skates. They were in constant motion, taking orders and clearing tables all at the same time. She sat down, waving as one sailed by her, collecting empty cups from the next table.

'Madame?'

Annie held up her index finger. 'A chocolate crêpe, please.'

He nodded and was gone again before she could draw breath. She'd never seen table service anywhere else quite like Paris. As she waited for her order, she wondered how Georgina was coping with a hangover in the cooking class. She smiled, thinking of her accent that always sounded royal. Tomorrow they would be up to their elbows in egg whites learning to make real French soufflés; now all she had to do was figure out how much money was left to pay for it.

Chocolate from the crêpe was still smeared across the plate. She looked down at it, debating how she could run her finger across the porcelain without being seen. As she put out a finger the waiter slid her bill on the table. She flinched, glancing around at the other tables. Licking her plate in public, especially Paris, wasn't the done thing no matter how much she loved chocolate. It seemed she'd picked up some bad habits from living alone.

She counted out several coins, thinking of Muriel and what had happened on the back verandah that terrible day. She tried to recall what she'd said in the kitchen afterwards, but the exact words were a blur. All she could remember was something about ringing when the real Annie returned.

If Muriel were sitting there now, she would tell her she could never go back to the person she was before. She wanted to, but it was impossible. She would tell her it felt like she'd walked through a storm and was covered in scars from where she'd been falling apart.

She looked down at her flowers on the table, thinking of the desolation she'd felt over the past years. Her daughters had thrown her a lifeline with the trip. It was now up to her alone to reinvent herself and begin again. The carrot of another trip was the only thing that would help her leave next week, but she didn't know how she could face what was waiting at home.

34

The entrance hall smelled musty when Mia opened the front door of her mother's house. It was more than a week since she'd been there and it looked bleak on the overcast Saturday morning. She didn't believe in ghosts, but the empty house made her uneasy as she stood listening to the antique clock ticking in the lounge room. She shivered, trying to cast off the feeling as she went down to the bedrooms.

The hallway was lined with her mother's art, many of the frames caked with dust. She wondered how they had been missed as she peered in each room, checking to see if anything else needed cleaning.

The brass bed in the master bedroom creaked when she sat on the edge, glancing around her. She'd changed the linen and dusted the bedside table, but the rest of the room felt off limits and nothing else was touched. Necklaces were in a jumble of beads on the dressing table in the corner and a pair of her father's shoes were underneath as if he'd just left them there. Her grandmother's velvet armchair sat in front of the bay window. A floral skirt was draped over the arm and piles of dust-covered paperbacks were stacked on the wide windowsill.

She could feel her parents' presence as she peered through the shadows at their black-and-white wedding photo hanging on the wall. Her mother's white gown billowed out like a meringue while her father's grey suit looked too big for him. They were laughing on the steps of a church and behind them their friends were throwing confetti. The frozen moment was their favourite photo taken on the day and they often commented about it, reminiscing about how young they had been.

She looked away. The sadness in the room was overpowering and she couldn't sit there any longer. She stood, glancing at the photo again before hurrying back to the kitchen to wait for Lucy. The ticking clock was the only sound in the house as she made a cup of tea, unsure why Lucy was so insistent for them to meet that morning.

Mia gaped across the kitchen table at her sister. 'You're doing what?'

'I just told you, how many times do I have to repeat it? I'm going to Italy and probably won't be back for ages.' Lucy folded her arms across her chest. 'You told me to do it so don't sit there acting so surprised.'

'I was talking about a holiday, not migrating.'

'I'm not migrating,' she snapped. 'I'm going on a working holi-day. I need a change; the shop has been going under for the past eighteen months.'

'I can't believe it.' Mia sat back in her chair. 'It's always seemed so glamorous.'

'What you see isn't how things really are.'

'It must be bringing in some money for you.'

'Not enough. Everyone wants to buy online these days. I've told you before. I can't go on; the rent is killing me.'

'I thought you were joking when you told me customers want to shop at home in their pyjamas. But if that's what they want, why don't you start an online store?'

'I couldn't imagine anything more boring. It would be like running a warehouse.' Lucy fidgeted in her seat. She wore a faded pair of jeans and a plain white shirt, her usual stilettos replaced by red sneakers. 'Anyway, I'm tired of the whole retail scene and even if I was making money, I wouldn't keep going. I'm over it.'

'What about Italy?'

'I'll be in Rome for a few days before heading up north.'

'Is that where Prue is?'

Lucy's face lit up. 'Yeah. She's still working at a vineyard in Tuscany. We've talked a lot this week. Work is available if I'm willing to do anything.'

'Is that legal? Aren't you supposed to have some kind of a work visa?'

'I'm one step ahead of you, kiddo. I've already applied for a working holiday visa and it should be sorted by the time I leave. Prue will help me with the other paperwork once I get there. I'm really excited. It'll be like an adventure,' she squealed, waving her arms. 'I'm going to break out and live the life I've always wanted.'

Mia shook her head at Lucy's theatrical display. 'Does this have anything to do with Dad?'

'Of course not. Don't be ridiculous.'

'I don't believe you. You've been too controlled for months. It seems like you're running away from your own emotions.'

'What's with you? I'm going on a working holiday and you're seeing things in this that aren't there.'

'When will you tell Mum?'

'I already have.'

'And?'

'She wasn't impressed.' Lucy sprawled back in her chair. 'By the way, she told me about George.'

Mia's eyes widened. 'Who is he?'

'George is some English granny she met on a boat. Her real name is Georgina.'

'Why did she let us think she was with a man?'

'According to her we've treated her like an old lady, and this was a way to let us know she isn't past it yet. A bit pathetic if you ask me.'

'She's actually got a point. We never considered her feelings about going to Paris. We just organised it thinking she was poor old Mum who couldn't help herself.'

Lucy ruffled her hair. 'Don't get all righteous. Remember Paris was your idea.'

'I know, but we never thought of talking it over with her. That wasn't fair.'

'If we hadn't taken charge she would've been still wringing her hands at home.'

'And having those nightmares we knew nothing about.'

'You're so full of it. Do we have to get into all of this again? Just drop it.'

'Mum can't win with you. You're so damn critical.'

'What did I just say? You're not listening.'

Mia put up her hand. 'Okay. So, back to your trip. What's happening about your apartment?'

'I thought you might like to rent it since it's close to a park. With the baby coming it would be better than that dogbox you're in near the railway line.'

'Is this why you wanted to meet me today?' Mia jumped up, glaring down at her. 'You're seeing me as a potential tenant?'

'You've got it all wrong.'

'What else could I be thinking?'

'I'm only trying to help you.'

'Oh sure, tell me another one.'

'Okay, if you don't want to rent it, you could buy it. It would be a great start.'

'It sounds like you have this all figured out.'

'Not quite,' Lucy grinned as Mia sunk back on her chair. 'I'm still making it up as I go. If you're not interested in the apartment, what about the leather couch at the shop? I could knock down the price for you.'

Lucy's offer didn't go down well with David. Mia watched his expression change from curiosity to annoyance when she told him, handing him a sheet of calculations Lucy gave her.

'Here we go again,' he said, tossing the paper on the coffee table without looking at it. It slid across the glass top, fluttering to the floor. 'When I first came on the scene, she was getting ready to open the shop. If I remember right, your parents had to back her to make her dream a reality. Your father was still trying to talk her out of it right up to that glitzy opening with all those so-called local celebrities.'

'What's that got to do with her apartment?'

'Don't you see a pattern here? She's lost interest in the shop and now we're expected to help out by taking the apartment off her hands so she can go on to her next big thing.'

'You're right, she admitted the gloss has gone off running a business. But it's a tough time in retail everywhere and the shop is losing too much money. She has to close, there's not much of a choice. The restaurant next door wants to expand and the owner's meeting her Monday to talk about taking over her lease.'

'When is the flight to Rome?'

'In two weeks.'

'Jesus, she doesn't procrastinate when she wants something.'

Mia leant back on the couch. 'She's always been impulsive, but her offer could actually help us. It would be a great buy. She isn't asking a lot for it.'

David's eyes narrowed. 'I can see it all now. Once the novelty of Italy wears off, she'll be back here wanting us to get out of her apartment.'

'If we buy it that couldn't happen.' Mia reached over and touched his arm. 'It makes sense; we don't have the deposit for a house in Melbourne, but we could swing an apartment. Even though it only has one bedroom, it could give us a foothold in the property market.'

'It sounds like you've already made up your mind.'

'Not quite,' she grinned, picking up the sheet of paper from the floor. 'I only need you to convince me it's all wrong.'

'Don't play that reverse psychology crap with me,' he said, looking down at Lucy's calculations. 'Let's see if she can add up.'

'I'll put the kettle on. Coffee or tea?'

'A beer sounds better.'

35

A text pinged on Annie's phone while she was dressing. The message from Mia pulled her back to the chaos Lucy was causing with her sudden decision. She looked out her hotel window, trying to gather her thoughts. Now Mia was thinking of buying her sister's apartment, not renting it. She must have misunderstood Lucy's plan. She glanced at the time on her phone; if she didn't get moving, she would be late for the cooking class. A reply to Mia's text would have to wait until later.

She checked her reflection in the mirror over the bathroom sink. Although she'd made an effort to look Parisian, nothing had changed. Still fat Annie from Melbourne, she thought, touching her new overshirt. She looked down at the matching loose-fitting pants. The shop assistant said the olive-green linen complemented her red hair, but the dark colour now made her feel uncomfortable.

She wiggled her toes in the black ballet flats she was wearing for the first time, hoping she looked the part for a big day out in Paris. She sighed; if only she had the figure to pull off Georgina's rock star style. She applied red lipstick and fluffed her curls. It was too late to change now.

She thought of how easy it had been to whip out her credit card to pay for the clothes in the little boutique across from the hotel. The sales assistant had convinced her a new leather bag and long silk scarf would complete the outfit and she hadn't hesitated to add them to her purchases. She'd been mesmerised as the young woman tied the scarf around her neck, showing her the different ways it could be worn. Her scalp had prickled while she listened to her French accent, watching in a full-length mirror how a simple scarf and the rich colour of the linen transformed her.

When she had handed over her credit card, it felt like getting something for nothing. She normally resisted paying for anything on credit, but now her world seemed to be turned upside down and nothing was quite the same as before. She read Mia's text again as she stepped out into the street, inhaling the aroma of something baking in the *boulangerie* across from the hotel. It was a beautiful morning in Paris and whatever was happening in Melbourne didn't seem important. She was still smiling as she turned towards the bridge with an unexpected feeling of freedom.

She started to sprint when she saw Georgina in the distance waiting outside the cooking school. Her new shoulder bag bounced against her hip on its long strap as she panted along the footpath.

'I'm sorry I'm late,' she gasped when she reached her. 'I should've left earlier.'

'Nothing has started yet,' Georgina smiled, opening the glass door. Annie followed her inside, still trying to catch her breath as they joined a group in the small reception area. The others all seemed to know each other, and she was relieved she wasn't alone. Georgina turned her back to them, leaning towards her. 'The chef is a bit of a pain, but he really knows his stuff,' she whispered, 'and he's gorgeous.'

'French?'

'*Oui*.'

'Ah, that explains everything,' Annie giggled.

A voice from the top of the stairs interrupted them. 'Welcome to Délicieux Paris. I'm Philippe, your chef this morning.'

Everyone in the room stopped talking and Georgina grinned at Annie.

'Our manager isn't here today and I'm doing the paperwork for her,' he explained. 'If you follow me, I have the class list upstairs.'

The students climbed the stairs as Philippe disappeared into the main kitchen on the next floor. When they reached the top step, Annie stopped, patting her chest. 'The last thing I need is more food. I've got to get rid of this weight,' she panted, handing Georgina an envelope. 'That's the money for the class.'

Georgina slid it into her handbag and laughed. 'Don't even think about dieting while you're in Paris. You can do that when you get home.'

'Make sure your egg whites aren't stiff,' Philippe shouted over the noise of the electric mixers. 'If they become too firm, your soufflés will be the wrong texture.'

Georgina peered into the mixing bowl before looking across to Annie. 'What do you think, should we turn it off?'

Annie nodded.

Georgina turned the dial and the egg whites stood up in stiff peaks.

'Oh no, here he comes,' Annie whispered as Philippe walked down the length of the table towards them. 'What should we do?'

'Stop worrying; no one is going to get in trouble for overbeating a few egg whites.'

Philippe glanced at the glistening peaks and shook his head. 'Ladies, you weren't listening; your egg whites shouldn't be so firm. We aren't making meringues today.'

Annie winced and Georgina pulled back her shoulders, facing Philippe over the mixing bowl. 'So, what would you suggest?' she asked, her British accent more pronounced than usual.

'There's no choice,' he grinned. 'You must begin again. Separate more eggs, but this time try beating by hand.' He reached across the table and grabbed a whisk from a large jar of utensils. 'Try this,' he said, handing it to Georgina. He smiled at the horrified look exchanged between her and Annie. 'It's better to get it right, don't you agree?' He folded his arms across his chest. 'Although it will be a lot of work, whisking gives you better control. I had more success in the beginning of my career by doing it this way.'

Annie leant across the mixer when he walked away. 'I feel like I'm in a domestic science class at high school,' she whispered.

'This is absurd. I don't know why he's getting all worked up about texture,' Georgina snapped.

'I guess we're getting our money's worth. If nothing else, we'll know how to beat an egg white when we leave here today.'

Georgina shrugged, handing Annie the whisk. 'I'll get the eggs.'

* * *

They took turns whisking and by the time their egg whites were the right texture, their arms were aching. 'I can't go on,' Annie moaned, putting the whisk beside the bowl. 'My arm feels like it's going to drop off.'

'This reminds me of a gym,' Georgina muttered. 'Can you imagine how firm our arms would be if we made soufflés like this every day?'

'I'd rather have tuckshop arms.'

'What are they?'

Annie stepped back as Philippe returned to their end of the table. 'I'll translate later,' she whispered.

'How did your whisking go?' he smirked at them.

Georgina jutted out her chin. 'Perfect.'

He glanced at the mixture and grinned. 'Well done; now fold your melted chocolate into the egg whites.'

'Melted chocolate?' Annie gaped.

'Yes, for your soufflés. Your chocolate should be ready.'

'We never got beyond the egg whites,' Georgina scowled at him.

Someone across the room waved and Philippe turned away. 'Read the recipe,' he called out over his shoulder.

'God,' Annie whispered. 'I never expected this would be so hard.'

Georgina's eyes narrowed as she watched Philippe across the room. 'Soufflés are an art form and we shouldn't be expected to get it right with one lesson. Where in the hell is the chocolate?'

Their soufflés wobbled when Annie took them out of the oven. 'They're sensational,' she said, looking down at their creations. 'I can't believe they actually rose.'

Georgina touched one. 'They smell delicious, but I'm not sure if it was worth all that work.'

Philippe tapped a spoon on the table to get everyone's attention. 'It's time to taste your soufflés,' he said, sliding a tray of shot glasses on the table. 'I've already put out several bottles of liqueur for you to try,' he continued. 'Measure out a shot to pour on your soufflés after you've cracked the top. Of course, they'll be just as delicious without the liqueur; it's purely up to your individual taste.'

Georgina was already pouring out two shots. 'We can't miss this,' she said, handing one to Annie.

The soufflés oozed when they cracked the tops, the aroma of chocolate and liqueur a heady mix in the warm kitchen. Annie looked around the table to see what the other students were doing. A German woman next to her tipped the liqueur down a small hole burrowed in the top of her soufflé. She scooped out the molten mixture and grinned.

'*Wunderbar*,' she said, holding up her spoonful.

The other students were attacking their soufflés as if they hadn't eaten for days, gulping down the chocolate concoctions while they rolled their eyes. The silence around the table was punctuated with moans and gasps of pleasure as they devoured their creations.

'I've died and gone to heaven,' one woman announced to no one in particular. She licked her lips and Annie could see a dribble of chocolate on her chin.

Philippe stood at the end of the table counting out recipe cards. He smiled as he listened to them, his head bowed over the growing pile of cards.

Georgina nudged Annie's elbow. 'This sounds like an orgy,' she whispered.

'Is that first-hand knowledge?'

'Hardly; only too many films,' she grinned, scraping her bowl. 'French of course.'

Philippe handed out the recipes before they left the kitchen. Georgina waved away the card he tried to give her. When it was Annie's turn, she felt her face flush as she looked up into his dark eyes. Many of the students shook his hand as they left, and two women kissed his cheek. He looked tired and now bored.

'It was great,' Annie said, following Georgina down the stairs. 'I'm so glad you invited me. Why didn't you take a recipe?'

'I'm over Philippe and I've had enough soufflés to last me a lifetime. I won't fit into anything if I keep this up.' She stopped and looked up at Annie on the step behind her. 'Speaking of clothes, you look really nice today. Is the linen new?'

'I went shopping yesterday,' Annie explained. 'The assistant in the boutique helped me, but I'm feeling strange in such a dark colour. I forgot to wear the scarf I bought to go with it.'

'You look quite smart,' Georgina said, touching the fabric of her sleeve. 'Although all those bright colours you usually wear are more you.'

'I've been feeling like a neon sign.'

'Nonsense,' Georgina said, opening the glass door. 'You always look creative. It's your own style.'

'You're very kind,' Annie said, following her outside, 'but somehow my style doesn't seem right in Paris.'

They stood on the footpath in front of the cooking school while

Georgina checked the time on her phone. 'Do you feel like lunch before we head to the gallery?'

Annie shook her head. 'Not right now, but I'd love some water. All that chocolate has made me thirsty.'

'We can buy some water on the way. It'll take about twenty minutes to get there and we can have a late lunch afterwards. How does that sound?'

'Great; only take it a bit slower,' Annie said as Georgina started to stride down the street. 'I'm not as fit as you are.'

As they ambled along the Seine, Annie told Georgina about her daughters. 'I can't understand why Lucy's decided to throw away everything she's worked for.'

'Maybe it's because you aren't there to talk her out of it.'

'You don't know Lucy; she's very headstrong. She never listens to me.'

'I sort of get where she's coming from,' Georgina nodded. 'I was pretty headstrong myself when I was younger.'

'What did your parents think when you decided to stay in Paris?'

'They were livid, especially when I dropped out of university.'

'But they were there for you when you went home, weren't they?'

'I think it was more out of duty than anything else. They were shocked I was pregnant, and I can hardly blame them. I know they endured a lot of gossip because of me. It was a different world in those days. Unwed mothers were like lepers.'

'I remember; not many girls kept their babies because of the social pressure.'

'They tried to talk me into adoption, but they couldn't force me because I wasn't underage. I kept telling them Alain and I were getting married and everything would be okay.'

'It must have been hard for you.'

Georgina buried her hands in her pockets. 'There was this terrible tension in the house. My mother took care of me while I was so sick all those months, but when I look back on it now, I can see how tough it was for her. I was so caught up in my own misery, I didn't consider how she felt.'

'The misery can cloud everything. A friend pointed that out to me only recently,' Annie said, looking out across the river. 'I didn't see it at the time, but now I do. Somehow I feel like I'm coming out of the fog.'

Georgina stopped and looked at her. 'I'm glad you're feeling better. It shows.'

A man selling bottles of mineral water at the end of a bridge interrupted them. 'One euro, one euro,' he called out, holding up a small bottle.

Annie waved at him. 'This is on me, George, my shout. Do you say that in England?'

'Oh yes, I know what you're talking about,' Georgina said as Annie paid for the water.

They stood in the shade of a tree gulping from the bottles. 'Can you explain those padlocks?' Annie pointed to the middle of the bridge as a young couple posed for photos while they clipped a padlock to the siding. 'I've crossed that bridge a few times and can't figure it out. What are they?'

'They're called love locks. The fad started here a few years ago. Lovers put their names on the locks and throw the key in the river.'

Georgina finished her water. 'It's supposed to prove their love. If you ask me, the whole idea is rather silly.'

'Wouldn't it be lovely to be silly again?' Annie sighed, looking across to the bridge.

Georgina laughed. 'Annie Green, I do believe you're a romantic. But I hate to burst your bubble.'

'What do you mean?'

'The locks are too bloody heavy. They've already removed most of them, but they thought allowing a few would be okay. I've heard they're now considering banning them all together. The bridges could've collapsed if they had let it continue without any restrictions. You should've seen it before; the bridge rails were completely covered with love locks.'

As they began to walk again, she touched Annie's elbow. 'Now I have a question. What are tuckshop arms? You told me in the class you would translate later.'

Annie giggled. 'That's easy, let me show you mine.'

36

Annie peered at the water lilies wrapped around the curved walls of Musée de l'Orangerie. They were only a suggestion of the real-life water lilies at Giverny, but the misty quality of the colours fascinated her. 'I never imagined the canvases were so large. They're more like murals,' she said, examining the brush strokes.

Georgina dabbed her eyes with a tissue. 'The first time I saw them I could hardly drag myself away,' she sniffed. 'Sorry, I don't know why I'm getting so sentimental today.'

Annie turned from the water lilies and looked at her. Georgina's cheeks glistened with tears. 'Are you all right?'

'I can leave if I'm embarrassing you.'

'Hey, you're with the drama queen of the Seine. A few tears can't embarrass me.'

'We better move on before I make a complete fool of myself,' Georgina said, her voice hoarse as she rubbed a mascara stain on her cheek.

Annie followed her into an identical room, her heart fluttering as she looked at more large canvases. She was bent forward studying one of the panels when Georgina touched her arm.

'I need some air. I'll wait for you in the foyer.'

She straightened up, glancing over her shoulder. 'I'll come with you.'

Georgina put up her hand. 'Really, I'm fine. I'll go freshen up and meet you near the gallery gift shop. Take as long as you like.'

A feeling of unease gnawed at Annie as she watched her walk away. Something was wrong and she didn't know what it was. She shivered; it was like waiting for a storm, making it impossible to concentrate on the exhibition. As she turned to leave, a large tour group crowding around one of the paintings blocked her way out. The visitors' expressions of wonder were almost childlike as their guide pointed to the water lilies. While the guide talked, she edged along a wall at the back of the group until she could break free.

The foyer was nearly empty with no sign of Georgina. She waited for a few minutes near the entrance before she went into the gift shop, trying to shake off the feeling of dread. Her feet throbbed from the long walk to the gallery and she was now limping around the shelves stocked with souvenirs similar to the ones she'd seen at Giverny. She chose two calendars before joining the queue in front of the cash registers. The service was quick and when she went out to the foyer again Georgina was sitting on a long wooden seat.

'I'm sorry I left you in there,' she said when Annie sat beside her. 'I thought I'd be okay, but there's a bit more to it than the paintings.'

Annie studied Georgina's drawn face while she listened to how Alain had introduced her to Monet's artwork soon after she decided to live with him in Paris. 'Now I can't see a water lily anywhere without thinking of that period of my life.'

'Do you come here on every trip?'

'Hell no; it would stir up too many memories. I hadn't been back in years until that day we arranged to meet here.'

'And I stuffed it up and went to Giverny instead.' Annie said, hugging the bag of calendars. 'It seems like a long time ago now.'

'That's what happens here. You can lose track of time. After Paris releases you from its grip, you're never the same again.'

'I know; it's already changed me.' They fell silent as another tour group streamed into the gallery. Annie patted Georgina's arm, still trying to ignore the uncomfortable feeling now giving her goosebumps. 'I'm sorry; I didn't know the gallery had such significance for you.'

'How could you? Anyway, I suggested it since you appreciate Monet's work so much. For some reason, I feel more nostalgic today than I did two weeks ago.'

'Maybe it's because we were talking about Alain the other night.'

'I'm not sure,' Georgina shrugged, 'but for some reason, he's been on my mind a lot lately. It's strange; I honestly don't know what's going on.'

'Do you think you're just lonely? It can make you weepy when you least expect it.'

Georgina sat up straight. 'Hardly, I have a very full life.'

Her British accent was now more pronounced. Annie had heard the same tone a few hours before when Philippe questioned their cooking skills. She'd unwittingly hit a raw nerve with her question and knew better than to say any more. It was clear she'd witnessed the vulnerability Georgina was hiding under her sophisticated veneer, although commenting on it went too far.

They sat in silence before Georgina finally spoke, avoiding any eye contact as she stared straight ahead. 'You know, you have this annoying habit of using your own experience as a water level for everyone else's life. Don't forget we're all different. You may be sad and lonely, but I'm certainly not. If you keep nurturing your grief, you'll always be stuck in the past.' She stood, looking down at Annie. 'It's too late for lunch now so let's just forget it. I've got a million things to do and can't hang around any longer. I'm sure you don't need me beside you to enjoy the art.'

Annie blinked at the crushing words, the storm breaking all around her. The muscles in her face felt like they would snap from the strain of her forced smile. 'Not a problem,' she gulped, standing to face Georgina. 'I'll get something to eat on the island.' She knew she was starting to babble, but she couldn't stop. 'I loved the cooking class; thanks so much for organising it.'

Georgina took a step backwards, ready to bolt for the exit. 'I'm glad you enjoyed it all,' she said, her voice tight. 'It's been nice meeting you.'

Annie didn't know whether to shake her hand or kiss her cheek. Georgina looked so tense; she knew whatever she did would be wrong. She stood with her arms dangling by her side like a rag doll, her new shoulder bag strapped across her chest. She leant over and picked up the carry bag of calendars that had slid to the floor. 'It's been nice meeting you, too,' she croaked, no longer able to hide her feelings.

Georgina didn't seem to notice her distress. 'Enjoy the paintings and the rest of your time in Paris. I better go; see you.'

As she turned to leave Annie blurted out the very thing she didn't mean to say. 'Thanks for your analogy about water levels. Of course, you're absolutely right.'

Georgina looked startled, giving her a dismissive wave before turning towards the exit. A few minutes later Annie could see her through the large windows overlooking the road. She was running away from the gallery, her red boots flying over the footpath before she disappeared into the crowd crossing the road at the traffic lights. When she was gone, Annie sagged back on the seat trying not to cry.

Her clothes were now uncomfortable, the linen prickly against her skin. Even if her new shoes weren't killing her, she was sure she couldn't face another Monet painting. The soufflé churned in her stomach. She'd been dumped in an unfamiliar part of Paris and didn't know what to do next.

She thought of her conversation with Georgina in the bistro earlier in the week. Most of what she'd told her was unintentional as the wine loosened her inhibitions. She bit her lip, thankful she hadn't told her about the nightmares or her narrow escape on the hospital balcony. If she'd gulped down one more cognac, no doubt she would have blabbed everything.

Her cheeks burned; after all, Georgina wasn't a friend. They were only two strangers who had shared a few outings and would never see each other again. Her own neediness had clouded her perspective; she was too clingy. She tried to recall what she said about moving on and grief. All she could remember was crying and telling Georgina how hard life was without Leo. She shouldn't have mentioned any of it.

Somewhere inside, a small voice told her to think of some of the other people she'd met on her trip. There was Bill on the tourist bus in London with his poignant advice; the young lecturer on the plane encouraging her to go to art school; Ed with the kind heart, so concerned about her after the bookshop reading. And she couldn't forget Emilio and Rachael showing her how to bluff her way in a French restaurant or Colette encouraging her to explore Paris.

They were a passing parade, touching her life in some way. She thought about the sign in the bookshop near Notre-Dame, noting strangers could be angels in disguise. All of these people had been like angels when she'd felt vulnerable and she couldn't let Georgina's harsh words overshadow their goodness.

She slumped on the seat for a few more minutes before trying to put weight on her toes to spare her throbbing heels that now felt like they were bleeding. She slowly limped down to the river to get her bearings, preparing herself for the painful trek back to her hotel. All she needed to do was keep walking and not cry, she told herself, but as Notre-Dame appeared in the distance she was searching her shoulder bag for tissues.

37

Georgina sprinted along the Champs-Élysées. The contents of her handbag thumped as she ran. She kept running until she was out of breath, sucking in air as she bent over, clasping her knees. While she gasped, she wondered how the past could creep up on her like that, making her cry in public. She'd made a spectacle of herself, but what she'd done to Annie was worse. Once her breathing returned to normal, she bowed her head as she walked along the edge of the footpath, trying to keep out of the way of the tourists swarming around her. While she walked, she could still see Annie's hurt expression.

She'd been a lot of things in her life, but never cruel, at least not until now. She didn't know why she'd turned on Annie of all people. She'd told her more in the last few days than any of her closest friends. Although they had only just met, it seemed like she'd known her for years. She slid on to a seat under one of the trees lining the long boulevard. Annie was right; she was desperately lonely and she'd lashed out at the one person who knew all too well how it felt.

She pulled out her phone and took a deep breath, not knowing how she would apologise. Annie's nasal voice was a whisper when she answered.

'It's George; I want to apologise.'

Annie was sniffing. 'I really don't want to talk right now.'

'I don't blame you, but I want you to know what happened had nothing to do with you. I'm so sorry; you didn't deserve that kind of treatment. I've been a first-class bitch.'

'I was only trying to be sympathetic, not judgemental. God knows I've found out first-hand loneliness is considered a real stigma these days.'

'I know that. Can I meet you somewhere and apologise in person?'

'I'm already on the way back to my hotel.'

'I can't let you leave like this,' Georgina gulped, fighting back her own tears.

'George, you don't have to say or do anything. You made it clear I assumed too much, thinking by sharing a few sad stories we were friends. I should've remembered it's always easier to tell stuff like that to complete strangers.'

'But we aren't strangers, not anymore. It feels like you're a dear friend and now I've messed everything up. Please let me make it up to you.' She could hear Annie's sharp intake of breath and then a moan.

'Sorry, I didn't mean to do that.'

'Are you okay?'

'These damn new shoes are killing me and I can hardly walk. I've got more blisters.'

'Let me grab a taxi and pick you up. We could have a coffee while you rest your feet. After that I promise to leave you in peace.'

'I have to admit that sounds tempting.'

Georgina could hear the change in Annie's voice.

'I was debating how I'd make it back to the hotel. I'm down from the Louvre along the river facing in the direction of the island. I'll look out for you.'

'I'll be as quick as I can. Don't go too far.'

'I can't, not with these blisters.'

38

They went back to the little bistro in the Marais to lick their wounds. Georgina overcompensated with another apology and Annie reassured her several times all was forgiven.

'It's okay, George; people often say the wrong thing. Sometimes they make up afterwards, sometimes they don't. It happens.' She thought of Muriel. Although they were talking again, she would still have to work on mending their friendship. 'If you ask me, I think you've covered up your real feelings for too long. I guess it's your British stiff upper lip thing. You shouldn't be so stuffy, although most of the time you dress like a rock star. And that's a compliment so don't take it the wrong way. I wish I could look like you,' Annie smiled across to her.

Georgina held up her glass as a waiter went by, speaking to him in French.

'Did you order more wine?'

Georgina grinned.

'You know we only intended to have coffee and some lemon

tart. I think the waiter remembers us staggering out of here last time.'

'Rubbish,' Georgina said, looking around the bistro. 'None of these waiters look familiar.'

'I wonder why?' Annie laughed, flexing her sore feet under the table.

The waiter returned with their wine and Georgina's smile faded when he walked away. 'I want to tell you why I was acting so strange today.'

'You don't have to repeat what I already know. Alain's unfinished business. You need to find him.'

'Do you think I should?'

'Why not? You've got nothing to lose.'

Georgina fingered the stem of her wine glass. She looked tired, the fine lines on her face more pronounced than usual. 'I don't know why I've left it so long, but I guess it's because I knew John wouldn't be happy with me if I went looking for his father.'

'This is your life; he doesn't have to know what you're doing. He does need to know, though, how much Alain still means to you.'

'I'd decided to never come back here again, but it seems turning my back on Paris isn't the right answer, either. I have only just figured that out.' She looked at Annie and shook her head. 'I'm like you. I can't seem to move on, and I guess I won't until I let Alain go. I just want this to be over.'

'It won't be until you find him.'

'I know that now,' Georgina sighed, 'especially after what happened in the gallery. Everywhere I turn in Paris there's something to remind me of him. It seems he's still a part of my life, whether I like it or not. I only have to look at his grandson's dark eyes and crooked smile. Patrick is the image of him. You're very perceptive, you know. I'm lonely, lonely as hell, but I was also lonely when I was married to the wrong man.'

Annie nodded. 'You've never said much about him.'

'William was twelve years older than me when we married. I met him where I worked in PR. He owned the company and was divorced with two daughters. They were teenagers and he didn't want more children. He was good to John, though, and I was grateful for that. He had plenty of money and treated me like his princess. The problem was, I didn't want to be anyone's princess.'

'Except Alain's.'

'That's how it always was,' Georgina said, fidgeting with her bangles. 'I tried to make it work, but the spark wasn't there. We were married for nearly twenty years.'

'And then what happened?'

'It fizzled out. I think William was sick of trying to make me love him and he was getting older. He gave up in the end.'

Annie's hand shot to her chest. 'He died? I thought you were divorced.'

'I meant he gave up on me. We divorced five years ago. We're like old friends these days. John sees a lot of him and still treats him like his father. He's very loyal to William and any talk of Alain being his real father annoys him.'

'Why is life so complicated?' Annie sighed.

They sat in silence, all the tension between them in the gallery now forgotten. Georgina glanced at the waiter standing near their table. 'Do you want to ask for a menu? We haven't eaten anything since the soufflés this morning.'

Annie shook her head. 'I'm too tired to eat and I need to do something about these blisters.'

'What about lunch tomorrow?'

'I'm going to the Louvre, but lunch first would be lovely. I can go to the gallery afterwards and this time I wouldn't expect you to come with me.'

'That sounds like a plan. Have you heard of the Palais-Royal?'

Annie had an image of the Canadian with the buzz cut. 'Isn't it near the Louvre?'

'You're starting to know your way around,' Georgina grinned.

'We drove by it when we picked up someone for the Giverny tour.'

'Well, there's this fabulous restaurant close by that I know you'd love. Scenes from a few films have been shot there. It's a bit touristy, but well worth a visit. Would you like to go?'

'Sure, you can tell me about the films over lunch.'

'I'll make a booking and meet you in front of the Palais-Royal. The restaurant's only a short walk from there. It wouldn't be far to go back to the Louvre afterwards.' She reached for Annie's hand. 'It will be a nice way to say goodbye for now.'

'Pardon?'

'You're coming back, aren't you?'

'How do you know that? I've only just decided.'

'It's written all over your face when you talk about Paris. You look like you're in love.'

Annie laughed. 'Maybe I am.'

'Come on, let's get you to your hotel,' Georgina said, pushing back her chair.

Annie put up her hand. 'Wait, I almost forgot to give you this. I originally planned to give it to you at the gallery.' She reached in her shoulder bag and pulled out a small parcel wrapped in white tissue paper.

Georgina unfolded the layers of paper, lifting out a tiny pen and ink drawing of the Seine. 'It's beautiful. The detail is incredible. Thank you so much.'

'I did it earlier in the week. I thought you would like it since we met on a river cruise.'

'I'll always treasure it.'

Annie beamed at her from across the table. 'You encouraged me to keep sketching. It rescued me.'

'It seems we've rescued each other,' Georgina smiled, her eyes glistening with tears. 'I know exactly where I'll put this after I have it framed.'

'I don't expect you to frame it.'

'Of course I will,' Georgina said, dabbing her eyes with a tissue. 'I'll ask my brother to help me choose the right one. Did I ever tell you he owns an art gallery in Notting Hill?'

'I didn't even know you had a brother.'

Georgina nodded, tucking the drawing into her handbag. 'I always stay in Stephen's apartment when I'm in Paris. I think he would be very interested to see this.'

'It'll probably give him a good laugh.'

'Nonsense; stop doubting yourself.' She put money on the table. 'My shout this time,' she smiled as Annie slipped her shoes back on. 'I'll order another taxi out the front.'

39

It looked like all of the city was at the Paris Métro Station. Annie pushed through a crowd milling around a ticket office, cringing as she thought of the exasperated woman in the booth at the river cruise. She glanced across to a row of ticket machines near her. Tackling a machine seemed easier than going through that again. All she needed to do was get through this part, she thought, and the rest would be easy.

She marched to the end of the nearest queue, determined to meet the challenge. When it was her turn at one of the machines she froze, staring at a touchscreen. She swallowed her rising panic.

'Is there a problem?'

She looked around into the inquisitive eyes of a young woman standing close behind her. 'Sorry, I won't be much longer. This is my first time in the Métro.'

'If you like, I can show you what to do.' Annie smiled and the young woman stepped forward. She spoke with a thick French accent, but her English was perfect. 'You need to touch the screen before following the options. There are different languages, so choose the one you want.'

Annie touched the screen and the instructions changed to English. She chose the type of ticket she wanted and the price appeared on the screen.

The young woman nodded her encouragement. 'Now you can put your coins in the slot,' she smiled.

Annie opened her wallet, fishing out the required money. There were a few mechanical sounds as she fed in the coins before her ticket dropped out of another slot at the bottom of the machine like a bottle of soft drink.

'How good is that!' she laughed. 'Thanks so much.'

'I'm sure you'll master it next time.'

'I'm curious,' Annie said, tilting her head. 'How did you know I'm a tourist?'

The woman smiled. 'When you live here, you just know.'

A man standing behind them cleared his throat and they looked around to a growing queue. 'Sorry, I'd better go. Thanks again for your help.'

The woman nodded and Annie turned towards a metal turnstile. She studied what the other commuters were doing before validating her own ticket and walking through a gate onto a spacious concourse.

She followed a group hurrying down to the next level and when she reached the bottom of the stairs, she faced a maze of tunnels lined with white tiles. She looked back to where she'd come from as an older woman picked her way down the stairs. A floral baseball cap was pulled down over her grey bob and she wore blue cargo pants with a matching blouse. Annie smiled at her pristine white sneakers; she looked like an American, but she wasn't sure.

'Excuse me, do you speak English?' she called out when the woman was closer. She stopped, looking down at Annie.

'I sure do,' she smiled, her American twang reverberating off the tiles. When she reached the bottom of the stairs, she leant over and rubbed her knees. 'Lord, I should've taken a taxi,' she drawled. 'These stairs are killers.'

'I hope you can help me. Do you know which train line goes to the Palais-Royal?'

The woman stood up straight and adjusted her cap. 'I was only thinking the same thing myself.'

'Is that where you're going?' Annie asked, searching her face for an answer.

'That's the general idea. I've always wanted to see the Colonnes de Buren.'

Annie shook her head. 'Sorry, I'm not sure what you mean.'

'They're a famous art installation of striped columns inside the courtyard at the Palais-Royal. It's now looking like going by train may not be such a good idea. My knees aren't what they used to be.'

Annie glanced across the station, unsure of what to do.

'I speak French, though,' the woman continued. 'Let me rest for a minute before I ask someone for directions.'

'That would be great.'

The woman slipped off her small backpack, smiling at her. 'How long have you been in Paris?'

'Almost three weeks, what about you?'

'I only arrived yesterday morning and I'm beat. I got it in my head I'd pretend to be French. I didn't want to go on one of those bus tours with all those smug couples, but now I'm having second thoughts. To tell the truth I'm so tired from just getting here, I don't know how I'm going to do it.'

'Take your time,' Annie said, feeling like a seasoned traveller. 'The place grows on you and you'll soon find your way around. I only wish I could speak French.'

'I guess I'm lucky in that regard, I've always been good at languages. I also speak Italian.'

'It's a real gift.'

They stood watching the passing crowd for a few more minutes until the woman turned to Annie, handing over her backpack. 'You look honest enough, take care of this while I go ask for directions.'

She pushed her way through the throng in front of them, bailing up a tall man with a carry bag. He towered over her and their conversation was animated as he pointed to several signs. The woman looked like she was in her late seventies, but her mannerisms were of someone much younger. Age is only a state of mind, Annie thought, as the woman kept waving her arms as she chatted. She was smiling when she returned.

'Right, we're almost there, only a few more stairs before another tunnel.' She pointed down to a sign beside the next flight of stairs. 'That sign points the way. It's hard to see it from up here.'

Annie handed her the backpack. 'Thanks so much. Do you want to walk down to the platform with me?'

'No thanks, I'll just mosey along; I've got plenty of time. Anyway, you look like you're on a mission.'

'I guess I am,' Annie laughed. 'I'm meeting a friend for lunch.' When she reached the next flight of stairs she looked back at the

American. '*Au revoir,*' she called out and the woman put up her thumb.

She began her descent again, hanging on to the metal handrail. When she reached the platform, she had a sense of being deep in the heart of Paris. Red bucket seats stretched along the platform and above them was a colourful mural of some long-ago revolution painted on the tiled wall. Classical music echoed through the tunnels.

She smiled; this was nothing like Melbourne. Only the French would stage concerts in their public transport system. She glanced up to the *sortie* sign at the end of the platform, thinking of Ed's funny story about his first trip on the Paris Métro. She was still thinking about him as the next train rattled through the underground station.

When it screeched to a stop, the crowd waiting on the platform surged forward and she was caught in the crush, carried along with them as they pushed into the nearest carriage. There weren't any seats left when she squeezed inside, forcing her to stand near the glass doors. She craned forward to see if there were any vacant seats further down the carriage, but they were all taken.

An old man sitting across from the doors put up his hand to catch her attention. He pointed to where he was sitting, motioning for her to take his seat. She shook her head; she couldn't take the place of someone a lot older than herself. He smiled and she could see most of his teeth were decayed. His long white hair looked dirty and he needed a shave.

She turned away, trying to pinpoint why he seemed so menacing. The train accelerated, the noise of the metal wheels grinding on the tracks deafening as it hurtled to the next station. She could still feel his eyes on her while she stared out at the flashing lights of the underground, thinking of the warning signs she'd seen about pickpockets in public places.

Annie didn't see the old man stand while she braced herself in the rocking carriage. When she felt a tap on her arm, she spun around. He was next to her, pointing to his empty seat. An old canvas bag was propped against it. She could smell his breath as he grinned at her. It was a foul combination of garlic, tobacco, and something else that could have been wine. He didn't speak and she suspected if she didn't take his seat, he'd hound her all the way to the Palais-Royal. It seemed easier to accept his offer and she nodded her thanks. She handed over his canvas bag, sitting down while he leant against a handrail.

She swayed with the rhythm of the carriage, conscious he was standing close to her. His presence was overpowering and she could now smell him, his body odour worse than his breath. His clothes were stained and he kept fidgeting with his frayed jacket. She looked down at the floor, hugging her shoulder bag. Even though it was strapped across her chest, she half expected him to reach down and rip it from her.

She wasn't sure what made her look up. When she did, she was eye level with the open fly of his trousers partially covered by the front of his jacket. She glanced away as he moved even closer. The swaying carriage made a loud grating noise and pitched sideways. His leg brushed against her arm as she was nearly jolted out of her seat. When she righted herself, their eyes met. He smiled down at her, making it clear he was enjoying her discomfort.

She felt her face burning; the old bugger knew his fly was open. She was trapped, her embarrassment his cue to casually open his jacket to expose his bulging penis covered with a rash. The other passengers standing next to the old man couldn't see what was going on under his jacket.

She was like a coiled spring ready to leap from the train as soon as it stopped again. When it clattered into the next station she bolted, nearly knocking the old man sideways as she leapt out on the platform. She could see him laughing at her through the open doors, thrusting his hips back and forth while he hung on the handrail. By now his jacket was buttoned over his offending crotch.

She began to run, her sore heels forgotten in her rush to get away. She didn't stop until she reached the street, safe in a crowd of tourists. Her pulse roared in her ears as she looked back at the station to make sure he hadn't followed her. As she stood trying to catch her breath, one thing was certain: she wouldn't be using her return ticket.

40

Georgina couldn't stop grinning. 'It's not funny,' Annie complained, wobbling along the cobblestones behind the Palais-Royal. 'What a waste of money. I only went on the Métro to avoid taking a taxi, but ended up using one anyway when I got off at the wrong station.'

'You won't forget your first ride on the Paris Métro in a hurry.'

'It makes me sick thinking about him, especially with that disgusting rash.'

'What rash?'

'I forgot to tell you. Not only did he stink, but his penis was also covered with red spots right up to the groin.'

'A spotted dick,' Georgina spluttered.

'Very funny; only someone from England would say that.'

'Don't Australians have that dessert?'

'No, thank God.'

'He was only an old fart. Try to see the funny side of it.'

'Actually, he looked like a scarecrow, when I think of it,' Annie smiled. 'All he needed was the straw coming out of his clothes.'

'But in this scarecrow's case, it was more than straw coming out of his fly.'

They began to laugh, hanging on each other for support as they made their way along the cobblestones. A man walking towards them took evasive action and crossed to the other side of the street, making them laugh even more. When they reached the restaurant, Georgina adjusted the lapels of her jacket.

'Shush, we have to stop,' she giggled, pointing up to the name of the restaurant embossed in gold on a black panel over the door. 'Don't forget this place has been immortalised in film.' She sucked in her cheeks and rolled her eyes, sending Annie into another fit of laughter.

'Yes, Madame,' she croaked, 'no more laughing.'

They both took deep breaths, battling to contain their giggles. As Annie turned towards the door, she saw a film poster in the front window. 'Is that one of the films?'

Georgina studied the poster. 'It must be the latest one shot here. They keep a scrapbook of them all. I'll ask a waiter to show you later.'

The restaurant was busy, the hum of the lunchtime crowd punctuated by clinking glasses and cutlery scraping across porcelain. A mosaic floor with an intricate swirling design glowed in the mellow light under the chandeliers.

'I've booked a table next to those potted palms in the back, but we better wait here for the maître d'.'

A man in a black suit hurried towards them. 'Is that him?'

'It looks like it.'

'*Bonjour,*' he trilled, and Annie felt like a movie star.

* * *

They were sitting on leather banquettes trimmed with brass rails running along the top of the backrests. A gold framed mirror above their table reflected the soft lighting.

Annie looked around at the opulence. 'It's all so beautiful.' She touched the silver cutlery. 'I keep expecting a celebrity to walk in,' she grinned.

Georgina took a few olives from the bowl on their table. 'Apparently, it happens here a lot. By the way, I've decided to leave a day early and ditch tomorrow's cooking class. I don't know what made me book three.'

Annie drew her attention from the antique furnishings, looking across to her. 'Would this have something to do with Philippe?'

'What do you mean?'

'You said yesterday you were over him.'

'I couldn't help it; he was so precious about everything and all those silly women were acting like teenagers. Did you see that young Italian fawning all over him? He encouraged her.'

Annie popped an olive in her mouth, slowly chewing while she thought of the right thing to say. If she started analysing the chef, their conversation could turn to what happened later in the gallery and she didn't want to churn it all up again. It seemed better to play low-key, even though she thought Philippe was charming.

'I didn't notice,' she said. 'I was too preoccupied with the egg whites.'

'It was ludicrous to make us whisk by hand.'

Annie took another olive before she answered. 'I guess in the end it was worth all the extra work. The soufflés were delicious.'

'I rang this morning and cancelled my booking for tomorrow. Thankfully, the school is open seven days a week and I spoke to Sally about it. She's the one who organised a place for you in the class.'

'What did she say?'

'She gave me a refund which was nice considering I didn't ask for one. I told a white lie and said I was called home. It seemed the only tactful way out without saying her man was a pain in the arse.'

'Are they a couple?'

Georgina nodded. 'She more or less told me. I could tell by the way she looked at him they were together. It's an old cliché. A girl on a holiday for the first time in Paris meets a young Frenchman and never goes home again. You know the rest.'

Annie decided to play it safe and not ask any questions, but the puzzle of what had happened at the gallery now made sense. Philippe must have reminded her of Alain and was the trigger for her meltdown. The comments later about loneliness had pushed Georgina over the edge. Monet's paintings were only a small part of it.

The waiter appeared with their order of poached salmon, carefully placing the dishes on the table in front of them. '*Bon appétit*,' he smiled.

Annie took a forkful of the fish glistening with butter sauce. 'What time are you leaving tomorrow?'

'Early; I managed to change my train ticket.' She cut a piece of the succulent fish. 'Which brings me to something I want to ask you.'

Annie looked up, her fork held out in mid-air. 'What?'

'Would you have time to make a detour to London before you head back home? It seems a shame not to and I've got plenty of room. There's a whole floor of extra bedrooms.'

'It sounds like you live in Buckingham Palace.'

'Hardly, I'm in one of those old white terraces in Kensington. So, will you come?'

'I don't know what to say.'

'Say yes.'

Annie sat back on the banquette, trying to calculate how she could afford to extend her trip. If she accepted the offer, she would have to finance London with her credit card. The thought of a maxed-out card was depressing enough, but not as much as what was waiting for her in Melbourne. She took a deep breath and smiled. 'That would be wonderful, I'd love to stay.'

Georgina seemed relieved. 'Good; that's all I needed to know,' she said, turning her attention back to her meal.

'The thing is, I didn't organise this trip myself and I don't know how I can change the itinerary,' Annie backtracked, while Georgina ate. 'I'm scheduled to fly home directly from Paris.'

'It's not hard to make changes. Your airline will charge a fee, but it's definitely doable. The easiest way would be to book a train ticket back to London and get your flight home changed to leave from Heathrow. The concierge at your hotel will be able to help you. How long would you like to stay?'

'Would a week be too long?' Annie gulped.

'Why don't you stay for two? It would give us plenty of time to do some sightseeing. You wouldn't be imposing at all and I would love the company. It would be nice for you to have an English Easter.'

'That's so generous.'

Annie's racing mind had already sabotaged her appetite. She swallowed the last of the salmon, unable to taste the fish. When their plates were whisked away, she was fighting a hot flush. It started its familiar route from her constricted chest, creeping up towards her face. She patted her forehead with a linen napkin as red blotches spread across her neck. If she didn't get some air soon, she would fall apart there on the banquette.

'George, where are the toilets?'

'Over there,' she pointed to the side of the restaurant.

Annie heaved herself up, her shoes digging into her sore heels. She winced as she manoeuvred around the table.

'You'll get a surprise when you go in,' Georgina grinned up at her.

'What do you mean?'

'You'll see.'

'I won't be long,' she whispered. The last thing she needed was a surprise.

Their waiter smiled at her while she hurried across the mosaic tiles, trying to hide her flushed cheeks with her hand. When she opened the door of the women's toilets, she faced a large area with a row of cubicles. A sitting room to her left had a red velvet couch and ornate basins with gold framed mirrors. Crystals from a chandelier bounced flashes of light around the room.

Across from her, a flat screen television mounted on one of the walls was showing a film. The scene screening had obviously been shot in the restaurant with three actors in animated conversation over a meal. In the background was the table where she just had lunch. The surprise Georgina had warned her about was like a circuit breaker. She shoved her hands in the pockets of her overshirt as she watched the scene play out, her apprehension forgotten with the distraction.

A display cabinet near the television was stacked with souvenir porcelain from the restaurant. She peered through the glass at the cups and saucers discreetly branded with the name of the restaurant. She smiled to herself; she couldn't leave today without buying something.

She could still hear one of the actors talking as she walked over to a basin to wash her face, patting off the last of her makeup with a linen hand towel. A full-length mirror was on the opposite wall and she turned, looking at herself in the linen outfit she'd decided to wear again. Her expression was showing more excitement than anxiety.

It may have been the soft lights or a trick of the eye, but she could see for herself how different she looked. She wasn't sure if she'd lost weight from all the walking or if the design of the French clothes covered a multitude of figure faults. Whatever it was, she felt good about herself for the first time in almost two years. She tilted her head, smiling at her reflection. It now seemed silly to work herself up about an offer to stay in an exclusive part of London. Of course, she could use her credit card; everyone else did.

She fluffed her curls and applied a new layer of lipstick, examining her skin in the mirror. The hot flush had gone, leaving her with a healthy glow. Behind her, the actors were still in the restaurant. She smiled at them before she went out the door.

* * *

Annie bought a cup and saucer before they left. The waiter handed them to her in a small carry bag while Georgina smirked beside her. 'You think I'm being a typical tourist, don't you?'

'I was only thinking of you lugging them all the way back to Australia.'

'I wanted something to remember Paris by. I've hardly bought anything, and this is unique.'

'What about what you're wearing?'

Annie glanced down at her clothes as they stepped out on the street. 'I forgot,' she grinned. 'No wonder I'm almost broke.'

Georgina stopped, grabbing her arm. 'Do you need money?'

'It was only a figure of speech. I'm all right,' she shrugged, playing with her curls.

'Are you sure? I can give you a loan to tide you over.'

'No really, I'm absolutely fine. Thanks anyway.'

'When you come back again, I'll organise for you to stay in Stephen's apartment. It wouldn't cost you any more than a small contribution for the electricity.'

Annie shook her head. 'Why are you doing all of this?'

'All of what?'

'London and now a Paris apartment; I can hardly keep up with it. Is this some sort of atonement for what happened yesterday?'

'Absolutely not,' Georgina fidgeted, flipping her scarf over one shoulder. 'Don't be so prickly.'

'Me prickly?'

'Touché,' Georgina laughed, linking her arm through Annie's as they began walking again. 'I know you'll enjoy the Louvre. Don't forget, though, you'll only scratch the surface today. There will be plenty of time to see the rest of the collection on your next trip, but don't miss the Mona Lisa.'

'I have to confess that painting is the main reason why I'm going,' Annie grinned.

When they reached the corner of the Palais-Royal, they stopped to listen to a string quartet serenading the afternoon crowds. The sun was warm on their backs as they stood enjoying the classical music drowning out the traffic noise. A young man in a black suit was wandering through the crowd selling the quartet's CDs.

'Do you want one?' Georgina asked.

'No thanks; I have stacks of them at home. Leo's collection takes up nearly a whole bookcase.'

They didn't wait to hear the end of the recital, but they could still hear the music as they walked away. The vast plaza in front of the Louvre was swarming with tourists when they reached the glass pyramid.

Georgina looked at Annie. 'I guess this is it. You have the Louvre and I have to pack.'

Annie bit the side of her lip, bursting into tears. 'I hate goodbyes,' she whispered, wiping her eyes with the back of her hand. 'I know it's ridiculous, but I can't help it. I've been like this ever since that last goodbye to Leo.'

'This is only *au revoir*; it means goodbye until we meet again. It's not final.'

Tears were streaming down Annie's cheeks.

'Don't forget the new you,' Georgina lectured, wagging a finger in her face. 'No more tears. Anyway, I'll be seeing you in London.'

'But we'll never be here together like this again. Paris has changed my life and now this special time with you is about to become only a memory.'

'Isn't that how life is? We can't hold on to anything; it's all made up of lots of passing moments and only our memories keep those moments alive. Have you ever read any Hemingway?'

'No,' Annie sniffed, taking a tissue out of her shoulder bag and blowing her nose.

'Buy a copy of his memoir about Paris. It might help you when it's time to leave.' Georgina smiled. 'Text me when you've made those changes to your itinerary and don't forget I'll meet you at the station.'

Annie nodded, her bottom lip still quivering as she reached out and hugged her. 'See you soon. *Au revoir*,' she whispered before turning away. As she walked, she remembered what Georgina had told her about the City of Light, unsure how she would feel when Paris released her from its grip at the end of the week. She glanced back at the crowded plaza before she went into the glass pyramid, but her friend was already gone.

41

Annie's phone rang while she was trying to decipher the evening news. Georgina's voice was a hoarse whisper. She strained to hear her, grabbing the television remote to turn down the sound.

'George, is that you?'

'Something terrible has happened.'

'What's wrong?'

'You told me I would never get over Alain until I found him again, so what am I supposed to do now? He's dead.'

'Oh no, I'm so sorry.'

'I found out this afternoon.' Her voice trailed off and Annie could hear her crying.

'What can I do?'

'Nothing. I only needed to hear your voice.'

'Does John know?'

'Not yet, but it won't mean much to him. He calls Alain the phantom.'

She sat on the bed listening to Georgina's voice choked with emotion while the weatherman on the television silently pointed out the temperatures across France. 'How did you find out?'

'Through his sister, Mathilde. It took me two days to track her down after I came home from Paris. She lives in Provence. Oh, God, why did I wait so long? All these years I secretly hoped he would walk back into my life one day. I've been such a fool.'

'Did she give you any details?'

There was a long silence and she held her breath while she waited for Georgina to speak again. When she did, her measured words were chilling. Alain had been killed in a motorcycle accident two months after Georgina had returned to England all those years ago. He'd been on his way to spend Christmas with friends in Normandy. The roads were icy after the first snow of the season and he'd skidded into a car on the outskirts of Paris. Georgina started to cry again when she told Annie there had to be a closed coffin at the funeral.

'He died like a dog in the gutter,' she sobbed, 'and he's buried in Paris.'

'I can't believe it,' Annie whispered, trying to control her trembling hands. 'It's so tragic. How are you?'

'I feel numb. I must be in shock.' She could hear Georgina blowing her nose before she spoke again. 'It gets worse.'

'Oh my God.'

Georgina gulped back tears as she spoke. 'Mathilde said Alain wrote to me after I left Paris, but when there was no reply to any of his letters, he started binge drinking. He was drinking the night of the accident.'

'What happened to his letters?'

'That's what I've only just figured out.'

She explained how her father had offered to post her letters to Alain on his way to work since she was too ill to go out. It was obvious to her now they never had been posted and Alain's letters never given to her. Even her letters to Mathilde had never been sent.

'My mother always waited to collect the mail as soon as it fell through the slot in the front door,' Georgina sniffed, 'but I never made a connection between her vigilance in the entrance hall every morning and the letters I was waiting for from Paris. When I was well enough to start posting the letters myself, Alain was already dead.'

She began to sob while Annie listened, the phone jammed to her ear. When the crying subsided Georgina's voice was croaky. 'The landlord of Alain's little attic room didn't return my letters and I had no way of knowing what happened. My whole life has been a lie.'

'Why would your parents do that?' Annie asked, pacing the room as she talked.

'Simple. They disliked the French and their unwed daughter had disgraced them.'

'But wouldn't they want you to marry the father of your child?'

'A Frenchman? You have to be joking. All they wanted was for me to give in and have my baby adopted so the whole episode would disappear. Except they didn't count on falling in love with their little grandson.'

'Did you tell Mathilde about John?'

'I was too distressed. I'll ring her back tomorrow. I'm not even sure if Alain told her I was pregnant, but she needs to know. I owe her at least that; John and Patrick are all she has left of her only brother. I'll also tell her how we were betrayed by the two people I least expected to ruin my life and destroy his.'

Annie blinked back tears. 'I wish I was there to give you a big hug.'

'I really need one right now.'

'I'll cancel my train ticket.'

'Why?'

'You don't need me there; I'd only get in the way.'

'Oh, Annie, I need you here more than you know.'

The sun was warm as Annie sat on the pew in front of the bookshop near Notre-Dame, thinking about Georgina. The unsettling phone call had kept her up most of the night. She couldn't shake the images of Georgina searching faces in the crowd and Alain in a lonely grave. She raked her fingers through her curls; she'd never been to the cemetery since Leo's funeral and would now have to face her own reality. She would take flowers there when she returned home.

She opened the paperback she'd just bought, searching for what Hemingway had written that would help her say goodbye to Paris. She was flipping through the pages when she heard someone calling her name. She looked up into Ed's smiling face and dropped the book.

'What's this?' he asked as he stooped down and picked it up. 'I thought you said you wouldn't be buying more books while you were in Paris.'

'I couldn't resist Hemingway,' she smiled, taking the book from him, 'especially after a friend told me it was important to read this.'

'Only if you've fallen in love with Paris,' he grinned, sitting beside her.

'It seems I have,' she laughed.

'That explains why you look happy. What was wrong with you after the reading?'

'Am I that transparent?'

'Yeah, you are.'

'It's a long story you probably wouldn't want to hear. Anyway, I only came here to say goodbye; I'm leaving in a few days. The girl at the counter inside said you usually come in at this time and I'm glad I waited.'

'Let's go have a coffee and you can fill me in on what you've been up to,' he said, stretching out his long legs.

Annie smiled across to him feeling like she was with an old friend.

It took two cups of coffee each and a plate of pastries between them to share their latest adventures in Paris. Annie reassured him her anxiety at the reading had nothing to do with him, finally revealing what had happened in her life over the past two years. She kept the emotion out of her story, surprising herself; it was the first time she'd talked about Leo without crying.

She tried to keep the conversation light after that, telling him about the soufflé class and the flasher on the train. He laughed when she told him, telling her writing at the bookshop was no match to what she'd been doing. She thought he'd edited the description of his days in Paris because she was old enough to be his mother, but she didn't say anything as he kept talking.

'I'm leaving earlier than I originally planned, so I'm glad you stopped by,' he said, taking another sip of coffee. 'I've done everything I wanted to do. Anyway, there's someone here trying to get too close.'

Annie thought of the young woman pouting outside the bookshop after the reading. 'The woman who writes poetry?'

He nodded. 'I can see what's coming next and don't want any part of it.' They sat in silence while a waiter put a fresh bottle of water on their table. 'It's been good having a project after what happened back home,' he continued, fidgeting with his cup. Lines etched his forehead as he told her how he'd fled to Paris after a broken engagement, throwing in a secure teaching job to follow his dream of seeing the world and writing about it.

'Bec was really pissed off with me, not to mention both sets of parents,' he said, rubbing the back of his neck. 'In the end, I couldn't be the person everyone else wanted me to be. All I wanted to do was travel, but Bec's idea of seeing the world was watching a few travel documentaries on her laptop. She refused to even consider travelling with me.'

He filled their glasses with more water. 'I was already over it all when she hauled me into a department store to put our names on the bridal register. There was this drama about whether to have plain china or something with a pattern. I ended it in front of the teacups, but sometimes I regret how it happened. I think she hates me now.'

Annie sat back in her seat, looking at the emotion written all over his face. 'Didn't you tell me the last time we had coffee that you're going to Italy next?'

'Actually, it's tomorrow now. I'm going to Rome first.'

'I know someone like you,' she said, telling him about Lucy and her job offer in Tuscany. 'Apparently, the owners of the vineyard are always looking for help. It may be worth investigating. I'm afraid I don't have any other details, but Lucy does.'

'Could you give me her number?' He pulled out his phone and handed it to her. 'I would be interested in hearing more about it. Give me your number, too.'

'What am I supposed to do with this?'

'Just tap the numbers in with the contacts.'

Ed grinned at her as she stared down at the phone, shaking her head. 'Do you have a pen? Smartphones are beyond me.' He fished one out of his shirt pocket and she scrawled across the back of a paper napkin. 'Lucy's leaving for Italy soon. I've missed all the excitement. She closed her shop and bought a ticket all in the space of a few weeks. I told her she should wait to sell the business, but she seemed in too much of a hurry to even consider it.'

'Sounds like she isn't interested in china patterns, either.'

'Definitely not,' Annie said, pushing the napkin across the table. 'I'll let her know you may be contacting her.'

By now the café was crowded and waiters were hovering with the lunch menus. 'I better let you go. Anyway, I have to start packing,' she said, taking out her wallet as they stood. 'This is my shout.'

Ed blinked at her and she laughed.

'That's Aussie slang for paying the bill. You paid last time.' She put a few notes on the side of her cup and picked up her book from the table. 'Let me know how your travels go, I'd like to keep in touch.'

He smiled, looking down at her. 'I forgot to give you my details; here, I'll write them in your book. I'm sure Mr Hemingway wouldn't mind.'

'What does he say about Paris?' she asked as he printed in the flap.

'Once you've been here, it stays with you for the rest of your life no matter where you go.'

Annie's face lit up. 'Now I know why my friend said I should read this. Maybe I'll buy another one of his books before I go home.'

'This one is a good read; I'm sure you'll like it.' He handed it back as they began walking towards the bookshop. When they reached the corner he leant over, hugging her. 'Take care, Annie from Australia; I'll be in touch.'

'Safe journey,' she whispered, before he walked away. She watched as he was swallowed in the crush of the lunchtime crowds while she stood on the footpath blinking back tears.

Annie's phone rang while she walked along Pont des Arts. She turned her back to a couple next to her entwined in each other's arms when she heard Mia's voice. 'Darling girl,' she laughed, 'what was that lecture you gave me about international calls?'

'I want to give you an update about things on the home front and texting seems too hard.'

Annie looked out to the river, trying to summon up some enthusiasm. 'What's going on now?'

'David and I met with Lucy today and told her we weren't buying her apartment. We couldn't fall in line with her urgent schedule and in the end, we didn't want to.'

'I thought it all sounded a bit far-fetched, but you know our Lucy. How did you get around it?'

'It wasn't easy, especially when we told her we wouldn't rent it either. It seemed pointless to go to another rental property. She really hammered us, only giving up when it was obvious she couldn't wear us down.'

'When is she leaving?'

'A week after you get back and to tell you the truth, I'll be glad to see her get on the plane.'

'Mia, I won't be home on the weekend, so I'm going to miss having Easter with you all. I was going to text you both later today. George has asked me to stay with her in London and I've changed my itinerary. I know I should've told you sooner, but I've been waiting for the confirmation of a new flight. I needed to ask for help from the concierge at the hotel, so it hasn't been straightforward.'

'How fabulous. Where does she live?'

'Kensington. She went home this week to some sad family news and I'll be able to give her a bit of moral support.'

'It sounds like you two have really bonded.'

'I guess we have. I'll be there for another two weeks so I'll miss seeing Lucy.' She took a deep breath. 'And there's something else I need to tell you. I'm selling up when I get back.'

'Oh, Mum, what a big step.'

'I've thought about it for months. I can't tell you how hard it is living with all the memories. Now I'm here, I can see how important a fresh start will be. If I don't do something, I'm afraid I'll never recover.'

'It makes me sad thinking of it. It'll always be home to me.'

'But darling, you have your brand-new life. I can't spend the rest of mine keeping the flame burning for what used to be. Anyway, we can talk more about this when I get home. This call must be costing you a fortune.'

'No, please, this is too important. Don't go.'

They talked for a few more minutes while Annie walked along the bridge surrounded by young lovers and tourists taking photos. After she said goodbye, it felt like a weight had been lifted from her shoulders. Talking about her plans made them seem more real.

Her neighbourhood in inner Melbourne was almost unrecognisable because of the pace of development over the past few years, as everyone around her cashed in on the hot property market. Now, she would do the same thing. Selling up was the only way she could rescue herself. There was no job to go back to, only the house.

The kindergarten where she'd worked had kept her job open for a few months after Leo's death, but she never could find the strength to return. When she'd run out of excuses why she couldn't go back, they had paid her out and thanked her for her long years of service. By then her will to go on had been diminishing with each passing day. Looking back on that time from where she was now, she wondered how she was still standing. It was a sobering thought as she walked back to the hotel.

Annie wheeled her suitcase out from the corner of her hotel room, pulling off the airline tags. She thought of the young man at the airport in Melbourne looping them on while he chatted to her about Paris. At the time, she was convinced she would never see her suitcase again as it disappeared on a conveyor belt at the side of the check-in counter.

She took out her tote bag from the wardrobe, running her hand over the shabby leather. There seemed no reason to keep something that would always remind her of the nightmares. She folded it over, pushing it into the small bin in the bathroom. Like the tote bag, her old life didn't fit anymore.

The courage to make a decision about the house had came to her at Notre-Dame. Over the past weeks she had often called in to sit on one of the wooden chairs near the back, reflecting on how her life had changed. She never prayed, convinced God wasn't listening, but the cathedral radiated peace and a feeling of comfort she couldn't explain even to herself. She lit a candle for Leo at each visit and when she returned, there would only be a puddle of wax where it had been.

She glanced at the tote bag in the bin. If she lit a candle every day for the rest of her life it would never change anything. Keeping the house like a memorial to her life with Leo would be like lighting the candles. He was gone and the house couldn't bring him back. She had to move on, but it didn't mean that the life they once shared would be forgotten.

42

Lucy stood in the middle of her bedroom staring at the open wardrobe. The metal rail sagged from the weight of her clothes. She groaned, asking herself what she would do with it all. She couldn't take it with her and if she stored it, everything would be dated when she came back.

The enormity of what she was doing started to sink in. She closed the wardrobe doors, thinking of Mia's negativity and her mother's annoyance. It had all seemed simple enough when the idea had first come to her, but for some reason everyone else didn't get it. It wasn't as if she was unloading a husband and skipping the country; she was only trying to close a failing business.

She patted the invisible weight pushing on her chest. Of course, it wasn't only the shop, it was how everything had changed with no way to control any of it. No tears, she lectured herself; this will be a grand adventure not a great escape. She flopped backwards on the bed and started to cry, hot tears running down her face. 'Dad, why did you have to go and fucking die on us,' she sobbed.

* * *

Lucy could hear her own footsteps echoing in the shop. She walked around the empty space thinking about the first time she'd seen it. Her father had met her for the inspection and she could still picture him leaning against the wall trying to talk her out of leasing it.

Standing in the shop now, it seemed as though nothing had happened since then. Not opening the business with all its highs and lows, not his illness or the aftermath of his death. None of it. It was as if time had been wound back and she was seeing the property for the first time three years ago. He was right, she thought, Toorak was out of her league.

She looked back at the front window. Her father had suggested the name of her business and although she had resisted in the beginning, *Lulu's* had stuck, becoming her signature brand. He'd given her the nickname when she was a child and now the elaborate script stretching across the plate glass was the only thing left. Even that would be gone after the window cleaners arrived in the morning. She glanced around at the shell of what once was. It all looked so forlorn.

The boutique across the street had bought her unsold stock and the restaurant next door had snapped up the industrial style table she used as a counter. She threw in her prized leather couch as part of the deal to thank the restaurant owner for taking over her lease. The only things she kept were the display cubes her father had made and her mother's large painting. The red hibiscus canvas had been a gift to celebrate the opening, becoming the focal point of the shop.

Lucy thought of the cubes and painting now stacked in her old bedroom at her mother's house. She'd been ferrying boxes to the house all week, stacking the room with remnants of the life she was leaving behind. The bedroom turned out to be the perfect storage solution; she only needed to run the idea by her mother when she returned home at the end of the week. There could be no reason why she would refuse her. Her eyes brimmed with tears as she stood in the middle of the empty shop; it felt like abandoning an old friend. She took one last look around before locking the front door.

The noise and fumes of Toorak Road dampened her emotions as she hurried to the pedestrian crossing on the corner, trying not to look back. Get a grip, she lectured herself; there had been enough sadness without getting all warm and fuzzy about a shop.

While she waited for the lights to change, she glanced across to her hatchback in a fifteen-minute parking space on the other side of the street. She frowned, now realising what she'd overlooked, muttering a string of obscenities as she stood on the kerb wondering how she could sell her car on such a tight schedule. An old woman standing next to her puckered her lips as she listened, but Lucy was in no mood to apologise to anyone. She sprinted across the street when the lights turned green, leaving the old woman to fret about the younger generation as she shuffled behind her.

Traffic was heavy as she drove home from Toorak. She thought about what home really meant, pondering the question as she manoeuvred into the next lane. For her, it was still the place where she'd grown up. It was the old woodshed where she and Mia had searched for the tooth fairy when they were little girls. It was the back verandah where she'd played board games with her friends on school holidays, the place where she could talk to her parents about anything, the place where she'd learnt what it meant to be part of a loving family. Home was her parents' house.

She thought of the modern block of apartments where she was now living. Her cramped apartment on the top floor would never feel like home, but it was all she had whether she liked it or not.

She was still surprised Mia and David had rejected her offer to buy it. When she'd met them a few hours before, she'd known what their decision had been as soon as they walked into her apartment like two strangers. David had done most of the talking while Mia sat beside him like a good little wife. She had seemed caught in the middle, not chipping in until the conversation started going in circles.

Lucy stared into the traffic; it didn't matter to her one way or the other who bought or rented the apartment. She was genuine in her concern about the baby, but Mia wouldn't listen, accusing her of offering them the apartment for selfish reasons.

When she'd reminded them South Yarra would be a better place to bring home the baby rather than their apartment in the western suburbs, Mia had called her a snob. It surprised her how they had already slipped into the roles of traditional parents, not willing to take any chances. She couldn't see why it was so hard for them to organise a home loan in two weeks.

The cardboard boxes lined two walls. They were backbreaking to lift, the distraction taking Lucy's mind off the tense discussion that morning. Her arms were aching as she tried to wedge a smaller box under the bed. It kept hitting something and she reached underneath, pulling out a small painting of a blue wren.

She smiled down at the bird caked with dust, thinking of how it once presided over their family meals from its perch on the dining room wall. She propped it next to the hibiscus canvas, wondering if Mia's old bedroom could be used for the overflow of boxes. The real estate agent suggested she lease her apartment as a furnished property to attract a higher rental price and she warmed to his idea, the plan solving her dilemma of what to do with it all since Mia had let her down.

She thought about the shop as she sat on one of the boxes. Technically, she could still trade out of the financial stress with a few simple changes like selling online, but the idea of fiddling with figures bored her. She enjoyed the thrill of taking risks, the heady feeling of walking the high wire. Sometimes she fell and there wasn't always a safety net, but most of the time the risks she took made her life more exciting. After three years the shop had lost its lustre and it was time to move on.

The only complication was her hatchback. She thought of her mother's old bomb parked in the garage. She treated it like a cherished friend, even giving it a name. Somehow, she would have to convince her to get rid of Bertha and buy the hatchback.

She was still stacking boxes when a key turned in the front door. She froze as she listened to footsteps in the hall. Before she could even climb over the boxes, Mia was standing in the doorway with her hands on her hips.

'What's going on in here?' she demanded.

'Fuck, you scared me.' Lucy picked her way through the maze of boxes to face her sister. 'I didn't know you were coming around tonight.'

'I bet you didn't. Why is all your stuff in here?'

'This is my bedroom and I can do whatever I want.'

'That's stretching it; you haven't lived here for years.'

'Yeah, whatever. So why are you here?'

'I'm watering the pot plants.' She looked across to the boxes. 'Have you asked Mum about this?'

Lucy shrugged.

'You haven't, have you? Well, dear sister, I have a big surprise for you. I just talked to her a little while ago.'

'What, tonight?'

'It's still morning in Paris. She's changed her itinerary. George has invited her to stay in London. She also told me she's selling the house when she gets back.'

'She can't do that; she's lived here forever.'

'She doesn't think she can face all the memories anymore.'

'What about my things?'

'You might have to ring a few storage places in the morning,' Mia smirked.

'When will she be back?'

'In two weeks.'

'But I'll be gone by then.'

'Oh dear,' Mia grinned.

'This is our family home. How can she do this to us?'

'Well, she is, and you better get used to it. You warned her about the rabbit hole and she listened. She even mentioned it to me.'

'What did she say?

'She said to tell you she isn't Alice anymore.'

43

The little café throbbed with music as waiters in black uniforms and long white aprons bustled between the tables. Many of the early diners were tourists like Annie with carry bags of souvenirs and guidebooks piled on their tables. She sat savouring her last night in Paris, taking in every detail for later when it all would be only a memory.

The lights of the city were beginning to glitter across the river and the evening traffic had slowed to a crawl. As she gazed out at the passing parade from under a striped awning, she could hear a rumble in the distance that seemed out of place. She looked up expecting to see a sudden approaching storm, but the sky was a benign shade of blue in the fading light. The persistent sound became impossible to ignore as she tried to eat. Other diners were also reacting, checking their phones and looking out to the street.

The first sign of looming danger was the distinct smell of smoke and wailing sirens. She craned forward over her plate while fire trucks forced through the heavy traffic, sounding their air horns. Pedestrians scattered as cars straddled kerbs to get out of the way.

A palpable tension fizzed between the tables. Diners stood, trying to see what was happening. Several waiters went out to the street, followed by a stream of people. Annie grabbed her shoulder bag and hurried to join them. From her vantage point in the street, she had a clear view across the river to Île de la Cité.

At the end of the island where it juts out into the Seine, Notre-Dame was blanketed in billowing smoke. The rumbling sound was louder now, resonating from deep inside the cathedral.

The growing crowd swarmed around her on the footpath. Several people reached out towards the cathedral, unconsciously trying to stop what they were seeing. She stood shoulder to shoulder with them, riveted to the spot in disbelief.

The cathedral windows glowed from inside as if someone had turned on its lights. Flames broke through the plumes of smoke, fanning out along the roof and shooting skyward like a licking tongue in the twilight. Within minutes the spire became transparent in the fire, a bell outlined in the inferno.

When she thought it couldn't get any worse, the spire buckled. In one agonising moment, it seemed to survive in that distorted position, but then it toppled, disintegrating into the flames along with the skeleton of the roof. Scaffolding that had been put up for the cathedral's renovation tilted in the firestorm.

Gargoyles with gaping mouths were silhouetted against the orange flames like a scene from the gates of hell. Above it all, the sky was pierced with red as if the very heart of Paris had been torn open, exposed and bleeding for all the world to see while Notre-Dame burned.

As she squinted into the haze, her nose and throat tingled from the rancid smell drifting across the river. In the middle of the chaos a woman's lilting voice rang out with a mournful hymn, followed by an emotional chorus. Although the French words had no meaning to Annie, they touched a deep, unknown well inside of her and she began to pray for the flames to stop. She prayed to the god she thought had betrayed her. It felt like a homecoming, a strange awareness that she wasn't alone. If ever there could be a rebirth of her fractured soul, it seemed to be happening as she stared at the horror across the river.

Dusk had faded to night, but the sky was still lit up above Notre-Dame. Plumes of smoke and flying embers danced under the emergency spotlights. Firefighters waded through puddles of water, dragging long hoses around the smouldering cathedral. An eerie hush had descended on the night except for the tolling of church bells all over the city.

Île de la Cité was closed to the public, forcing Annie to walk back to Île Saint-Louis the long way around. Over the past weeks, she'd used the square in front of Notre-Dame as a shortcut on her walks around Paris. The cathedral and its garden had become her base camp, the place where she would sit in contemplation before setting out to explore the city. Now, life had again taken an unexpected turn.

Sombre crowds swarmed around her as she walked, all facing the disaster scene across the river. When she reached Pont de la Tournelle, she stopped by a pocket of people praying on their knees. She leant against the stone balustrade of the bridge, listening to the bells tolling for the charred cathedral still standing under the spotlights.

* * *

Colette was alone in the foyer when Annie reached the hotel. She looked around when Annie came in, her face pale against her black uniform. 'Madame Green, are you okay?'

Annie slumped on one of the couches, trying not to cry in front of her. 'I've just come from Notre-Dame. I saw the spire go.'

Colette was standing ramrod straight with her hands in her pockets, fighting to maintain her usual businesslike manner. She was dishevelled with ash scattered across one of the sleeves of her blazer. 'I saw it all from the bridge,' she said, her voice tight with emotion.

'I'm so sorry. I know how much the cathedral means to you all.'

'It feels like our mother is wounded.' Her eyes were glistening as Annie stood, reaching out to her.

Colette stepped back, keeping her professional distance as she tried to regain her composure. She smoothed her tousled hair, adjusting the lapels of her blazer. 'You look exhausted. Let me organise some coffee and dessert for you. I'll have it sent up to your room,' she offered.

Annie was too rattled to maintain any kind of detachment after what had happened. 'But what about you? Who is taking care of you?'

Colette looked startled. 'I have my family, but tonight all of Paris is family. There is no need to be concerned for me.'

'I can't help it,' Annie whispered, fidgeting with the top button of her cardigan. 'I never imagined my last night here would be like this. I wanted to hear the Notre-Dame bells in the morning one last time. I'll miss them.'

'We all will, but we will rebuild again. This is what we do.' Colette's voice cracked as she spoke and she began to weep, covering her face with her hands. This time she let Annie hug her.

Dawn was breaking over Paris. Annie looked out at the pink sky with an empty feeling, trying to grasp what had happened the night before. The street below her hotel window was deserted except for a man walking his dog. She picked up her shoulder bag; there was one last thing she needed to do.

Downstairs the reception desk was closed. She left her key by the phone and walked out into the cool morning. The stench from the fire still lingered as she walked over cobblestones smeared with white ash. When she reached the bridge that linked the two islands, several people were already there taking photos. The scarred cathedral rose defiantly in front of them, dominating the landscape like it always had for more than eight hundred years.

Annie walked as far as she was allowed, standing in front of the fluttering red-and-white plastic tape blocking the end of the bridge. She bowed her head, silently saying goodbye while policemen with guns stood sentry on the other side of the tape. When she turned to leave, she noticed a tiny piece of charred timber at her feet. She picked it up, slipping it into her pocket. As she walked away, she looked back at the cathedral. Birds were circling above the towers while church bells tolled in the distance like they had the night before.

* * *

Annie shook Colette's hand when the taxi arrived. She wanted to hug her, but thought better of it, knowing it would only rake up the emotions of the night before. 'I'll be back again,' she smiled. 'Thanks for everything. I hope you're feeling better today.'

'Yes, I am,' she nodded. 'We look forward to seeing you next time.' The phone rang, interrupting them and she smiled before turning to answer it.

Annie glanced around the foyer, unable to tear herself away as Armand wheeled her suitcase outside. The gardenias were still in bloom on the polished table. Their sweet scent was mixed with the aroma of fresh coffee. As she lingered there, she thought of Hemingway. He was right; all of this would stay with her for the rest of her life no matter where she was.

When she finally went outside, Armand was talking to the taxi driver. She opened her wallet, handing him a note. 'I never gave you a tip that first day. This is for all your help.'

She knew he didn't understand what she said, so she smiled, and he took it. He adjusted the collar of his uniform, nodding his thanks. The taxi driver put her suitcase in the boot while she slid into the back with the new red tote bag she'd bought the day before. She could smell his aftershave when he sat behind the steering wheel.

'Gare du Nord?'

'Yes, I'm catching the nine o'clock train to London,' she said, buckling her seat belt. She glanced out the rear window as the taxi inched down the cobblestone street. Armand was standing on the footpath waving to her and she waved back, willing herself not to cry.

All of the shops were still closed. Cleaners in green and yellow uniforms were sweeping the street with brooms while water flowed along the gutters. The café on the corner was open and a lone waiter walked towards a couple at a table out the front, a tray held high above his shoulder.

When the taxi rattled over Pont Marie, Annie rolled down the window looking back at Île Saint-Louis, wishing she could wrap up the little island and take it home with her. In the distance she could see the towers of Notre-Dame and blue sky in the space where the spire had once stood. The river shimmered as a tourist boat glided across the water. She leant out the window trying to hear the music on the boat, but it was too far away. Tour buses were already doing laps of the city. She rolled up the window trying to put a lid on her emotions. This was *au revoir*, she kept reminding herself; she would be back again one day.

As they drove towards the station, the streets so foreign three weeks ago now looked familiar. She shook her head remembering her fear that first day. When they passed the Louvre, she thought of Georgina's phone call. They never guessed what was coming when they had said goodbye in front of the glass pyramid. She could still hear the anguish in Georgina's voice, unsure of how her friend would face the truth that had eluded her for so long.

Georgina was still on her mind when the taxi stopped in front of the station. She clambered out while the driver put her suitcase on the footpath, paying him with the last of her euros. As he drove off, she looked across to the taxi rank at the side of the station. She was back where it all began.

44

The train stretched along the tracks like a silver snake. Annie found her carriage halfway down the platform, heaving her suitcase on board. It seemed lighter than before and she guessed all the walking had made her fitter. Behind her, several passengers waited with their suitcases outside the luggage compartment while she jammed her bag in an empty space on a bottom shelf. She nodded as she brushed past them on the way out, half expecting to see the arrogant young man with the long fringe. Before she went to find her seat, she took one last look out the open door, breathing in Paris.

'Au revoir,' she whispered. 'Au revoir. Merci.'

The carriage was nearly full when she found her seat, sinking into the thick upholstery. She glanced around at the other passengers; there weren't any children. It seemed the return journey to London would be uneventful.

Twenty minutes later the train was gliding through the suburbs. The further it went, the Paris of the guidebooks melted away, replaced by another version of the city tourists hardly ever saw. Annie gazed out at shabby high-rise buildings and grimy streets clogged with traffic. The last time she'd passed these outskirts she'd been too distracted by the wild children in her carriage to notice what was right in front of her. Now the other Paris with all its warts was flashing by her, unlike the frothy confection she was familiar with.

Within minutes it was all erased like it never existed, left behind as the train sped through the countryside. Green fields with the occasional small town streaked by while Annie's thoughts slid back to when she'd travelled through France three weeks before. Layers of time peeled away as she looked out at the scenery, thinking of her great-grandfather. These fields were where he'd fought as a young soldier in the war that was supposed to end all wars.

She thought of his tarnished World War One medals she'd inherited when her mother died. They were still in a black velvet box that hadn't been opened in years, tucked away in the back of her wardrobe. She took out the charred piece of timber from her pocket, turning it over in the palm of her hand. If only he were still alive so she could tell him how much the country he'd once defended meant to her.

Annie ran her hand along the rough surface of the balcony railing, looking down at a rose garden bathed in morning sun. Lucy and Mia waved to her from under a peppercorn tree. Before she went back into the hospital, she glanced over her shoulder at the Eiffel Tower.

Her buzzing phone brought her back from the dream. She jumped, disorientated as she automatically reached for it, smiling when she heard Lucy's voice.

'How's it all going?'

Annie stared out the window at the suburbs of London gliding by. 'I'm glad you rang, I must have nodded off.'

'I hope you weren't having one of those nightmares.'

'No, they're only dreams now.'

She closed her eyes with the phone jammed to her ear, realising what she couldn't see before: she'd survived. All of it.

'You sound distracted.'

'Sorry, I'm not quite awake.'

'Where are you?'

'I'm still on the train. It's slowing down so I guess I'll be in London soon.'

'I heard about Notre-Dame. It's been all over the news here.'

'I saw the whole thing last night. I was having dinner across from the cathedral when the fire started. I'll never forget it.'

'Oh, Mum, if I'd known, I would've rung you. What a thing to happen on your last night there. Do you think what's left can be saved?'

Annie thought of Colette. 'They'll rebuild. That's what the French do.'

'I've heard from Ed, that American you texted me about. He's interested in some work at Prue's vineyard.'

'I didn't think he would contact you so soon.'

'He's already in Rome and wants to meet me when I get there.'

An unexpected image of Ed with her daughter in a Roman café made her grin. 'How amazing,' she said, unsure if she'd unwittingly played matchmaker by scrawling Lucy's number on that napkin. 'You both have a lot in common, I'm sure you'll like him.'

'Yeah, I thought he sounded pretty cool. By the way, Mia will be ringing you soon. I talked to her only a few minutes ago. She has some news for you.'

Annie sat up straight. 'Is something wrong?'

'Everything's okay, but I won't spoil her surprise. She's wanted to tell you before, but now she can't wait any longer. I have to fly; someone is coming soon to look at my car and I need to clean it out. Fingers crossed it gets sold.'

'It has to, there's no room for it in my garage. Accept any offer to get rid of it.'

Lucy ignored the comment. 'Enjoy London. Love you.'

The call ended abruptly before Annie could say goodbye, making it obvious Lucy didn't want to discuss the consequences of not selling her car. She thought of their conversation the day before, remembering the relief in her daughter's voice when she'd told her the boxes could stay until the house went on the market. For once Lucy didn't challenge her, even when she'd made it clear she couldn't part with Bertha.

Annie slipped her phone back in her shoulder bag and stared out the window. The train was moving into St Pancras International and everything looked familiar. She put her tote bag on her lap while she waited for the train to stop, wondering what Mia wanted to tell her.

Hemingway's memoir sat on top of the other souvenirs inside the bag. She touched the cover, thinking of what he'd written about Paris. When she stepped out of the train, she could see Georgina sprinting across the platform in her red boots. Annie waved, the tiny wheels of her suitcase vibrating on the cement as she rushed towards her.

POSTSCRIPT

Months after Paris, Annie walked along a Melbourne street lined with trees sprouting new spring leaves. She stopped in front of the café she'd run out of on Leo's anniversary, trying to blink away the memory. If she'd ended it all later that day, she would never have gazed into her granddaughter's blue eyes only minutes after she was born. Life would have moved on and she would have missed it all.

She stood debating whether she should go in and buy a treat for Mia or keep walking. Inside, she could see several customers talking over their coffee at a table near the window. She took a deep breath and pushed open the glass door.

No one was behind the counter and she rang a bell next to the cash register. When there still was no service, she rang it again. A waitress in a black apron backed out of the kitchen, laughing as a young man followed her.

'Stop it,' she said when he whispered in her ear, 'we're at work.' They kept their backs turned to the counter while they continued whispering. Annie recognised her, clearing her throat and they looked around.

'I'd like a bag of chocolates, please.'

'What ones do ya want?' the waitress whined without a flicker of recollection.

'The ones with soft centres.' The waitress ignored her, distracted with the young man now clearing a table. Annie rolled her eyes. 'I can see nothing has changed. Any chance of a bit of service?'

The waitress dragged her attention away from the young man and looked back at Annie. 'What did ya say?'

'I'd like the chocolates with soft centres.'

The waitress shrugged, plonking a cellophane bag on the counter.

Annie handed her a note. 'You know, it's a good thing you aren't in a café in the City of Light,' she laughed, scooping the chocolates into her shoulder bag.

'Where's that?'

'Paris.'

'France?'

Annie grinned. 'That's the one. But, I'm afraid if you were trying to hold down a job there, you probably wouldn't last five minutes.'

She turned, skirting around the display of imported tea near the counter. When she reached the door, she glanced over her shoulder at the waitress. She was still gaping at her from behind the cash register.

A charity street stall had been set up on the corner near the café. Annie manoeuvred around the bargain hunters, making a beeline for the baby wear on a trestle table. A white cardigan caught her eye. She touched the embroidered rosebuds on the collar.

'It looks too big, but has plenty of room to grow into,' she said to an old woman sitting behind the table.

'Is it for a special baby?'

Annie stood a little taller. 'It's for my granddaughter. She was born yesterday.'

'Oh my, how lovely. What's her name?'

'Rosie, after my mother. I'm so touched my daughter and her husband chose it for their little one.'

'A beautiful old-fashioned name. Is she your first grandchild?'

Annie nodded. 'I'm already besotted with her.' She looked down at the cardigan. 'I'll take it.'

'I made that one,' the old woman beamed, tucking it into a pink carry bag.

'What exquisite work. I'm on my way back to the hospital now and will bring it with me.' The old woman took her money, folding it into a biscuit tin with her gnarled fingers.

'Say hello to Rosie for me,' she said, handing the bag across the table.

Annie smiled. 'I sure will.'

She pulled out her key ring of Notre-Dame as she walked back to her car, the silver souvenir now a treasured icon. She was still smiling when she reached Bertha.

Acknowledgments

The idea for this book started on a rainy day in Paris when the character of Annie appeared and wouldn't go away until her story was told. I would like to acknowledge all those who helped me on the journey to publication since that rainy day. I'm indebted to Shaun Wilson and Tammy Honey for their support in helping *Ticket to Paris* come to fruition. Petra Poupa gave me the confidence to keep working on the manuscript after her insightful assessment, later polishing final drafts with meticulous editing. Jo Chehab read the first draft as it was being written, always giving her generous input as the project developed. Pamela Anthonee in Paris gave me invaluable help during my research trips there and later checked the French dialogue. Athalie Moss allowed me to use one of her experiences in Paris for Annie. Barbara Keppler Cowan in the United States helped shape the narrative with her perspective. Grace Aanensen, Jenny Macaulay and Helen M. Dalton also contributed important feedback. Helen Christie made the work shine with her creative design skills. Pauline Hopkins proofread the final pages with her skilled eye for detail. Thank you all for helping me reach the finishing line with your valued expertise and encouragement along the way. And finally, I'm grateful to the late Peter Wilson who taught me to never give up.

9 780648 955399